CHRISTINE THORPE

FAIRFIELD
Gardens

A BETTER, GENTLER WORLD...
WHERE NOTHING CAN REALLY GO WRONG

FAIRFIELD
Gardens

A BETTER, GENTLER WORLD...
WHERE NOTHING CAN REALLY GO WRONG

G2 rights ltd

G2 rights ltd

Fairfield Gardens
Copyright ©Christine Thorpe 2012

First edition published in the UK in March 2013
© G2 Rights Limited 2013
www.G2rights.co.uk

All rights reserved. No part of this work may be reproduced or
utilised in any form or by any means, electronic or mechanical,
including photocopying, recording or by any information
storage and retrieval system, without prior written permission
of the publisher.

Print Edition ISBN: 978-1-78281-027-8

The views in this book are those of the author but they are general
views only and readers are urged to consult the relevant and
qualified specialist for individual advice in particular situations.
G2 Rights Limited hereby exclude all liability to the extent
permitted by law of any errors or omissions in this book and for any
loss, damage or expense (whether direct or indirect) suffered by a
third party relying on any information contained in this book.
All our best endeavours have been made to secure copyright
clearance but in the event of any copyright owner being
overlooked please go to www.G2rights.co.uk where you
will find all relevant contact information.

G2 Rights Ltd, Unit 9 Whiffens Farm, Clement Street, Hextable, Kent, BR8 7PG

INTRODUCTION

I was born in England and moved to Australia with my husband almost forty years ago. We have two children and live in Sydney, where I still work as a teacher. I have always been interested in writing but only ever managed letters to family and friends overseas.

Then in 2005 I was diagnosed with leukaemia. During my recovery, following chemotherapy, I made the decision to enjoy every single day and to do whatever pleased me most. So I started writing: poems, my brush with serious illness and memories of my childhood.

Then I started working on a fictitious story loosely based on the village in the UK where my brother lives. I had absolutely no intention that it should develop into a book, but the characters became so real that I did not want to stop. One day someone suggested that I might get it published and I thought "Why not?"

I do hope others will enjoy reading Fairfield Gardens as much as I enjoyed writing it and be encouraged to follow their own dreams.

Christine Thorpe

November 2012

CHAPTER 1

Stepping out of the door, past the tiny wheelbarrow filled to bursting with shining daffodils, Joy suddenly stopped with a gasp of delight. This was Easter morning and the day was heart-stoppingly beautiful. There was a real warmth in the early sun and small fluffy clouds, like children's drawings, hovered in the pale blue sky. As if on cue, all the daffodils in Fairfield Gardens had sprung open overnight. Easter was early this year and everyone had feared the worst, with those of a pessimistic nature predicting snow and the more optimistic saying it would surely rain after days of cloudy, dry conditions.

Joy locked the door, then turned again to savour the view and try to store it in her memory for future delight; rather like Wordsworth remembering his daffodils, she thought with a smile.

Fairfield Gardens was a small cul de sac of only eight houses, modern cottages built five years earlier to blend in with the village of Fairmead. Several of the older residents had been horrified when they had discovered that the long-lost son of much-loved Farmer Hawton had been discovered living happily in Australia and, on hearing of his father's demise, had immediately sold one of his fields to a developer, while renting the remainder of the farm to the neighbouring farmer. Much to everyone's relief, the little detached houses were built of the local red stone with steep roofs, small windows and dear little porches. All had cottage gardens, as befitted their ambience at the front and rather large grassed areas at the back. On the outside the houses appeared to be three or four hundred years old, but on the inside all was modern convenience. No one wanted to live without a shiny kitchen and bathroom.

On this Easter Sunday morning, Fairfield Gardens was looking its best. The houses stood almost in a circular pattern, with three down each side and two at the far end. The road ran around a delightful little grassed island which had three large elm trees growing in the middle, thankfully saved by the developer, a constant source of delight to the residents. The trees themselves were beautiful in every season and the wildlife fascinating to those who cared to observe, from squirrels and nesting birds to ants scurrying up and down. This tiny oasis, known locally as Hawton's, was oval in shape and today the grass was almost hidden by masses of daffodils in full bloom.

Suddenly Joy was shot out of her reverie by the first sharp peal of the church bells. Taking three steps down her gravel path, she hurried through the little white gate and turned up the Gardens to the road which ran along the top.

The church of St Mary–in–the–Mead was only a short distance along Bridge Road. A small part of the original Norman structure remained, but the rest had been added on over the centuries and Joy always felt that its patchwork quality gave it a most homely feel. Indeed, she felt so comfortable and at ease that she had been attending regularly since arriving in the village the previous autumn. On that memorable day, she had slipped in towards the end of the afternoon for a moment of peace after the bedlam of moving and sat transfixed behind a pillar while listening to the gloriously soaring notes of evensong and the mellow tones of the vicar reading the lessons. Though she had never been a regular churchgoer, from that day on she had gone almost every week. She was looking forward to this Easter service with high anticipation.

★ ★ ★ ★ ★

Others in Fairfield Gardens were also preparing for church. At number four Liz Norris was attempting to hurry along her three noisy boys. Going to church was not their idea of a fun-filled Easter, but Liz and Tom were determined to 'bring them up right' and thought church would be a civilizing influence, even if only on high days and holidays. Sam, Joel and Dan were all named after Old Testament characters, but their biblical names didn't seem to curb their high jinks and Liz rather dreaded to think what they would get up to when they became teenagers in a few years' time.

At the moment, however, her thoughts were entirely on the present and the effort to get her four 'menfolk' out of the door in time. And it certainly was an effort. Indeed, everything these days seemed to be an enormous effort. Even previously enjoyable occupations, such as gardening and having a cup of coffee with Megan at number eight, seemed beyond Liz's capabilities. The thought of returning to her little job as cleaner at the village school filled her with horror.

Though everything in her wanted to return to bed and the bliss of closed eyes and inertia, Liz was made of stern stuff.

Rallying all her willpower, she managed to chivvy her brood out of the door and down the path only a few moments after the bells had started ringing. She saw Joy turning into Bridge Road but could not summon the energy to catch her up or even call good morning. Oblivious to the daffodils and the glorious morning, she focused on each step in the knowledge that very soon she could sit and doze in the warm, sun-filled church.

The occupant of number six was already in church. He had arrived there long before anybody else because he was the Vicar, Paul Adamson. He had been living in Fairfield Gardens for the last four years, since the Diocese had sold the large and rambling vicarage at the far end of the village, along with its even larger and more rambling gardens, to be converted into an old people's home. Though run by a private firm, the name had been kept. St Mary's Home was still under the wing of the church, pastorally at least. Paul Adamson had been thrilled to move out and even more thrilled to find a dear little house in Fairfield Gardens, with all mod cons and only a couple of minutes from the church.

About the same time, as if to celebrate the new house, Paul had found a wife. He was already forty and had never even had a serious girlfriend before. Though he had a cheerful, kindly personality, at heart he was an academic and loved nothing better than to hide himself away in his study, reading anything and everything voraciously. But he was a conscientious vicar and tried to be friendly to all who lived in Fairmead, not just his own parishioners. As a result of this inclusiveness he had spoken pleasantly to a young lady he had never seen before while waiting to be served in the village stores. Sophia was petite and slim, with shoulder-length curly hair of a slightly reddish tinge, which stood out like a halo around her face and seemed to emphasise her large, child-like eyes. Paul was smitten. He was immediately infused with the certain knowledge that she was the one he had been waiting for all these years.

Sophia was oddly moved by this man in a clerical collar, with rimless spectacles adorning his long, thin face and a shabby black suit clothing his tall, slightly stooped body. His gentle kindliness touched a chord in her gentle heart and from that moment on they became firm friends.

It didn't matter one iota to Paul that Sophia was much involved in Eastern philosophies and did yoga and meditated every day, nor that she occasionally visited a Buddhist centre in Mansford. Her parents had moved to Spain for the sun, so at the age of twenty-eight, while working in a homewares shop but not particularly liking it, Sophia had decided to make a clean break. She had sold her miniature flat in Mansford and gone to stay with her aunt and uncle in Fairmead, intending to use that as a base while looking for a job and accommodation in a more rural setting. On her very first morning, while getting a paper for her uncle, she met Paul.

Needless to say, the good people of Fairmead were initially perplexed by Sophia's leaning, not to mention the fact that she was a vegetarian. However, in a very short time her kindness and gentle ways won them over, as did the fact that she seemed to have no objection to attending St Mary's or joining in village activities. So, when the marriage was announced, there was almost universal approval. Only a few die-hard oldies shook their heads and wondered to each other whatever was the world coming to that a vicar could marry someone with such outlandish views. But even they admitted that she was probably kinder than most other people they knew.

On this beautiful Easter morning, Sophia arrived at the church only ten minutes after Paul. While he was busy in the vestry, she cast an eye over the piles of prayer books and hymn books, then lingered on the glorious flower arrangements that she and two other ladies had spent all yesterday afternoon labouring over. The white and yellow flowers poured over the church like a blessing, as did the morning sun after what had seemed an eternity of cloudiness.

So far the church was still quiet, the only choir being the spring songbirds outside. Sophia sat in her favourite spot, in the front pew, in a pool of morning sunlight and closed her eyes. She had already meditated earlier, when the sun had been barely peeping over the hawthorn bush at the bottom of the garden, and she had taken a chair out to enjoy the unaccustomed sight, so now she simply allowed the warm sunshine to wash over her and let her thoughts run as they wished.

In fact there was only one thought in her mind, and it was more of a glorious symphony than a product of the intellect. Yesterday she had received the most wonderful news imaginable. After almost four years of marriage, she was finally expecting a baby. Although she and Paul had always spoken positively of 'when we have a family', she had begun to feel it might never happen, and she knew that Paul was becoming conscious of his age as the years passed. Both had more than enough to keep them occupied with church and parish affairs.

Paul had his books, and she had her few hours each day helping at Fantastic Flowers, the small garden centre out on the Melbury Road. She had even acquired a dear little puppy, of uncertain lineage, from Megan next door, and she loved to curl up in her special armchair, reading a good book with the puppy's warm, furry body wedged in beside her. But still there was a great longing for a baby of her very own and now, wonderfully, gloriously, it was going to happen.

She had rushed into Paul's study as soon as she had received the doctor's call, unable to contain herself. Although she had not given him the slightest clue, just in case it was all a mirage, he had known the reason as soon as he had seen her beaming face. His smiling face equalled hers as he loped over to give her the biggest hug he could manage without actually crushing her. Later that evening both of them had wandered over to the church, as if floating on a cloud, to give thanks, each in their own way.

As Sophia sat luxuriating in her happiness, little Miss Whitehead tiptoed in and found her way to the organ. She loved the old church and tried to attend every service she could, plus the weekly choir practice every Wednesday at 7.30 pm. She was not only the organist but the mainstay of the choir, never having been known to miss except for incapacitating illness. In the most dire weather, she would be the first (and sometimes the only) person there.

As a young woman Miss Whitehead had dreamed of becoming a nun, but her parents were older and as an only child, it was her duty to care for them. She did this for many years, and they both lived to a ripe old age. When her mother finally died, she was left completely on her own, all cousins and wider family having left the area years ago. She had been about to retire from the office job in Mansford, where she had worked for forty years, wondering what was to become of her. One lunchtime, she had slipped into the large city church of All Saints and put her dilemma to the Lord. That very evening, in the local paper, she saw an ad for new houses being built in the nearby village of Fairmead. Usually a conservative, practical person, she had thrown caution to the wind and rung the developers' number as soon as she could the next day.

In an amazingly short time and with no fuss at all, she had sold the large terrace in Mansford for an incomprehensibly large sum, and moved into number ten Fairfield Gardens. She loved the new house, with its old-looking exterior and modern, labour-saving interior, as soon as she saw it. She loved looking out to the front at the three beautiful trees on Hawton's and she loved all the neighbours in the little Fairfield Gardens community. Most of all, she loved having St Mary's church so close. Mr Adamson was the kindest of vicars and said he would leave a little side-door open for her, if she would like to pop in the church during the day for a little peaceful time. To Emily Whitehead, this was heaven. Every day she would slip in for an hour or so.

Emily was never bored. She was either in the church or out visiting the old people in St Mary's Home or the housebound of Fairmead. Her quiet smile was welcomed everywhere. She knew that the years were passing for her too and some time in the future she would be the one who needed visiting. For the present, though, she would continue to be thankful for her many blessings and to bring as much pleasure to others as she could.

To this end, a year after arriving in the village, she had volunteered to play the organ and run the choir. The very old lady who had played the organ for years had suddenly died, with no successor, and no choir had sung since a makeshift one had been hurriedly put together for the previous Christmas Eve service. Emily could play the piano well and had occasionally attempted the organ in her city church. The Vicar was thrilled to have a volunteer, and over the weeks and months she had improved tremendously. As for the choir, nobody ever felt they were forced to sing, but somehow Emily's gentle ways drew people in and now a grand total of ten sang most Sunday mornings - five women, two men and three children. Three of the ladies, including Emily, and one of the men even managed to gather for Evensong on Tuesday and Thursday afternoons. Paul Adamson thought privately that it was a miracle how beautifully they sang and thanked God for the arrival in Fairmead of Emily Whitehead.

Having arranged herself quietly at the organ so as not to disturb dear Sophia, she began gently to play a piece of much-loved Bach while waiting for the choir and congregation to arrive.

CHAPTER 2

The first choir member to make an appearance was Isabella Blackett, accompanied by her husband William. Sophia opened her eyes and stirred as Isabella bustled in. It was impossible for Isabella to be quiet even if she tried, which she was doing now. She was a round, red-faced, motherly woman who loved wearing the most garish outfits because she said they made her 'feel good'. Today's ensemble consisted of all the colours of the rainbow and many more besides, or so it seemed. Though she lived next door to Emily, they could not have been more different; small against large, quiet against loud. 'Even our names are opposites' Isabella laughed, with tears in her eyes, to all and sundry.

But little Emily Whitehead had made a big impression on Isabella when they had moved to Fairfield Gardens four years ago and she thought the world of the older lady. Almost without knowing what was happening, she had found herself joining the choir and, amazingly, enjoying it. Her rich, deep voice was an asset and everyone, from the vicar down, had made her feel so welcome.

However, only part of Isabella's mind was on her choir duties this Easter morning. Almost all her considerable family were coming for lunch and the meal loomed large in her thoughts. The little house would be groaning under the strain of accommodating so many, though fortunately it was a lovely, sunny day and the children would happily play outside. The old family home in Mansford had been ideal for their family but once Susie, the youngest, had left for university, Isabella and William had decided to sell up and move to something smaller and easier to manage. Never ones for nostalgia and ever the optimists, they had seen number twelve Fairfield Gardens advertised in an agent's window and on the strength of the photo, decided that that was the house for them.

There would be fifteen adults for lunch and Isabella had lost count of how many children. In the last three months, two more grandchildren had been added and, although she laughed at how many there were, in reality she loved everyone of them, knew their likes and fears and favourite toys and treated each as if he or she were the only one. She was not only Granny to all her own grandchildren but Granny Isabella to most of Fairmead's children. Sam, Joel and Dan from across the road were always popping over to see her, and without fail she would stop what she was doing, find a sweetie each for them and settle down to play Snakes and Ladders or toy cars, or just read them a story from the box of books in one of the kitchen cupboards.

Isabella's husband was several years older than she was and somewhat quieter. William loved all the children quite as much as she did, but in a less demonstrative way. He was also looking forward to seeing their large family but, not having the concerns of lunch, his mind could focus on his church duties.

About the same time as Isabella had joined the choir,

William had become churchwarden, rather against his better judgement. He had recently retired from his busy life as an accountant and a member of several boards of directors and was looking forward to a quiet life with no children and no responsibilities in his new home in the country. He might have known he would be busier than ever living in a village. Starting off as churchwarden, he soon progressed to member of the church council, unofficial keeper of the church accounts, chief member of the School Friends Association, member of the Village Affairs Committee, Cub Master and sundry other roles too numerous to mention. Golf and gardening were still pleasures he enjoyed but time for them was limited. In addition to everything else, Isabella had fallen under the spell of Megan's puppies and brought one home before he could protest. After five minutes, William too had been bewitched by the tiny nondescript bundle and Scrappy had merged into the family. Isabella fed him and cuddled him endlessly, but it was William who took him for walks, morning and evening, and attempted to teach him some basic rules.

As his wife hurried across to the organ, William turned to the piles of books, certain that they would all be needed on this special Sunday. Sophia joined him, giving him a wide smile and whispering Easter greetings. Then she picked up one of the piles and joined him at the church door, just in time for the first parishioners to arrive. The good people of Fairmead never seemed to be rushed, and although the bells had been ringing for several minutes, the first-comers were only just arriving, while others could be seen strolling along Bridge Road.

Joy Taylor had actually arrived before William and Isabella

but had gone straight through to the vestry to make sure all was in readiness for Paul. She knew he would be there already, head buried in his prayer book, but she was taking her role as acting verger very seriously and moved around so quietly that the vicar was hardly aware of her until he suddenly glanced up. Then he jumped up, almost knocking the chair over. He wished her a very happy Easter and thanked her sincerely for her good work, as everything had been in apple-pie order when he arrived.

Joy, in her capacity as one of the teachers at the village school, had been asked rather shyly by Paul if she would be the temporary custodian of the vestry for a couple of weeks while old Bill Hughes from St Mary's Home went to stay with his daughter in Mansford for Easter. Joy was only too pleased to accept the role, especially as it was school holidays and secretly, Paul was pleased to have such a competent helper during the Easter ceremonies. Dear old Bill, though very willing, was not particularly suited to the job; he was eighty-two, very deaf and walked with the aid of a stick.

Seeing Paul's wide smile had increased Joy's happiness on this glorious morning. When she moved out into the church and saw Sophia's matching smile, she had an intuition that they must have had some wonderful news and felt sure that by the time they left everyone in Fairmead would know what it was. The instantaneous nature of the village grapevine still amazed her.

As Joy took her place, she began to notice some of the children from the school and smiled kindly at each one as she saw them. Though she was enjoying the Easter break, she would be pleased to return to her class of little ones when school resumed.

The bells had been pealing merrily for the last ten minutes, but now they suddenly ceased. The silence was a shock to the system. For many years now there had been no bell-ringers and the four old bells in the tower had been locked away, gathering dust, mice and the occasional stray bird. Fewer and fewer villagers were willing to turn out on cold winter nights to stand in a freezing tower learning to ring the bells. In the end the vicar and leading parishioners of the day decided to stop ringing the bells on Sundays permanently. Although few had been willing to make the effort, almost everyone had missed hearing them ringing cheerfully before Sunday Service, and even non-churchgoers had complained that it wasn't Sunday without the bells. Eventually the Village Affairs Committee had decided to raise money to install loudspeakers and a tape of a famous Cathedral's beautiful bells. The Vicar readily agreed, and the money was raised at the next Village Garden Party. Since then, the bells had been heard every Sunday, with an extra five minutes added for Christmas and Easter.

As the last peal was sounding, Molly and James Standing walked briskly up the church path and accepted hymn and prayer books from Sophia and their neighbour, William, with smiles and thanks and Easter greetings. Entering the church, they nodded and smiled at friends already settled, then hurried over to the organ, where Emily Whitehead was still quietly playing. Both husband and wife had fine, strong voices and were invaluable members of the choir. They were almost the last to arrive and just had time for a brief hello to all before

Emily played a last lingering note, then turned to smile in her gentle way at her fellow choristers. They were quietly arranging themselves and their hymn books in their assigned places. Even Isabella was trying her best to be organised. In her wildly-coloured Easter outfit, every move she made was visible to the whole congregation. But Granny Isabella was loved by young and old, and all looked at her with an indulgent eye.

Molly and James also loved Isabella and thought themselves extremely fortunate to have such good neighbours. They had moved to number fourteen Fairfield Gardens two years ago, when James' job had been transferred from London to Mansford. The large pharmaceutical company he worked for had a smaller plant in Mansford and his promotion had depended on his moving there. Both James and Molly had been loath to leave the capital but decided that a change might be good for them after fifteen years of married life in a garden flat in London. The firm was generously helping them to relocate and several weekends had been spent travelling to Mansford looking for a new home. On these occasions, they had stayed at the King's Head in the centre of Mansford, driving out in different directions each time. On the third weekend, they had driven through Fairmead on a Saturday morning and stopped at the Village Stores for a soft drink and bar of chocolate to sustain them. It had been a beautiful June morning, with sunshine, wispy clouds and loud birdsong, far too beautiful for them to stay cooped up in the car, so they abandoned their search and went for a walk around the village. Though they had never lived in a village before they were completely bewitched by the lovely houses glowing a golden red in the bright sunshine and when they saw the little notice in the Village Stores window proclaiming the availability of number fourteen Fairfield Gardens, their minds were made up. Without having seen the house or its environs, they had already decided that this was to be their new home. The drive to Mansford every day was no hardship to James, who had spent fifteen years, twice a day, on the manic London Underground, and the house was everything they had dreamed of.

Now, two years later, they wondered how they had ever survived in the big city. They were involved in village affairs, deeply attached to the church and loved every one of their neighbours in Fairfield Gardens. Their lives in London had been dominated by work, but as the months passed in Fairmead they found themselves slowing down and their priorities changing. Family and friends became much more important. James' family lived in Scotland, not far from Loch Lomond, and Molly's were in the beautiful Lake District. They now began to visit their families at other times besides the obligatory Christmas and Easter. They phoned more often too, and the couple experienced a sense of belonging they had never felt during the London years.

But this Easter was different; they had not driven north the previous day, as was their custom. Today little Cathy and Mark were finally coming to stay as their foster children.

No children had ever appeared on Molly and James' horizon. Being immersed in work and London life, they never seemed to have time to discover the reason. Now in their early forties, they had begun to wish they had a family of their own.

They were always included in Isabella and William's gatherings and loved every one of their children and grandchildren, but it felt quiet when they returned home. When Paul had mentioned one day at choir practice that he and Sophia had started visiting a small children's home on the far side of Mansford, they both had the same thought, though they both kept it to themselves for at least a week. Then, while they had been weeding in their little front garden one fine Saturday the previous October, Molly had not been able to keep her idea to herself. She had been amazed when James had said he was harbouring exactly the same thought.

So at the first possible opportunity, they contacted the children's home and after much bureaucratic delay, including interviews and visits by social workers, they finally met Cathy and Mark, sister and brother, aged five and seven. Their parents had been killed three years before in a freak holiday accident involving a ski lift. The children had been staying with their grandma, a widow living in Mansford. She continued to care for them with much love, but sadly she had heart problems and no longer felt able to cope. The other grandparents, though willing to help, lived in a small flat in New Zealand and there were no aunties or uncles. Their grandma, therefore, had decided that it was best for the children to find good foster parents, and in January they had gone to live at the children's home. They saw their Grandma every Sunday and were able to continue at their same school, but their schoolwork suffered and they became withdrawn.

At the end of January they met Molly and James Standing for the first time. The first meeting was a little strained, with the adults trying to appear friendly but not pushy, while watching the five children playing in the garden of the home. Cathy and Mark seemed to stick together and did not really mix with the others. A few days later the children were asked if they would like to go to the nearby park with Mr & Mrs Standing and they agreed, without much enthusiasm. However, from that inauspicious start had emerged a happy couple of hours for all concerned. Cathy and Mark had enjoyed playing on the swings and slides before eating a huge ice-cream each, despite the freezing weather. Then, to warm up, the four of them had kicked a ball around, thoughtfully bought by James two minutes before picking up the children. This was followed by a walk round the lake feeding the ducks with bread brought by Molly.

After this enjoyable trip Cathy and Mark were eager to see the Standings every weekend and soon began calling them Auntie Molly and Uncle James. Each Sunday they all went to visit Grandma for an hour and then went back to Fairfield Gardens for a roast dinner.

It wasn't long before Molly and James asked if they could foster the children and this was arranged in double quick time, to everyone's satisfaction, including Grandma's. Of course, the sudden acquisition of a family had entailed quite major changes in the Standings' ordered way of life. Rather to her surprise, Molly had become the owner of a very small business. While in London, she had worked for many years in a very high-class salon, attending to the hair of the rich and famous, and even in Mansford, she had worked long hours in a large establishment. But the previous Thursday she had worked her last day and was about to embark on a new and much smaller enterprise as Fairmead's first resident hairdresser. She had no premises and was planning to offer a home-visit service.

Her ads in the Parish Newsletter and the Village Stores window were greeted with much enthusiasm by older ladies and busy mothers who never seemed to have the time or energy to go regularly to Mansford for their hair needs. Eventually, Molly thought, she would extend her service to nearby villages and possibly set up her own salon, but for the time being this would be ideal, allowing her to work only school hours and still have time left for the extra work involved in having two young children around the place.

Even while she was finding the place in her hymn book, half her mind was thinking pleasurably of the children's bedroom, filled with new furniture and quite a number of new toys, many given by friends and neighbours. She and James had decided to let the children sleep in the same room, at least for a while, to help them settle in and feel less strange.

CHAPTER 3

As Emily settled herself at the organ and began to play the first rousing Easter hymn and the choir readied themselves, Megan Todd and her four children almost fell into a pew near the back. They were favourites with the whole village and the people around made room for them with broad smiles.

The three older girls were all dressed the same, in pretty pink dresses and white, frilly socks, which was an amazing change from their usual tomboy jeans or shorts. This was the main reason why they were so late arriving at church. Megan had had to exert all her authority, plus much bribery and corruption, to get them to wear the pretty outfits. Sally, Jenny and Amy were triplets and always stuck together. Usually, they were easy-going, placid little girls, but this morning they all agreed that they wanted to wear their new candy-striped T-shirts and red shorts. Megan insisted that these were to be kept for tomorrow's Easter Fayre - always provided the weather held, she thought to herself.

But prevailing on the girls to wear their pretty new dresses was only part of Megan's pre-church duties. She also had to feed, change and dress her fourth little daughter, two-week-old Angie, full name Angela but known as Angie from birth. The baby looked like an angel, with downy fair hair and big blue eyes, and most importantly, she behaved like an angel, eating and sleeping regularly and hardly ever crying.

For this mercy, Megan was certainly grateful. Angie had been born two and a half weeks early, only 31 hours after her father, Jack, had set off for the airport on his way to New York for an important business trip. His return had been scheduled for a few days before Megan's due date. But Angie had decided to arrive before then and it had been panic stations to get Megan's mother up from the South Coast where she ran a small bed and breakfast with her husband. She had driven overnight to take charge of Amy, Sally and Jenny and half an hour later Megan had been driven to Mansford Royal by her good neighbours Isabella and William Blackett. Megan's mother had stayed to help until last Thursday but then needed to return to her hard-working husband to prepare for the Easter rush.

So for a few days Megan had tried to keep the ship afloat, with the help of just about everyone, young and old, in Fairfield Gardens. At regular intervals during the last couple of days, someone or other had called in with offers to have the girls over to play or take them to the green or walk the dog, Bonnie, or just to bring over a casserole or cake.

Megan knew she was blessed with wonderful neighbours and she had really wanted to go to church this Easter morning. She had so much to be thankful for, not least the fact that Jack would be arriving back this very evening. His business partner, Dave, would drop him off about six o'clock before returning to his own home in Mansford. The trip had been longer and more exhausting than anticipated, but all the negotiations had been successfully concluded and now Jack was longing to return home to Megan, his three darling girls and now a welcome addition, not to mention the dog, who adored him and was always restless when he was away. He was also looking forward to a week's well earned holiday and a chance to get to know his little Angie.

As the first Easter hymn rang around the old church, Megan caught her breath and began to relax. As she glanced around, she realised with pleasure that the two people who had made room in the pew for the little family were her neighbours from number sixteen, Louisa Ward and Kate Manning.

The two ladies were, in fact, sisters-in-law, though they had been friends from the time they had both started at Fairmead School many years before. As young women, they had pursued different careers. Kate had moved to London and taken up nursing, while Louisa had risen in the retail world, to become chief buyer for a chain of fashion stores. In her time she had travelled throughout Europe and occasionally made forays into Asia. But eight years before, her world had been turned upside down. First a slight stroke had forced her to abandon her high-pressure job, and this blow was followed by an even worse one when her dear husband of thirty years had died suddenly of a heart attack.

Her only son was living in California with his wife and family, and although they had asked her to live with them, she had no desire to leave the country of her birth. She felt a great need to return to the village where she had been born, so once all her affairs had been settled she had gone to Mansford to stay with Kate, who had returned a couple of years earlier to take up a position at Mansford Royal Infirmary. Her husband had been Louisa's brother, but he had died as a result of a work accident when they had been married only five years. Kate had been left to raise their daughter alone, helped by the compensation she received and her nursing, which she loved.

Now Chloe was pursuing a PhD at Oxford, something to do with the environment, and was aiming to save the world. She kept in touch with her mother as much as possible, phoning twice a week and visiting at least once a month, but Kate missed her rather intense personality and was very pleased when Louisa asked to stay.

Louisa was never one to sit and mope. When she had read in the local paper that the Village Stores in her very own village of Fairmead was about to close through falling patronage, she had wasted not a moment before driving over to see things for herself. The stores were housed in the front parlour of an old cottage on the High Street, round the corner from St Mary's Church and three doors down from the Farmer's Arms. The old lady who ran the Stores had her living room across the central passageway, in what had once been the bedroom. An old-fashioned kitchen and an even more old-fashioned bathroom had been added at the back some time in the nineteenth century. The toilet was in the tiny washhouse in the back yard. There was no upstairs and old Bessie lived and slept in the same room. Now she had been persuaded to move to the modern luxury of St Mary's Home, and the Stores was to close.

Being a businesswoman at heart, Louisa had weighed up the pros and cons and decided she would take on the challenge. She had made Bessie an offer that brought tears of gratitude to the old lady's eyes, and within a couple of months the transformation of the Stores had begun. The old-world charm was kept but the stock was vastly increased. Walking a fine tightrope, Louisa managed to cater for both locals and passing tourist trade. She kept her prices competitive and soon people were willing to stay in Fairmead for some of their shopping rather than doing it all in the Mansford supermarkets.

Five years before, she had opened Bessie's former living quarters as a charming bijou café, employing two local ladies to make coffees, lunches and afternoon teas. Many Fairmead residents had become regulars, and at weekends people would drive out from Mansford and surrounding villages to enjoy the hospitality of Louisa's Café.

About a year after opening the café, Louisa and Kate moved to number sixteen Fairfield Gardens. It was further for Kate to go to work, but the thought of living in a delightful village again after so many years in cities was overwhelming, and neither of them ever regretted the move.

Initially Louisa had only intended to stay with Kate for a month or so, but the ladies got on well together and Kate made it so obvious that she was delighted with the company that the visit became permanent. Now established in Fairfield Gardens, they could not be happier. Louisa was in her element running the Village Stores and Louisa's Café, and Kate loved her job on the children's ward at Mansford Royal. From the moment she had first entered the large London hospital as an eighteen-year old-many years before, she had known that this was what she had been born for. She had loved her husband and daughter dearly, but nursing was her passion.

Now in her early fifties, Kate had no desire to retire for many years, but of late she had been finding night duty rather a strain and had put in a request for permanent morning duty, which had been granted. She had been told this welcome news only yesterday and was now starting a few days' holiday before returning to her beloved children. On this joyous Easter Sunday, her thoughts were full of thanks for the lifting of the burden of night duty, for the darling children on her ward, for Louisa's friendship and for all the dear people of Fairmead.

As she and Louisa shuffled along to make room for Megan and her little ones and the first hymn got underway, Kate's gaze rested on Liz Norris from across the road at number four. For once the boys were behaving themselves, looking like angels, with hymn books open and voices straining, though Kate noticed, with a smile, that Dan's book was upside down. Their father Tom, a large, muscular man who ran a small construction company, looked a little self conscious, holding his hymn book at arm's length and singing heartily.

But Kate's attention was drawn to Liz. Kate had not seen her for a couple of weeks and to her practised eye, she did not look well at all. Though she was standing and holding a hymn book, her eyes were closed and she was not singing but holding on to the pew in front. She looked pale and had lost weight. Kate's concern rose. She knew she must have a word with her after church and persuade her to see Dr Miles when he next visited the village on Wednesday morning.

CHAPTER 4

The Easter morning service was all it should have been. The choir excelled itself, the vicar and readers spoke well, the magnificent flowers were a feast for the senses, sunlight and birdsong flooded in from the open doors and shafts of multi-coloured light from the stained-glass windows playfully slid around the church. As the joyful, concluding hymn was soaring on high, Joy Taylor slipped out into the entrance porch, as quietly as possible, and switched on the church bells' tape once again. This was usually old Bill Hugh's job, but she had volunteered to take responsibility in his absence and was so anxious that all should go smoothly that she set them going before the last hymn had finished, to everyone's enjoyment, especially the children's, whose excitement level rose tenfold with all the noise.

While everyone was preparing to leave, Paul made a quick dash from the vestry, down the side path, and was in place at the church doors to greet the first leavers. Though the church had been lovely, the glorious morning took everyone's breath away as they emerged and, unlike previous Sundays, no one was in a hurry to leave. The only person who was not in the highest spirits was Liz. The boys were racing around the churchyard as though they had been in prison for years and

Tom was soon in an animated conversation with two of his friends from the Farmer's Arms Darts Club. Hardly anybody noticed as she slipped away, which was most unusual in Fairmead, except that today there was much to take their attention, particularly that of the ladies.

Megan's little Angie was like a magnet for the womenfolk. Though everyone in Fairfield Gardens had been helping since the baby's birth, this was her first excursion to church, and all wanted to admire her in her little pink and white Easter outfit. She had been asleep in her mother's arms during the whole of the service, but as she emerged into the bright sunlight, she opened her blue eyes and gazed serenely out at all her admirers. Megan thought she probably had about half an hour before the next feed and relaxed as she enjoyed the attention.

Molly was also the focus of much attention. To everyone's delight, she was about to become a foster mother in only an hour or so, and there was much advice and many offers of help at any time. Cathy and Mark were already known to all and everyone wished the new family well. Isabella, particularly, thought they needed 'fattening up' and felt that they were rather too quiet for children their age, but she had every confidence in Molly and James and had asked them to pop over during the afternoon, so the children could play with her own contingent of grandchildren.

At that thought, Isabella remembered lunch and reluctantly made moves to leave. But, being a most sociable person, she found it hard to drag herself away. In no time she was deep into conjecture with half a dozen Fairmead ladies as to Sophia's 'condition'. It was generally agreed that such radiance could mean only one thing and that the first to find out for sure would immediately let the others know.

Although just as interested in these absorbing affairs as all the other ladies, Kate was also aware of Liz's swift departure. Making apologies for having to hurry away due to the imminent arrival of Chloe for Easter lunch, she left the busy churchyard and was soon turning into Fairfield Gardens and walking up the Norris' front path. Liz was surprised but pleased to see her and ushered her into the lounge, apologising for the mess and saying that she had not got around to tidying up.

Kate knew she only had a few minutes before Tom and the boys returned and came straight to the point, telling her friend that she did not look at all well and should see Dr Miles on Wednesday. Liz put up no resistance, saying that she felt so tired that maybe she was coming down with something. Her eyes filled with tears and she confided that she was afraid she had heart trouble because she was finding herself gasping for breath when climbing stairs or doing anything only moderately strenuous. She was feeling cold, even on this warm spring day. Kate was more alarmed than ever, but kept her suspicions to herself. With a professional smile of confidence, she offered to go with Liz to see the doctor, as she was on holiday for a week, and arranged to call over at nine o'clock. Tom would have gone to work and Kate said she would ask Isabella to have the boys for an hour.

Naturally, Isabella would have to be told and the whole village would know almost instantaneously. But they probably knew already, thought Kate, though they most likely thought it was a touch of flu and not what she feared it might be.

⋆　⋆　⋆　⋆　⋆

The afternoon proved a happy one for all in Fairfield Gardens. Even Liz was comforted by Kate's calm presence and enjoyed a peaceful few hours dozing in a deckchair in the back garden, while Tom took the boys to his parents for lunch and Easter eggs, giving flu as the reason for his wife's non-appearance.

Joy and Emily had been asked for lunch by Sophia and Paul. Old Bessie, from St Mary's Home, was also invited, as was a vicar friend of Paul's. Bessie was the life and soul of the party, recounting many funny stories from her years at the Stores, and all had a most enjoyable time. Joy and Emily would never have dreamed of asking Sophia about her condition but Bessie plunged in, saying that you would never know unless you asked, and Sophia, after a little initial embarrassment, was only too happy to share the good news.

Megan had Jack's mother and two sisters over from Mansford and was extremely happy to have the help. The girls loved their Nana and aunties and the feeling was mutual. After all had held Angie and cooed over her, she obligingly fell asleep in her pram in the back garden, oblivious to the excited shrieks of her sisters as they found their Easter eggs and played in the new Ladybird tent given by their doting relatives. Jack's family were planning to stay until he arrived home in the evening, so Megan was able to relax and rely on other pairs of eyes.

For once Louisa's Café was closed, despite the many day-trippers driving through Fairmead on this beautiful day. Louisa was adamant that Easter Sunday and Christmas were days for church, family and friends and that she and her loyal staff needed the time off, though secretly, she paid them as if they had worked the Sunday. Now she and Kate were enjoying their well-earned rest and being waited on by Chloe, who insisted on cooking lunch for her mother and aunt. The meal was slightly more exotic than they were used to but neither dreamed of saying anything, so pleased were they to have Chloe to themselves, chatting about friends, life at university and hope for the future.

That day Isabella and William's house was the loudest in Fairfield Gardens, if not in the whole of Fairmead. By noon, most of their large family had arrived and parked cars stretched around the Gardens and out into Bridge Road. The family tradition was that all Easter-egg giving was to be celebrated with the whole clan at Granny and Grandpa's, after the huge lunch. The children were, therefore, consumed with barely-contained excitement and ran around in a fever, getting under everybody's feet. Though Isabella had had this lunch on her mind earlier in the morning, it was by no means her sole responsibility and she knew that it would all work out splendidly, as it always did on these occasions.

As usual she had cooked an enormous piece of beef, which had had been left in the oven on a fairly gentle heat while she and William had been at church. With years of experience, she knew that it would be perfect by the time they returned home, as indeed was the case today. The remainder of the lunch was provided by their various offspring. By means of much phoning and emailing during the previous couple of weeks, they had all agreed who was to bring what. The frantic contacting of each other was probably unnecessary, as they usually brought the same each time, but it was part of tradition and, as such, an honoured part of every Christmas and Easter.

Like all the residents of Fairfield Gardens, Molly and James were thinking with pleasure of the day ahead as they left the churchyard. But their pleasure was tinged with a great deal of nervousness. This was the first day of a new life and the end of many years considering only themselves. However, they had little time for misgivings, as they had promised to collect the children at twelve sharp before taking them for their weekly visit to Grandma, and they knew they would be eagerly awaited.

Cathy and Mark had no doubts at all about going to live with Auntie Molly and Uncle James. The ladies who looked after them at the Home, and the other children too, were very nice but it wasn't the same as having your own home and family. Grandma was the best in the world, but she wasn't well and couldn't play with them or take them out. Mark could remember their own mummy and daddy because he was a big boy of seven, but Cathy couldn't remember much and he had to keep telling her things before he too forgot. It seemed such a long time since they had all lived together. But today, all their thoughts and chatter were about staying in the lovely house in Fairfield Gardens and leaving their clothes in their new bedroom and playing with all the new toys Auntie Molly and Uncle James had told them about and going for tea with Granny Isabella and her hundreds of grandchildren.

Mark could almost tell the time, at least when it said o'clock, and all morning he kept running to the big old clock in the hall to check the time. They had said goodbye to the others earlier, when they had left to go on a picnic with Jane.

Only Edith was left to look after them for the remaining time. Usually a quiet boy, he had almost driven her insane, asking the time every five minutes.

At a snail's pace, the clock moved up towards twelve o'clock. A good twenty minutes before the due time, Mark and Cathy were standing in the hall wearing their Sunday best, with their cases and bags ready and waiting. Then, to their immense relief, ten minutes early, Auntie Molly and Uncle James' car came up the drive and the children rushed outside to meet them.

The sight of Mark and Cathy, with their beaming smiles and madly waving hands put any lingering doubts to rest. Molly and James knew, without a shadow of a doubt, that they were doing exactly the right thing for all of them.

CHAPTER 5

The next day dawned dry and sunny but much colder, with a wicked little wind. Everyone said to everyone else how lucky they were to have had such a magnificent Easter Sunday and at least today was dry for the Fayre. The Easter Fayre had been held on Easter Monday for more years than anybody could remember, on the village green in all weathers.

Fairmead was fortunate to have retained a small patch of common land more or less in its centre, just off the High Street. Some trees grew along one side, thoughtfully replaced from time to time by worthy villagers. These days it was the Village Affairs Committee who lobbied the local council to supply saplings, which were then planted ceremoniously by the children from Fairmead School. There were now six young trees, planted the previous summer, and the children were honour-bound not to go near them. The mature trees, however, were fair game, and every Fairmead child, boy or girl, had swung on their branches, made tree-houses and climbed up as far as possible, many times, as had their parents and grandparents.

Under one of the trees was a bench, much frequented by Fairmead's older residents, particularly the more mobile from St Mary's Home. Bessie Crabtree and Bill Hughes were to be seen there holding court nearly every morning between ten and twelve.

In winter, covered in frost or snow, the green looked magical and many snowmen had been built there over the years. After rain, however, it became a quagmire to be avoided by the adults at all costs, while the children were irresistibly attracted. Before winter was even over, snowdrops and then crocuses turned it into a fairyland, and now Easter daffodils were nodding gaily in the stiff breeze.

Though some visitors did put in an appearance, essentially the Fayre was organised by Fairmead for Fairmead. Most of the Village Affairs Committee were also on the Easter Fayre Committee, but the duties were not very onerous, as the same people ran the same stalls year after year. It was a very traditional affair, which caused newcomers some frustration until they learned to relax into the village way. Once accepted as Fairmeaders, they were welcome to help on existing stalls for a few years and eventually establish their own stall, if they still wished to.

Tom Norris, William Blackett and James Standing were out early on this Easter Monday morning, helping to erect stalls and trestle tables with half a dozen other Fairmead men. Of the three, William was the only one whose mind was completely on the job. Tom was concerned about Liz, who seemed to have no 'get-up-and go' these days and looked even paler than was to be expected after a cold, dismal winter. She said she must be coming down with flu, and that was what he had told the family yesterday when they had gathered for Easter lunch. They had all been very kind and his mother had rung her during the afternoon and promised to call round next weekend, when she would surely be feeling better. But Tom wondered if it really was flu and was glad that she was going with Kate Manning to see Dr Miles on Wednesday.

James' thoughts were considerably more cheerful than Tom's. He had been more nervous than Molly about taking on the children full time, but from the moment they had seen Mark and Cathy jumping up and down with excitement as they parked the car in front of the Home, everything had been wonderful. There was a kind of inevitability about the children coming to them, as though all the years in London, the non-appearance of natural children and their moving to Fairmead had somehow been leading to this.

James shook his head to try and get his mind back to the job in hand, but it was no good. While listening with half an ear to William telling him a long tale about one of his sons who was a police officer, the major part of his mind was re-living yesterday. In his mind's eye he saw Cathy and Mark's delight at their new bedroom, their thrill at finding little Easter eggs all over the house and garden, their enjoyment playing with Isabella and William's grandchildren and the bedtime story he had read them before tucking them in. Despite a very busy and exciting Easter Sunday, they had been awake extremely early, but had played happily in their room until it was time to get up. Such good children, thought James. We are really lucky to have them.

At that very moment Molly was thinking the same thing, as she watched them eating their breakfast. Neither of them was a big eater. Mark was fairly easy to please, but Cathy was quite fussy and there were numerous things she wouldn't eat, fruit being a major dislike. Apart from that they were remarkably compliant and had beautiful manners, due mainly to their Grandma, who always insisted on best behaviour. Molly had commented on this several times during their weekly visits and she had replied that children and animals always give back what is expected of them. If you always insisted on politeness and good manners, that is what you will get. Molly had taken this wisdom to heart and was determined to keep up the good work. To this end she made a point of waiting for 'please', 'thank you' and 'excuse me' from the children and James had followed her lead.

Her musings were cut short by the sound of the door bell. It was Sophia, looking windblown, with her golden-red hair standing on end, as if she had had an electric shock. But her smile was as wide and sweet as ever. She was here to say hello to Cathy and Mark before departing to set up her stall at the Fayre. She knew the children quite well, having met them at the Home and at Molly and James'. When she heard they were still having breakfast, she said to give her love and she would see them later. Then she kissed Molly and made her way to the green in her usual unhurried way.

Sophia thought Molly looked happier than she had ever seen her. 'Motherhood must suit her' she decided, and hoped it would suit her too. This morning, for the first time, she had felt slightly queasy, but whether that was the result of her pregnancy or the aftermath of much eating yesterday, she couldn't tell. The Easter lunch had stretched into the evening and nobody had seemed inclined to leave. Joy and Emily had contributed to the feast but Sophia had excelled herself and produced not only the expected roast dinner but several delicious vegetarian dishes. Not wanting to upset her, the others had tasted the unknown food with some trepidation, but had all been most pleasantly surprised. It had been eight o'clock before the party had broken up. Paul's vicar-friend offered to drive Bessie home and both Emily and Joy were pleased to have only a few yards to walk. Paul and Sophia then sank gratefully into their armchairs, listened to ten minutes of Mozart and stumbled up to bed. After a dreamless sleep, both felt refreshed and ready for another busy day.

*   *   *   *   *

The excitement in the Norris house was tremendous, and Liz didn't feel up to coping. Tom had been wonderful and the boys had had breakfast, got dressed and even brushed their teeth by eight-thirty, when he left for the green. On his way, he had called in at Isabella's and asked if she would mind having the young ones until he returned in an hour or so. Isabella was swathed in a deep pink dressing gown and said nothing would give her more pleasure. So Sam, Joel and Dan raced over, without a backward glance at their mother and were soon deep into playing Snakes and Ladders with Granny Isabella, who seemed oblivious to the fact that she wasn't dressed yet. Liz breathed a sigh of relief and decided to leave the chaos in the kitchen, bathroom and boys' rooms and pop back to bed for five minutes. In two minutes she was fast asleep.

Joy was luxuriating in the fact that she did not have to get up for school. She lay in bed for a full fifteen minutes extra, but she couldn't relax and got up despite the fairly early hour.

She made a cup of tea and went to sit near the window in the lounge, looking out at her own neat garden and across to Hawton's, its golden bounty straining in the wind. Joy did this every morning, though on school days she was limited to five minutes. Hawton's was a beautiful oasis in every weather and, every day without fail, Joy blessed her good fortune in securing such a delightful place to live. She always added a heartfelt thanks for a job she loved so much.

Joy's childhood had been eventful. Her mother had left when she was only two and her father had moved many times, furthering his career. He had always taken Joy with him, to the USA, Singapore and even India, for a short time. There were also many extended trips to Europe. Joy's father was very fond of her but was a busy man and she had been cared for by many nannies and maids over the years.

She had also attended many schools, being taught in several different languages. Far from impeding her learning, this state of affairs had greatly enhanced it and she had no trouble at all gaining a place at university. But, unlike her father, she was not ambitious and she longed only for two things: to put down roots and to teach small children. Being essentially concerned with his own affairs, her father was quite happy for her to do as she pleased.

She had gained her teaching degree with flying colours and was immediately snapped up by an expensive private school in London. Joy had stayed there for three years, but was not totally happy, so when she had seen the advertisement for a position at Fairmead School, she had applied that very day. Miss Browning, the Head Teacher, couldn't believe her luck that such a well qualified and obviously dedicated teacher would want to teach in a small village school. Joy had started the previous September, teaching the twenty-four youngest children and loving it from the first day. At first she had boarded with an elderly couple who lived near St Mary's Home. Then, in early October, the dear little house in Fairfield Gardens had become available. A phone call to her father had secured the necessary funds and she had moved in a few weeks later.

Though Joy was the newest member of the Fairfield Gardens community, she felt at home straight away. Within two days, she had met every person, from oldest to youngest. Some of the younger end wondered what it would be like having a teacher living next door, but they weren't too worried as she was generally considered to be fair but kind.

One of the first people to call round and offer help on the day she moved in was Sophia. They were already firm friends through church and school and it was Sophia who had told her about number two being for sale, before it was even advertised. The second person who had called to offer welcome and help was Miss Whitehead, or Emily, as she insisted on being called. Despite the difference in their ages, the two became immediate friends. Emily never intruded on Joy's privacy but always seemed to be available whenever she needed someone to talk to and her quiet peace always lifted Joy's spirits.

It was Emily whom Joy saw now, as she sat enjoying her cup of tea and the lovely view of Hawton's. Emily smiled and waved as she passed, probably on her way up to church, thought Joy with affection, before all the Fayre activity really gets underway. Joy and Emily had agreed to be on the plant stall and the previous week almost every household in Fairmead had left their contributions near Joy's and Emily's front porches. In effect, everybody would be exchanging their plants for someone else's, but all money raised was going to an orphanage in Africa which was supported by St Mary's Church and was generally agreed to be a good cause.

Megan and Jack had been woken at five by Angie and then at six by Sally, who had 'accidentally' wet her bed. She did this sometimes when overexcited, but Megan tried hard not to get cross; after all Jack was home to help her now. She got up to sort things out. As she did so the other girls woke up and any thoughts of returning to bed were ended. She told them firmly to play quietly and not disturb Daddy because he was very tired, but inevitably, their spirits woke him a third time and he crawled out of bed for a strong cup of coffee.

After the previous day's tussle about clothes, the girls were wonderfully unconcerned about having to wear a tracksuit over their red shorts and striped T-shirts. So excited were they about the Fayre that they were ready in half the time it usually took to get ready for school.

★ ★ ★ ★ ★

Louisa had taken only one day off over Easter. This morning the Village Stores and Louisa's Café were open for business by nine o 'clock. As far as the Stores was concerned, Easter Monday was always a major retail day, as many day trippers drove through the Village. Louisa had, however, generously offered to donate all proceeds from the Café, apart from her two ladies' wages, to the African orphanage. This was most appreciated by the Easter Fayre Committee and the vicar, and a large notice proclaiming this fact was stuck in the window.

Louisa expected to be very busy and had asked Isabella and William's youngest daughter, Susie, to help out in the shop so she herself could help in the café. As students are always in need of money Susie was only too pleased to work for a little cash, which she could spend in the evening with her friends in Mansford.

Being on holiday, Kate did not get up as early as Louisa. Chloe had stayed overnight and when mother and daughter finally emerged, they enjoyed an unaccustomed chat, just the two of them, over an enormous cooked breakfast, Chloe was in the last stages of her PhD and was planning to work for an environmental agency in a country Kate had hardly heard of. She was extremely proud of her daughter but sometimes found herself wondering rather wistfully if Chloe would ever marry and give her grandchildren. These thoughts were never spoken out loud and, on this morning, all talk was of exciting plans.

At eleven o'clock, the vicar declared the Easter Fayre open and almost all Fairmead, well wrapped up against the sharp wind, clapped and cheered. With great good humour, the Fayre got underway. To most people's satisfaction, tradition had been adhered to and everything was exactly the same as in previous years. Isabella and two other ladies ran the cake stall and it was always the first to sell out. Anyone who bought a cake took it home immediately and then returned to the green.

The children spent their pocket money on the hoopla stall

and coconut shy and threw ping-pong balls to win goldfish, which inevitably died within a week. When their money ran out, they chased each other round the green and up the trees.

Some hardy souls had brought fold-up chairs and had a little picnic, but most had left food warming in their ovens or chosen to dine out at Louisa's Café. Everyone 'chatted for England', as Bessie wittily commented one year. It was as though people hadn't seen each other for a decade. A good time was certainly had by all.

By two o'clock, all the stalls were cleared and all the goldfish won. The women and children wandered off, still deep in absorbing conversations, but several of the men stayed to help Tom, William and James dismantle the stalls and tables and load them into Tom's van to be transported back to the school, where Miss Browning was waiting to supervise their storage in the Sports Shed. This was actually quite a large outbuilding and was a home for all those items too bulky to store in the classrooms. Miss Browning was adamant that it should have a clear-out every summer, in case it became merely a dumping ground. She allowed the village to store the stalls and trestle tables there, as the only other place would have been the church crypt.

To the great sadness, and indeed anger, of all in Fairmead, the village hall had been declared out of use. The building had been erected at roughly the same time as the school and was well over a hundred years old. For all those years, it had been perfectly adequate for the people of Fairmead, but eighteen months before the County Council, in its wisdom, had decreed that it was not suitable for people with disabilities. The toilets were too cramped and there was no wheelchair access. In vain, the Village had replied that any person in need was always helped and nobody had complained in over a hundred years. Yet despite petitions and letters to the local newspaper, the hall had had to close at the beginning of the year. A monster Christmas party had been the last important event held there and now the old hall was locked up and forlorn. One or two people had suggested that the proceeds of the Easter Fayre should be used to start a Hall Fund, but the amount required was so astronomical that the idea was soon dropped in favour of the African orphanage.

This problem weighed on William's mind as he helped to unload the stalls and tables. As an ex-accountant and experienced board member, he was not about to take this state of affairs lying down. He had spent many quiet moments wondering how the required funds could be raised. However, despite numerous phone calls to friends and business acquaintances, he had not so far had much success. The general opinion was that Fairmead could hire the hall in the nearby village of Oaklea and one or two had even hinted that they might be willing to consider buying, knocking down and building new houses, if permission could be obtained. William had hastily assured them that this was not an option and finished the conversation. Indeed, this was Fairmead's worst fear.

The hall was on the outskirts of the village about five minutes from Fairfield Gardens, along Bridge Road in the opposite direction to the church.

The Farmer Hawton of the time had sold a small piece of land, next to the road, to the people of Fairmead for a very reasonable amount, on the understanding that a village hall would be built. The fear now was that the present owner of the surrounding fields would sell, forcing the village to sell its own small plot. Fairmead did not want to lose its identity with large-scale development. Although the land was zoned for agricultural use at present, everyone knew the Council was under pressure from Government to build more houses and could easily change the use of the land.

Unknown to anyone, even Isabella, who knew most things going on in Fairmead, William had made contact with the present owner and laid all the cards on the table. He alone knew the outcome of these phone conversations, conducted well away from the village, in the office of his good friend Timothy Miller, of the law firm Miller Smythe Hitchin, at its prestigious address in Queen Anne Parade, Mansford.

CHAPTER 6

On Wednesday morning it was much warmer, but rain had replaced the wind. Isabella was up earlier than usual in preparation for the descent of Joel, Dan and Sam, who were coming at about eight thirty for a couple of hours while their mother went to see Dr Miles. She had not needed Tom to tell her that Liz was not well. The whole of Fairfield Gardens was aware, as were many others around Fairmead. She was also aware that Kate was to accompany her and knew that this must be more than a touch of flu.

William had arranged to go over the church accounts with Paul but Isabella was quite happy to entertain the boys, even on such a wet morning. She regarded them as three more grandchildren and was always more than willing to abandon housework in favour of playing.

Emily Whitehead was up at six, as was her custom. By eight o'clock she had washed the breakfast dishes, fed her old cat, Fluffy, and tidied her house, though as she kept everything as neat as a pin, it did not need much attention.

As she gathered together her raincoat and umbrella, she glanced out of the window and saw Kate hurrying up the path of number four. Emily was not in the habit of spying, but she knew that dear Liz was unwell and that her boys were going to

Isabella's while their mother went to see Dr Miles. She decided to keep that little family in the forefront of her prayers, as she made her way to the church.

Louisa's prayers were of a different kind entirely. She had just opened the shop, at eight o'clock sharp, and wandered into the small storeroom, only to find the unmistakable sign that mice had been there before her. Somehow, they had invaded during the night and targeted a packet of digestive biscuits. Louisa was extremely conscious of health regulations, particularly as the café was only next door.

Fortunately the tiny kitchen appeared to have avoided the menace. Swiftly she rummaged through her stock and found four mouse-traps. Then she plucked a packet of cheese from the cold cabinet and put a large lump in each. Although she did not feel her furry intruders would return during the day, she was taking no chances. Just as she had completed this task, her first customer arrived and the thought of mice receded, though it never completely disappeared during the day.

Molly had a slight dilemma as to what to do with the children on this horribly rainy day. James had left for work at seven thirty and the children were not yet back at school. Several ladies had already asked her for trims and perms, but she had told them she would not be working during school holidays and had made appointments for the following week. Cathy and Mark seemed perfectly happy playing with their new toys but Molly felt like going out. She was so used to getting up and setting off for work early that she felt restless.

As she was considering what to do, the phone rang and Megan's voice came on the line, with the sound of children's voices in the background and a baby's cry somewhere further away. She came straight to the point. Jack had been called back to the office urgently for a few hours, and Megan needed adult company, the girls were desperate to play with the new children. Would Molly be a saint and come over for the morning? This was an answer to her prayers, and Molly said they would be over in ten minutes.

Sophia had arranged with Joy to have a trip into Mansford to visit Rockman's, the largest bookstore in town. On the upper level was a delightful café where they would have morning tea. Usually, Sophia looked at books on Eastern philosophies, Buddhism and Zen, meditation and vegetarianism, but today she wanted to consult books on pregnancy and possibly buy one. Having no sisters and a mother in Spain, she felt in need of some up-to-date advice. Paul was to be shut away in their lounge with William, getting to grips with the church accounts. She knew this was the only thing he did not enjoy about being a vicar and it would make him slightly grumpy for an hour afterwards.

They were going in Joy's car, much to Sophia's relief, as she hated driving in Mansford in the rain. Joy was more than pleased to go out with her friend. She had been planning to do some gardening, but this was impossible in the wet and she was looking forward to perusing some of the gorgeous books in Rockman's extensive gardening section. There were also a couple of books for school that she had been meaning to buy for some time.

★ ★ ★ ★ ★

As soon as Kate had delivered the boys to Isabella's, she and Liz set out to see Dr Miles, who visited the village on Wednesday mornings. His surgery was a back room in the Farmer's Arms. It opened on to the backyard and most people forgot that it was even connected to the pub. As all the patients knew each other, there was not much privacy and symptoms had been well discussed before going in to see the doctor. Dr Miles' main surgery was in Mansford but he visited several local villages during the week. He also held an honorary position at Mansford Royal and was much respected by all. He was now in his early sixties and should have been taking things easier, but he was blessed with abundant energy and refused to slow down.

Liz and Kate were waiting before he even arrived. They sat in silence, Kate respecting the fact that Liz needed a rest after the exertion of getting the boys ready and walking over to the Farmer's. Several other patients arrived soon afterwards and the little waiting room steamed gently as they removed their wet coats.

Just after nine o'clock, Liz went into see Dr Miles, leaving Kate outside. Usually Liz was there with one of the boys, as they were always bumping and cutting themselves, but today she told him she was the one who was not well. He gave her a thorough examination and took a blood sample, asking her to come again next week for the results, but said he did not feel there was anything wrong with her heart.

Liz was reassured by his calm kindness and left feeling much happier. Dr Miles, however, was quietly very concerned. He decided to drop the blood into the Royal's lab that afternoon rather than wait for the regular collection from his Mansford surgery. He would ask for it to be given priority. He had also seen Kate Manning waiting with Liz and knew that she was also worried.

Paul went to open the door as soon as he saw William emerge from his house. The rain was torrential and William was soaked in no time. Paul took his coat and umbrella and insisted that he remove his shoes and socks and borrow a thick pair of his own.

Sitting by the warm fire, drinking a cup of scalding coffee, William thought how much more pleasant this was than the parlour in the old vicarage. He was glad that Paul and Sophia lived in Fairfield Gardens. As the two men got down to work, one with enthusiasm and the other with resignation, their previous thoughts began to fade. Paul had been reflecting happily on their wonderful news and William had been wondering whether to tell Paul about his contact with Anthony Hawton in Australia, but he had decided it was probably better to wait and see what would transpire in the next few weeks.

Molly had wondered if Mark would be overwhelmed by all the girls, but the five children got on splendidly. Mark and Cathy were quiet children and their presence calmed the triplets, who were beginning to feel restricted in the house. They had brought a couple of their new toys in plastic bags, and everyone shared them and played remarkably well. Molly nursed Angie while Megan made coffee and cut up fruit for the children. By twelve o'clock when Jack returned and it was time to leave, everyone was firm friends. Sally, Jenny and Amy had been invited to play at Cathy and Mark's on Saturday morning, while their mum and dad took Angie into Mansford to do some shopping.

★ ★ ★ ★ ★

Sam, Dan and Joel were also having a lovely time at Granny Isabella's. They did not want to leave, as it was more fun at her house. Isabella guessed that Liz would appreciate the rest and rang to ask if they could stay longer. Liz was indeed grateful and decided to pop to bed for a little while.

She was still asleep at three o'clock when Tom arrived home early from work. It was far too wet for outside work and he had spent the day attempting to get his paperwork in order ready for next week's dreaded visit to the accountant. He was a strong, practical man, ideally suited to building but not to keeping receipts and checking bank statements. Early in his career, he had been fortunate to make the acquaintance of Edward Dowling, a junior partner of William Blackett, whose quarterly advice was much appreciated. Many times he had saved Tom from the clutches of the taxman, but he was an unusually outspoken man who did not hesitate to admonish Tom on his tax account-keeping whenever he thought it was necessary.

At first Tom thought Liz and the boys were out, but her car was still there. Finding her just emerging from a little nap, he went to make a cup of tea. The two of them sat by the fire, enjoying the unaccustomed peace and quiet, while Liz told him about her trip to the doctor's.

Just as they were finishing their tea, the doorbell rang and, to their surprise, Dr Miles was standing there under an enormous black umbrella. Liz stayed by the fire while Tom bustled about, taking the doctor's wet coat and making another cup of tea. Liz was silent and sat very still, as though alerted by a sixth sense.

Once they were all settled, Dr Miles told them the reason for his visit. In his kindly way, he said that he had asked for Liz's blood test to be hurried through and wanted to tell her the result as soon as possible. He said he was glad Tom was there because the news was not very good.

The result seemed to indicate that Liz had an acute form of leukaemia. This was why she had been feeling so tired. It also explained why she had had a couple of nose bleeds recently and swollen ankles in the evening. Her red cell count was now very low and it was imperative she have a transfusion immediately. He had taken the liberty of informing the hospital that she would be arriving late afternoon or early evening.

Liz sat calmly, but Tom couldn't believe it and questions poured from him. Dr Miles knew that everyone reacts to bad news differently and that some need time for it all to sink in. Suddenly, Tom seemed to remember Liz and, putting his arms round her, he looked like he was about to cry. But, strangely, Liz felt vindicated. She now had a reason for her weariness and inability to cope. She was also, for some reason, pleased that it was not her heart. The very last thing she wanted was for Tom to break down. She needed everyone to be strong and positive. Her own mind was switching to organizational mode and, within five seconds, she had decided that Isabella could have the boys to stay, her parents in Devon should be rung, she would take her new nightie and Tom could have the two pork chops in the freezer for his tea.

As if in a dream, Liz kissed the boys and Isabella, put a

couple of things in an overnight bag and they drove off in the rain towards Mansford Royal. Dr Miles was to meet them in the main entrance and would speed their way through the formalities. Both Liz and Tom were deep in their own thoughts and hardly noticed any details of the journey.

Like wildfire, news of Liz's diagnosis spread through Fairfield Gardens and out into the village. How this had happened, nobody was quite sure. By early evening, Isabella was at the Norris' house collecting clothes for the boys, having assured them that they could bring over any toys and games they would like the next morning when it might have stopped raining. William was busy making up the beds in the room usually reserved for grandchildren. Dan had been close to tears when his mummy and daddy had driven off so hastily but Granny Isabella had said they would all go and visit mummy tomorrow afternoon and now he and his brothers were watching cartoons on television.

Isabella's heart was heavy for her friend. She knew that these days there were wonderful treatments for all sorts of ailments, but many years ago, her own little sister had died of leukaemia at only five years old. The memory weighed heavily on her. But as she left the Norris' trying to hang on to plastic bags and a colourful umbrella, she put on her usual smile and knew that she must be the strong one for Tom and the boys. Despite the serious circumstances, she could not help but be excited at having a family to look after again and had insisted that Tom have his tea with them every day, so he could see the boys before going to visit Liz.

Kate was not at all surprised at the news. She knew that Dr

Miles would tell her exactly what type of leukaemia it was when the hospital had carried out its own tests. Several years ago, while still at the big London hospital, she had worked for a while on the haematology ward and she knew that Dr Miles would trust her to be discreet with her knowledge. While, no doubt, everybody would rush to get details from the internet, she was the only one with first-hand experience.

Paul and Sophia were shocked when Isabella rang to tell them what had happened, not least because they had been so caught up in their own wonderful news that they had hardly noticed Liz's increasing lethargy. Paul rang Dr Miles immediately and took no comfort from hearing that not even Tom had realised how serious it was. He was filled with guilt and felt he had failed as a pastor and neighbour.

It was a good couple of hours before Sophia's calm commonsense could persuade him to stop thinking about himself and concentrate on Liz and her family. Feeling much more at peace, Paul strode through the rain to the church, entered through the still-unlocked side door and found his favourite nook. Then he bent his head and began to pray for Liz and all his sick parishioners. Soon he was totally absorbed and his prayer was widened to include the whole world.

Unseen by Paul, Emily was already there. She had returned home mid afternoon after visiting her friends in St Mary's Home. Usually, she stayed for afternoon tea at about 3.30, but it was such a dismal, wet day that she had left early and waded home in her rubber boots, swathed in an ancient raincoat and protected by an equally ancient umbrella. As she was sipping a hot cup of tea and enjoying the warmth of the fire, she had seen Dr Miles arriving at number four, then, a short time later, Liz, Tom and the doctor had emerged, gone over to Isabella's and all driven off, looking very subdued. Emily would never dream of interfering, but when she saw Isabella going over to collect things from the Norris', she was sufficiently concerned to get her still wet umbrella and go next door to see if anything was wrong. She was saddened to hear the news and went straight up to church to pray for dear Liz, at least an hour earlier than she would normally go for choir practice.

★ ★ ★ ★ ★

Joy was deeply engrossed in a gloriously-illustrated gardening book bought that very day in Rockman's. She and Sophia had had a lovely time looking at the books and having coffee in the charming café. They had even braved the wet to go for a wander round Selby's, Mansford's most prestigious department store, before enjoying an excellent lunch in their restaurant. It had been a most satisfying day. Joy had managed to obtain several interesting books for school and these lay on her desk, while she was curled in her large armchair in front of the fire with her new gardening book.

When the phone rang she sighed with slight irritation, wishing she had thought to move the phone closer, but when she heard Sophia's voice telling her of their neighbours' troubles all thoughts of gardening vanished and she asked immediately what she could do to help. Sophia felt that they could approach Tom and see if he would like them to tidy up for him and maybe ask Isabella if they could help with the boys' washing. Joy thought these were good ideas and returned to her book in a thoughtful frame of mind.

Megan and Jack were also very sorry when told, especially Megan, who was very friendly with Liz and often had coffee with her when the children were at school. She knew her friend was feeling under the weather and had thought she was staying away in case the baby caught anything. She herself had been so busy with Angie and the triplets and Jack being away that she had not had a moment to think of anything else except her own family. She felt quite devastated that Liz had not felt able to confide in her and was determined to visit her as soon as possible, which would be fairly easy while Jack was still on holiday. Jack said he would keep an eye on Tom's garden, especially his little vegetable patch near the back door. Having decided to help in these small ways, they were distracted by Jenny and Amy shouting and pulling each other's hair, while Sally looked on smugly, since both her sisters wanted to borrow her best Barbie dress.

Molly and James were probably the last in Fairfield Gardens to hear about Liz, because somehow the receiver had been left off the phone, possibly by Cathy, who liked to play at pretending to phone her imaginary friend, Lulu. Molly had caught her doing this twice already today and had decided to buy her a realistic toy phone the next day in Mansford. She thought she would buy Mark a toy car, which she knew he particularly wanted. She did not want the children to think they would get something every time they went shopping, but James had suggested telling them that they were little welcome gifts from everyone in Fairfield Gardens and, unless she thought of a better idea, that was what she would tell them.

Molly discovered the errant receiver when she went to answer the front doorbell. It was Isabella, who had been trying to ring with no success, and had popped round to make sure all was well. As she stepped into the lighted hallway, out of the dark rain, Molly could see that her usual cheerful smile was missing.

When she heard about Liz, she was most upset. Like others in Fairfield Gardens, she was dismayed that she had been so taken up with her own affairs. Though she felt quite nervous about having three extra boisterous boys in the house, she bravely offered to have them any time Isabella needed to go out or just to have a break. With her broad smile returning, Isabella thanked her heartily, privately thinking she and William could manage between them and she would spare poor Molly, whose only experience of children had come in the last few days.

Dan, Sam and Joel had been subdued during tea. Their father had not returned from the hospital, but he had phoned to say Mummy was fine and sent her love. She couldn't come to the phone because the doctors were finding out what was wrong with her. She hoped they could come and see her tomorrow. Granny Isabella had said of course they would all go tomorrow afternoon. They had got ready for bed, with no protest, and were now having a story on the sofa with William, who said he was more than capable of putting three little boys to bed and would enjoy its being just the boys while Isabella went to choir practice. He knew how much she enjoyed this outing and, despite the suspicion that his charges would not be able to sleep until their daddy returned, he robustly shooed his wife out of the door.

After informing Molly of the sad news, Isabella marched up the wet road, where she was just in time to catch her old friend, Jane Simmons from the Farmer's Arms, disappearing into the dimly-lit church. The turnout was small. Molly and James Standing had already asked Emily to excuse them, as this was their first week with Cathy and Mark. In future, Louisa had promised to come round and sit with them for the hour or so. If they were all ready for bed, she would give them supper and read them a story. Louisa had offered to do this, partly because she had become very fond of the children and partly because she missed her own grandchildren in America. She had visited them several times but it was not the same as having them on the doorstep. They were now about the same ages as Cathy and Mark, and Louisa liked to think that she could become an honorary grandparent to the dear little ones who had come to live next door.

The next morning dawned blessedly fine, though everything was still wet from the day before. It had become William's habit to take little Scrappy out for a morning constitutional about seven thirty before enjoying his own breakfast. In all weathers he would proceed up Fairfield Gardens, then turn left along Bridge Road, past the sad village hall and thence through Farmer Hawton's fields, by means of several public footpaths. He would double back, passing the church and emerging into the village itself near the green. He would usually be the first customer at the Village Stores and, with his paper under his arm, he would stride back home, anticipating the mouthwatering smell of frying bacon as he opened the kitchen door.

But this morning he was late setting off because, despite

falling asleep at a very late hour, the boys desperately wanted to accompany him. Scrappy was in his element with three exciting new playmates, and William felt that all his attempts at training had been in vain. Isabella had insisted that the boys wear their wellies and raincoats, in case of further downpours and, as these were still at their own house, William and the boys had had to go and find them. Tom had left for work just after six, but fortunately he had given the Blacketts a key.

By eight o'clock they were ready. William felt like the Pied Piper as he led all his charges down the garden path. When they had finally gone, Isabella attempted a little tidying up and then turned her attention to breakfast. She wondered how Liz was coping with hospital and tried to remember all Tom had told them last night, but it had been late and she had been very tired. He himself had been quite vague about such details as what kind of leukaemia it was, what the treatment would be or how long she might be in hospital. He did know that she had been given two lots of blood and, as a result, felt very much better and he had left her in a much happier frame of mind.

Kate, on the other hand, was much clearer about it all because she had spoken to Dr Miles during the evening. They were waiting for the specialist to give his opinion, but Dr Miles felt quite certain that it would require chemotherapy and, possibly, a bone marrow transplant. Kate sincerely hoped that that would not be the case and decided to see what Paul thought about organising a Prayer Circle for Liz. She knew many people in Fairmead would be only too happy to be a part.

Paul had had much the same idea the previous evening up at the church and was very pleased when Kate called in just after breakfast. He, Sophia and Kate agreed to door-knock everyone in Fairmead, whether parishioners or not. In addition, Kate would ask Louisa to put a notice about the Prayer Circle in the Village Stores window and Sophia would see that it was mentioned in the Church Magazine.

Emily was at that very moment in Church praying, particularly for Liz, and deciding that she would help on a practical level too. As she left the church, she saw William, the boys and Scrappy returning home in great good humour and her heart felt lightened by the happy sight. She decided to call in briefly to see Martha Turner, an old lady of ninety-six who lived in the High Street, before going to Isabella's. In about an hour she was in that lady's kitchen and had somehow persuaded her to allow her neighbour to help with the housework.

Just as Emily had started methodically tidying up, Joy and Sophia arrived to offer their services in the laundry department. They said they would wash and iron for Tom and the boys. Isabella was quite overcome and had to sit down. She knew that she wasn't quite as young as she used to be and, though the boys had been with them only a short time, she was feeling more tired than she cared to admit. She had also promised to take the young ones to see their mummy that afternoon and wasn't really looking forward to shepherding three very lively boys. Joy must have been a mind-reader because, as though it was the thing she most wanted to do in the whole world, she suddenly asked if she could go with them to see Liz. Isabella said she would love to have her company, though the boys were a little less keen to be seen with their teacher.

CHAPTER 7

After an overcast, though mild, few days, Monday was a perfect spring day, reminiscent of Easter Sunday. Everybody said wouldn't you just know it, on the first day back at school.

Megan had been rather looking forward to this day, with Jack back at work and the girls back at school, and was planning to try and catch up on neglected housework, at least when Angie was asleep. In fact it was quite hard to get back into the early morning routine. Jack was very good about getting his own breakfast and organising himself, but he left about seven thirty for an early meeting and Megan was left to try and hurry the girls along. Amy hated waking early and had to be almost tipped out of bed, which left her in a very grumpy mood, and this morning she seemed to be more uncooperative than usual. Jenny said she was feeling sick and didn't want any breakfast and Sally had wet the bed.

In the middle of all this commotion, Angie uncharacteristically started screaming to be fed, which was awkward, as Megan was still breast-feeding. Eventually the girls settled down and began to get dressed. Megan thanked her lucky stars that she had thought to lay out all their clothes the night before, despite arriving home late from Nana's. Order was restored and they managed to leave the house by quarter to nine.

The Standing household was considerably quieter, but tensions were running quite high. Molly was trying her best to appear calm and confident, knowing that Mark and Cathy were nervous about starting a new school. Luckily, they had met Miss Taylor, their new teacher, several times and liked her very much. They also knew quite a few of the children in their new class, but now that the morning had actually arrived, they were silent and strained.

James had arranged to start work late, so he could be there with Molly to take the children to school for the first time. The two of them, however, felt out of their depth. They had no experience of getting children ready for school and did not want to upset them by making them hurry. As a result, Cathy and Mark were still eating their breakfast at eight thirty and Molly was getting quite worried. Whatever would the other mothers think if she could not get her children to school in time on the first day?

James suddenly decided that enough was enough and, in his best managerial manner, told the children to brush their teeth and be ready in five minutes. This was exactly what Mark and Cathy needed, and thus directed, they were waiting at the front door by 8.38. Molly helped Cathy zip up her jacket and they emerged into the bright sunshine, just as Isabella was shooing the boys down the garden path.

Isabella might not have had as much energy as Molly, but she had vastly more experience of getting children off to school. She was enjoying having a family again and, even though William grumbled now and then about the mess and the noise, she knew that he was happy with the arrangement too.

The boys had been every day to see their mother, once with Isabella and Joy, the other days with their father. They all thought Liz looked really well, was quite lively and had some colour in her cheeks. However, they knew that this was something of an illusion, caused by the fact that she had had several blood transfusions which had greatly boosted her red cell count. Thankfully, the specialist had given his opinion that a bone-marrow transplant might not be necessary and chemotherapy might do the trick. This week there would be several tests to make sure Liz was fit enough to stand the strong chemo, then a start would be made next week. From that time on, the boys would not be allowed to visit for fear of infection. Liz's white cells would drop to zero for a time and she would be moved to a single room, while staff and visitors would have to wear gowns.

Poor Tom had thought that he might lose Liz and didn't know how he would carry on without her. Each evening, Paul had slipped next door for five minutes to see how he was and offer him any words of comfort he could. He never made Tom feel uncomfortable and was always welcome.

Once Tom heard the hopeful report from the specialist, he felt a weight had been lifted. In an amazingly quick time, he found himself settling into a routine. He was used to waking early, getting his own breakfast and leaving for work before Liz and the boys were up, so in that respect, there was no change. Now, in the late afternoon, after finishing work, he would go straight to the Royal to see Liz, leaving about five-thirty to go and have tea at Isabella and William's. He would stay and play with the boys until about seven thirty, having supervised bath time, which usually started about seven. When he got home he would force himself to do about an hour's paperwork before watching a bit of television, with heavy eyes. He was always dead to the world by nine thirty.

Much as he detested the business side of his work, he made a big effort to keep up to things. In the early days of their marriage, he had let it all slide in favour of taking on more and more building work, which he loved. The result was complete chaos, and almost the loss of his business. Liz had found him a wonderful, though expensive, accountant who patiently sorted through Tom's drawers and boxes and plastic bags of receipts, accounts and letters from the taxman. Eventually some order was restored. Tom was shown how to keep simple books and how to file the mountains of paperwork his business seemed to generate. Being completely computer-illiterate, he was happy to continue using pen and paper, and his accountant had promised to keep an eye on everything by checking once a quarter.

Tom was more grateful than he could say that the worry of the boys had been so competently lifted from his shoulders by Isabella and William. He knew that they were happy and well cared for. He also had the suspicion that the older couple were in their element having children around the house again.

On the first day back at school, Dan, Sam and Joel were up very much earlier than the other Fairfield Gardens children. They had solemnly promised, before going to bed on Sunday evening, that if they were allowed to go for the morning walk with Grandpa William and Scrappy, they would eat breakfast and get dressed with no arguments and be ready by half past eight. All had gone to plan, though it was nearer quarter to nine by the time they were completely ready, one of Joel's socks having disappeared mysteriously in the night.

As they hurried down the path, they saw Mark and Cathy pushing through their gate and ran over to greet them. Then they all proceeded at a smart pace up the Gardens. As they turned into Bridge Road they saw Sally, Jenny and Amy skipping along in front of their mother, who was pushing the pram.

All the Fairfield Gardens children arrived at the school gates in a noisy bunch and raced to be first into the playground. Molly and James were very relieved to see that Mark and Cathy had cheered up tremendously as soon as they had seen the other children and were now quite submerged in the milling throng, waiting for the bell to ring. Isabella was a little out of breath, having marched to school rather more quickly than she would have chosen, but she was basking in the happy feeling of being with other mothers in the playground again. It was several years since she had had the pleasure of chatting and gossiping in this way and it made her feel ten years younger. Megan was also enjoying being a centre of attention, with other mums admiring little Angie, who was looking cherubic and playing her part to perfection.

At exactly nine o'clock Miss Browning came out to ring the bell, accompanied by Mrs Evans and Miss Taylor. As the children began to form class lines, Molly and James collected Cathy and Mark and took them over to Joy, who smiled at them kindly and guided them to their places in the line. Cathy was near the front with the babies, with Dan behind her and a little girl she remembered from the Easter Fayre in front. Mark was near the back of the line, as he was now a big boy of seven. He was behind Joel but didn't know the girl behind him. He could see the triplets somewhere in the middle of the line and Sam was near the front of Mrs Evans' line.

As several mothers, including Molly and Isabella, blew surreptitious kisses, the children marched inside, following their teachers. The school consisted of three classrooms, only one of which had an exit to the playground. Every teacher for the last hundred years had wondered what the architect had been thinking of, as there was no corridor and children from the far classrooms had to tiptoe through the end room to use the toilets, which were at the far side of the playground. Miss Browning, as head teacher, had the room at the far end for the very good reasons that her children were the oldest and could be expected to move around quietly, also, as this room doubled as a staff-room, a corner could be set aside without little hands prying.

The middle room was Mrs Evan's domain and she ruled over the lower juniors. She was a large, happy woman, nearing retirement, and her class was a happy, quiet one. This state of affairs was ideal for Miss Browning on one side and Miss Taylor on the other. Joy had the room with the exit, as her children were much more likely to need the toilets urgently. She sometimes worried that her little ones made rather a lot of noise, especially when dancing was involved, but Mrs Evans always assured her that the old walls were so thick that she never heard a thing.

On this first morning back after the holidays, the children filed through to Miss Browning's room for assembly. It was quite a squash but was the only place available. The oldest children stood at their desks, while Mrs Evans' children stood at the end of each desk and the youngest ones stood at the front near the teacher's desk. Miss Browning had invited the vicar to lead an Easter-inspired assembly and he was already waiting as the children squeezed in. He loved this duty, the way the children looked at him with large, bright eyes and the way they sang the hymns with gusto. He also loved to catch glimpses of boys pinching each other in the back row or girls giggling at a private joke. But of course these shenanigans were not allowed to continue very long, as Miss Browning's sharp eye was everywhere.

As the last child settled into her place, Miss Browning raised her hand a fraction and chatting began to cease. In a remarkably short time, silence was achieved, the vicar introduced and the children welcomed back. Assembly had begun.

CHAPTER 8

Out in the playground, gossip continued apace. Many had not seen each other since before Easter and were eager to fill in the missing days. Molly, however, was not one of them, as she had her first hair appointment at 9.15 at the far end of the High Street. James was also in a hurry to be off, so they pecked each other on the cheek and, as in the old days, rushed off to their separate occupations.

The moment Molly turned out of the school gate, she slowed to a snail's pace in order to enjoy this glorious morning. She breathed in the clear air and said a heartfelt prayer of thanks for her present life, for the fact that she lived in a beautiful village, didn't have to face London's Underground, was still able to do a job she loved and, most of all, had a complete family to return to at the end of the day. As she progressed along the High Street, she thought of dear Cathy and Mark. Despite the upheavals of their lives, they were sweet, loving children and she knew that she and James would move heaven and earth to give them the best life possible. She also blessed their dear Grandma, who had given them a wonderful start and taught her so much about bringing up children. While she was at it, she said a little prayer for their parents, sadly only vague names, and thanked them for the gift of Cathy and Mark.

At this point her thoughts turned abruptly to the matter in hand. She knocked at the rather shabby door of an old cottage set in a slightly overgrown garden. As though she had been waiting on the other side of the door, Clarissa Jones opened it and greeted Molly with a toothless grin. She laughed and apologised. Her dentures had cracked the previous day and the Home Help lady had dropped them into the dentist's in Mansford for her. With the ice broken, Molly arranged Clarissa in a chair and unpacked her hairdressing equipment, knowing that she would not be leaving before she had had a good long chat and cup of tea.

Isabella was enjoying company every bit as much as Molly and was in no hurry to return home. William had been slightly evasive when asked what he would be doing in Mansford that morning; he was probably going to meet one of his many friends, who took extended business lunches as a matter of course, and he certainly needed the break after his sterling efforts with the boys. She could not have managed without him over the last few days and she certainly did not begrudge him a day out.

She herself had asked Emily Whitehead to come for coffee, or in her case a cup of tea, at 11 o'clock, both because she was extremely fond of the older lady and as a way of thanking her for her unobtrusive help since the boys had arrived.

Megan was also enjoying the unaccustomed freedom of being able to talk to adults without constantly keeping an eye on the children. Angie had fallen asleep in her pram and the dog was sitting quietly, its lead tied to the handle. As she talked animatedly to her friends she hugged to herself the delightful prospect of a day almost by herself at home, catching up with much neglected housework, and possibly finding ten minutes to peruse her favourite magazine, maligned by Jack as being total rubbish. With this happy thought in mind, she excused herself after about ten minutes and set off for the Village Stores to purchase her publication, keeping one eye on Angie who was still asleep but due to wake for a feed at any time.

She found Louisa surrounded by boxes of soft drinks, filling the cabinet with cans and bottles and gently tutting to herself, torn between her businesswoman's desire to make money and her desire for healthy living. Since her own slight stroke several years before and her husband's death from a heart attack, she had read extensively of the role of nutrition in preventing illness and adapted her own diet accordingly. When she saw Megan, she gladly abandoned cabinet-filling and settled for five minutes to discuss babies, a topic which was uppermost in her mind this morning after a more than welcome phone call from her son in America informing her of the glad tidings of another grandchild, due about the beginning of October.

★ ★ ★ ★ ★

Sophia's mind was also occupied with baby thoughts as she moved quietly round her beloved plants, rearranging them after the weekend crowds and watering each carefully. After a busy couple of days taken up with church affairs, she always enjoyed her Mondays at Fantastic Flowers. It was a peaceful day both for herself and the plants. Jim and Anita, the owners, usually took Mondays off, though they lived only five minutes away and could be there in no time if any difficulties arose. Sophia was in her element and always returned home feeling renewed in body, mind and spirit.

On this morning, it was such a beautiful day that she knew she would spend as much of it as possible out of doors. She was feeling particularly well and looking forward to her first hospital visit in a couple of weeks. She had bought a wonderful book in Rockman's last week when she had gone into Mansford with Joy on that dreadfully wet day. It was a comprehensive guide to pregnancy and she had devoured it in less than a week. Even Paul had been interested enough to read some of the sections, though she could have sworn he turned quite pale in places.

While Sophia was beginning her happy morning among the flowers, Kate's day was well underway. She had never had trouble waking in the morning, which was just as well, in light of her job. This morning she had risen at 5.30am, left the house at 6.15 and was on her ward by 6.55, there being virtually no traffic and plenty of parking in the hospital car park at that early hour. In no time she had familiarized herself with all that had happened during her absence and had plunged happily back into the work she loved most in the world. During the course of the morning she remembered Liz, who would still be undergoing tests in preparation for the start of chemotherapy. Her ward was not at all far from the children's ward and she made a mental note to pop in on her way to lunch.

At that moment Liz was thinking of her boys, rather than the imminent treatment. Having received several blood transfusions and being waited on hand and foot, she felt a different woman. The other three ladies in her room were pleasant but pleasingly quiet and Liz was rather enjoying the laziness of being able to choose between reading, watching television or doing a crossword.

Of course she knew that once the chemo started, it would be a different matter and she would feel extremely uncomfortable. She had carefully read the little booklet provided by the hospital and one of the nurses had told her, quite graphically, that she would feel as though she had been run over by a steamroller. She also knew that she would be moved to a single room and not allowed visits from the children, in order to limit the chance of infection. Even adults, staff and visitors, would have to wash their hands before approaching, wear a gown and be honour-bound not to come if they had even the slightest sniffle. So far, the boys had visited several times and she was hoping Tom would be able to bring them this afternoon, though she knew it would mean his finishing work a little early in order to pick them up from school. But she did so want to hear about their first day back and it was too much to expect dear Isabella and William to bring them. They were doing so much already and she didn't know how she could ever thank them enough. Others were also helping, she knew; Joy and Sophia with the laundry and Emily Whitehead, in her quiet way. Tom's family were also helping in many ways, though his parents were not too well themselves. Her own family had a smallholding ten miles the other side of Mansford and spring was a busy time for them, but her parents and two younger brothers had managed to visit yesterday and her mother would help as much as possible once she returned home.

But it was really no use trying to plot and plan. Liz was beginning to realise that the best way was to allow things to take their course and to relinquish trying to control everything, which could be quite difficult – after all, it was part of a mother's job description. On that thought, she lay back, closed her eyes and enjoyed the warm sun flooding through the window on to her bed.

Less than a mile away from the Royal, William was parking his car in the happy knowledge that he could stay all day if he wished and not get a ticket. He was leaving his car in the Visitors' Parking spot of Miller Smythe Hitchin, Solicitors, on Queen Anne Parade, and was to walk through the centre of town to the King's Head, where he would have an early lunch with his old friend Timothy Miller. He was, however, quite early for this appointment and, as it was such a perfect morning, he decided to take his newspaper and sit in Central Park, a delightfully green oasis in the middle of the city. He felt in need of some peace and quiet after the hectic morning. Sam, Joel and Dan had all woken extremely early and, with much laughing and jostling, managed to throw on old tracksuits and be ready to go with him for Scrappy's walk. This was no hardship at all on a gorgeous spring morning, but his breakfast was much delayed as the boys' needs took precedence over his and he was left frying his own bacon as Isabella set off for school. He knew she would linger there, making the most of the company, so having eaten a less-than-perfect breakfast, he had strolled up to the Village Stores for his paper, an hour later that usual, and taken it with him to Mansford.

After a satisfying assembly, Paul was also anticipating a most pleasant half hour taking Lady for a walk. Lady was rather a grand name for such a cuddly, friendly puppy and 'Heinz 57 Varieties' would probably have been a better one but there was certainly no doubting the fact that acquiring her from Megan was one of the best things he and Sophia had done. Unlike her brother, Scrappy, she was calm and placid and very easily trained.

Paul had never in his life owned an animal and had been somewhat dismayed when Sophia had brought her home. Now, however, he was as smitten as she was and took great pride walking her around the village. He also felt that little Lady had awoken dormant paternal emotions which were sure to be magnified many times in a few months' time when their child was born.

On this lovely morning, he had decided to walk along the stream near his old home. A narrow path wound along beside it and wild daffodils shone on both sides. These short, hardy flowers always touched a chord in Paul's heart and he marvelled at how they had survived for countless years untouched by human hand. Humming *Morning Has Broken*, one of his favourite hymns, he found Lady in his back garden, attached her lead and set off with a jaunty step.

Miss Browning, however, was by no means in such high spirits and her mind was seriously distracted from the spelling lesson she was giving to her seniors. For the last few days she had been desperately trying to find a replacement cleaner. Poor Liz would not be available for many months, if ever, and Miss Browning was at her wits' end. The office had been no help whatsoever, as it had been closed for the Easter holidays. When she had phoned that morning, a girl with an unforgivably bad phone manner had implied that the Education Office had much more important issues to attend to and she would be well advised to find somebody herself. This was going to be easier said than done, as the hours were few and the pay even less. It had been hard enough finding Liz, but she had turned out to be a real treasure, always reliable and always doing a good job.

Miss Browning wondered if the best way might be to put an ad in the Village Stores' window and pray that somebody local would like to oblige. In the meantime, she herself would have to perform the duties, on top of her own as class teacher and Headmistress. She couldn't ask Joy, as she knew she was already helping Isabella out with Dan, Sam and Joel's washing, and Margot Evans was a little old for that sort of thing. It was a problem she hoped would be solved before the end of the week.

In the room next door but one to Miss Browning's, Joy's mind was totally occupied by her little ones. They were starting the morning with activities and, in groups, were attempting to get to grips with such pursuits as playing Word Bingo, assembling large jigsaws, cutting pictures out of magazines and writing on small chalkboards. One group of slightly older children was sitting in a corner with Miss Taylor looking with interest at their new reading books. Two mothers were keeping an eye on things, though they had a definite tendency to focus most of their attention on their own children. However, Joy was far too good a teacher to let anything escape her notice and was constantly on the lookout for potential trouble. She kept a particularly watchful eye on the two Norris boys and also on the new children, Cathy and Mark. She felt privileged to know their circumstances and was willing to treat them in a more indulgent way than usual. She was slightly concerned about the report on Cathy and Mark, sent by their previous school, detailing their lack of progress, though stressing their exemplary behaviour.

As she had this thought, John Fyne kicked Tony Pearson's jigsaw, destroying it in an instant. Tony retaliated by punching John, but Miss Taylor was there in double quick time and chaos was averted.

★ ★ ★ ★ ★

Just before the end of school, William's car drew up outside the church. He had seen Paul disappearing inside and wanted a word with him before returning home. His friend was more than pleased to see him, as he had been just about to make a much-postponed start on clearing out one of the larger vestry cupboards.

Paul pulled out two chairs. Never a man for a great deal of small talk, William came straight to the point. Timothy Miller, his lunch companion, had been the bearer of good tidings. It seemed that the council had had a slight change of heart concerning the Village Hall and the alterations needed to make it disability-accessible would be less extensive and therefore, less expensive. A letter stating, the new requirements would be arriving in the fullness of time.

Timothy's news did not stop there. He had also had

communication with Anthony Hawton, whose father's estate had been handled by Miller Smythe Hitchin. The upshot was that old Farmer Hawton, who had lived all his life in Fairmead and loved the village, had bequeathed an amount of money to be used for the village as his son thought best. Timothy's suggestion was that the Hall alterations, and subsequent reopening, would be a very worthy use for this gift. He also mentioned that Anthony himself would be returning shortly to take up a new position in London and would be having a holiday in the area first, thus being able to supervise the undertaking himself.

Paul had known this was going to be a great day, from the moment the sun had woken him up. The reopening of the Hall would be a wonderful thing for the village. Since the New Year, meetings, clubs and activities had struggled to find suitable venues. Some, such as Ladies' Gentle Exercise, had managed in various members' homes. Others, such as Whist and Trivia Nights, had been allowed to use a classroom at the school. Others, such as Cubs and Brownies, had been cancelled altogether, due to their boisterous nature. This had been of particular concern to William, who as Cub Leader, believed strongly in the positive value of the Scouting Movement.

The Scouts and Guides were more fortunate, as their gatherings were held just this side of Mansford. It was however considered too far for their younger brothers and sisters.

William's thoughts were leaping ahead, still with the Cubs, and he was wondering if Joel and young Mark next door would like to join Sam when they reformed. Suddenly he realised that Paul was still talking about the building work for the Hall and that Tom Norris' name was being mentioned. Immediately, he clicked back into accountant mode. Costs were discussed and the two men agreed to put forward the possibility of asking Tom's firm to do the work at the next Village Affairs Committee meeting. This was scheduled for Thursday evening at St Mary's Home.

That evening another meeting took place, in Emily Whitehead's neat little sitting room. Many people throughout the village, including non-parishioners, and indeed non-believers, had pledged their support for the Prayer Circle and had promised to say a little prayer for Liz twice a day, about noon and six in the evening. The prayer, suggested by Emily, took only a few moments and it was just a question of remembering. A couple of the ladies had suggested a more formal prayer group to pray for Liz and all those unwell in Fairmead, and this was their first get-together. Emily was expecting five, including herself, and had arranged chairs in a semi-circle around the fire, which was gas but had pleasingly-real flames dancing unevenly, as the evening had turned decidedly chilly, with a rising wind.

Sophia was the first to arrive, followed immediately by Kate, who wasn't particularly religious but felt Liz needed all the help she could get and, through her years nursing, had often observed that those who were prayed for seemed to do better than others. As a result of this, she made it her habit to pray each day for the dear children in her care and had been pleased to support Emily's Prayer Circle. The last two ladies arrived together, unmarried sisters in their fifties. Both worked for the Library Service in Mansford and both supported every church association and activity. They were well known to the other ladies, as they were also in the choir.

In a few moments, all had settled into their chairs and relaxed in the warmth. For thirty minutes, they were enfolded in peace and tranquillity as Emily gently led them through prayers, hymns and silent reflection.

CHAPTER 9

By Friday morning Fairmead in general and Fairfield Gardens in particular were abuzz with the welcome news. The Village Affairs Committee had met the previous evening at the Vicarage, seated around Paul and Sophia's dining table, enjoying the warmth of their fire and relishing coffee and homemade oat biscuits. All six members were present and all knew what was to be discussed but, in time-honoured tradition, they feigned delighted surprise when William disclosed the information concerning the Hall.

He told them that Timothy Miller had known for years of Farmer Hawton's small bequest but, as it was entirely his son's decision how it should be used, he had felt unable to disclose either the fact of the bequest or the amount. With Timothy's tacit support, William had decided, as a desperate last resort, to contact Anthony Hawton and see if he could help in any way. Anthony was not hard to locate, as he was a successful lawyer in Sydney, and once or twice William had spied his name in *The Times*. Now that the Council had revised its requirements William felt the small bequest would almost cover the cost.

The all-important letter detailing the revised schedule of work had arrived that morning. Anthony had been sympathetic, but on the two occasions he had spoken to William he had been on the point of flying off to some distant part of the country on important matters and had felt unable to give his full attention to the Village he had left many years before. He had, however, promised to call Mr Miller when he had a little free time. This he had done the previous week, confirming the bequest and agreeing whole-heartedly that it should be used on the Hall. He had also added that his work would be taking him to London for a year. Before commencing, he would be taking a short holiday, visiting childhood haunts and reacquainting himself with his roots. He would be arriving in the second week of May and had already booked for two weeks at the prestigious Manor Hotel in Mansford.

Excited chatter broke out as William took breath and sipped his coffee, now grown decidedly cold. Paul offered to heat it in the microwave, and while this operation was under way, William coughed politely to gain attention and continued laying out his plans. He wondered what the others would think about asking Tom Norris to do the job. This suggestion was unanimously accepted and Paul said he would speak to him later that evening when he popped round for his regular five-minute visit.

The meeting then lost all semblance of formality and was succeeded by animated chat. After about ten minutes, Paul glanced at his watch and suddenly resumed his role as chairperson, as Sophia would say. He called the meeting to order and the last fifteen minutes were spent hastily getting through other business: the weekly roster for litter collection; the tending of the village green; the adding of Clarissa Jones' garden to the lawn-mowing list and the advertising in the Stores window for volunteers to form the Flower Show Committee. All items were dealt with speedily and the Village Affairs Committee turned out into the chilly night much pleased with their work.

Paul ran up the stairs to tell Sophia he was calling next door for a few minutes. She had decided to have a luxurious lingering bubble bath and read in bed while the Committee was hard at it downstairs. Though she still felt fit and well, she found that by evening she was quite weary and pleased to relax at home. Many evenings this was not possible, as she was the Vicar's wife and committed to so many organisations and activities, but whenever the opportunity arose she would welcome it gladly.

★ ★ ★ ★ ★

At number four, Tom was attempting to write invoices for several small jobs he had finished well before Easter. Though his mind knew that cash-flow depended on promptly-posted invoices, this duty often fell further and further behind. Liz had been so helpful many times giving him a hand, after the boys had gone to bed, though she had no office experience and had worked in a supermarket before Sam was born.

At the thought of Liz, Tom abandoned his invoice-writing. She had begun her eight days of intensive chemotherapy that morning, but had seemed little changed when he visited late afternoon. He always felt ill at ease in the hospital, being an active, outdoor man, and more than anything, he hated seeing all the tubes attached to his wife. But now she had been moved to a single room, he felt slightly less constrained, though in all honesty it seemed little more than a cell to him and he felt he would go mad with claustrophobia if he was in there all day like poor Liz.

Paul's knock startled him, but he knew who it would be and opened the door gladly. His friend's short visits were always most welcome. After hearing Tom's news with great sympathy, Paul told him of the outcome of the meeting next door, though, like the majority of Fairmead, Tom already knew about the Council's revised decision and Anthony Hawton's reappearance on the scene.

When he heard of the Committee's recommendation that his firm should do the work on the Hall, he was pleased, though not surprised, as Fairmead people always tried to give work to locals and Tom's work was always exceptionally good. Other quotes would, naturally, have to be obtained, but Tom's would be competitive and it was a foregone conclusion that he would be chosen.

As he was about to leave, Paul became aware of the jumble of papers on the dining room table and the lack of a computer. In his usual diffident way, he broached the subject of Tom's getting somebody to help with the bookwork, at least while Liz was away. This was something Tom had resisted through the years, insisting that such a small business could manage without help. However, in the last couple of years, work had increased as his good name had spread, and he now employed a third-year apprentice who could be left to attend to smaller jobs, though Tom always personally checked these on completion. He also had a first-year apprentice, two labourers and numerous contractors on call. It was all getting too much to handle, especially with visiting Liz every day and trying to keep the boys happy. He admitted as much, and Paul offered to put a notice in the Village Stores window for a person willing to do Tom's paperwork for a few hours a week.

Miss Browning's notice for a school cleaner had been answered within a day by old Bill Hughes' great-niece Felicity, who lived with her long-suffering mother just out of the village on Bridge Road. Felicity was in her mid-twenties and was rather slow. 'Not the full shilling' was how most Fairmead people described her. She had never kept a job for more than a week or two and most of the time she had no job at all. Miss Browning remembered her from schooldays and was very doubtful of her ability to perform even the simple duties of school cleaner with any degree of proficiency.

This assessment had proved correct. Felicity's cleaning skills were very poor and on Thursday morning, she had not turned up until ten o'clock. Miss Browning had had to open the toilets, when she glanced out of the school door and saw two Infants jiggling about in some distress and their mothers looking at their watches. When opened, the toilets were found to have been untouched since the previous afternoon. As a result Miss Browning was forced to terminate Felicity's appointment when she finally arrived. This severely disrupted the lessons of all three teachers, caused great hilarity among the children and resulted in Miss Taylor volunteering to attend to the toilets before playtime if Mrs Evans could supervise her little ones through the connecting door. Miss Browning sighed at the aggravation and wondered how long it would be before she found a suitable cleaner.

As she plunged up and down with the toilet brush, clad in an overall in a bilious green and pink rubber gloves, Joy chuckled to herself that at least her four years at university had equipped her to clean toilets. Then her thoughts turned to Mark and Cathy, who were lovely children but whose work was far behind that of the rest of the class. Even John Fyne, previously her slowest child, was considerably further ahead than Mark, though slightly younger. She had already consulted Miss Browning and decided to have a word with Molly and James, regarding extra help for the children.

By two o'clock on Friday afternoon, Molly was relaxing with her feet up on a little stool. If it had been warm enough, she would have had an hour pottering in the garden, but it felt damp and chill, though no rain had fallen all day. The forecast for the weekend was good, with sunny spells, so she was hoping for the best. After years in London, she loved her garden, though she was rather a novice in the art. Still, Sophia and Joy were experts and always willing to give useful advice. She had had a most successful week, with people ringing every day, requesting cuts and colours and perms. Whatever did one do before mobile phones were invented?

She was, however, used to long working hours and even with the added responsibility of Cathy and Mark she still seemed to have some time on her hands during the day. However, on her way home this lunch time, after visiting St Mary's Home and setting several ladies' hair in tight curls, she had called in the Village Stores both for a chat with her neighbour, Louisa and to buy more milk, which seemed to disappear at an alarming rate now they had the children. On her way out, she had caught sight of a notice written in the Vicar's scholarly hand, requesting bookkeeping assistance for Tom Norris.

Before deciding to become a hairdresser, Molly had worked in an office for a few months, and thereafter she had retained an interest in business and account-keeping. It was she who always dealt with the household bills and money matters, so the thought of filling in a few hours a week and helping Tom at the same time was very attractive. As she sat with her mug of coffee in her warm room, she decided to see what James thought and then speak to Tom in the morning.

As promised, the sun shone from early Saturday, though grey clouds were banked on the horizon. All in Fairfield Gardens made the most of it, getting their washing out early and mowing their lawns. The daffodils were still beautiful, though some were slightly past their best and weeds had sprouted during the previous warm weather.

Before enjoying a morning in her garden, Joy took the opportunity of speaking to Molly. She had seen James striding towards Bridge Road, in the wake of Mark and Cathy, who were carrying large balls, probably on their way to the green. Molly had emerged, wearing oversized gardening-gloves and a battered straw hat. She smiled when she saw Joy approaching, but was soon serious as she listened to what she had to say. She and James had known about the children's academic problems but to hear it confirmed was rather a shock.

Joy, however was full of reassurance, saying that she and Miss Browning felt that action now could avert trouble later. They proposed putting Cathy and Mark on a special learning programme at school and providing extra work for Molly and James to do with them at home. Joy stressed that no pressure at all was to be put on the children; it was all to be fun, with rewards and incentives, never punishments. She also said how well Molly and James were doing in helping them settle in and how wonderful it had been to see James heading off to play with them this morning.

With these words, Joy departed and Molly attempted to start her gardening. It was lovely to know that others were as concerned about the children as they were. She wondered if she should still speak to Tom, but knew that two or three hours office work would not affect Cathy and Mark. Last night James had thought it a great idea, so she was determined to ask Tom, when she saw him, if she could help.

CHAPTER 10

As Whitsuntide approached and the temperature rose, Fairmead sank into a sea of pink and white blossom, falling like snowflakes in the slightest breeze. The daffodils were all but gone and their glory was reduced to brown tatters. The good gardeners had already looped them down, holding them in position with twine. Others had simply cut them off, hoping for regeneration next year. Joy and Sophia had volunteered to keep Hawton's looking trim and cared-for and were often to be seen sipping and tidying, much to the pleasure of all in Fairfield Gardens.

Waiting for Sophia to arrive on this heavenly Saturday morning, Joy knelt and began dealing with the daffodils. Already buttercups and daisies were sprinkling across the grass and baby leaves were covering the elms. Though the birdsong was loud, it could not compete with the sound of the Fairfield Gardens children laughing and shouting.

Sally, Jenny and Amy had made a tent in their back garden, using an old clothes horse covered with Bonnie's blanket. This edifice was too small and unstable for three excited children, not to mention the dog, who was barking and chasing round hysterically. Not surprisingly, Angie, snoozing in her pram woke up with a start and began to scream. Their father emerged, none too happy to have his Saturday breakfast so rudely disturbed. Megan had set off early for Mansford, before everything got too busy. She was only doing the supermarket shopping, but always relished her few hours alone. Though she loved her husband and children dearly, she looked forward to her Saturday mornings.

Dan, Joel and Sam were back home for the weekend. Tom had worked every Saturday since Easter. but today he was taking the boys to the Whit Fair, held on some spare ground near Mansford Forest. In medieval times the Forest had covered a great area, but now, sadly, it was merely a small area of woodland maintained by the Council.

The boys had not been able to visit their mother for weeks, though they had spoken to her often on the phone. They had adapted to the situation remarkably well and Tom did not know how he could ever thank Isabella and William enough, or all the other neighbours who had helped over this traumatic time. Molly's assistance with his paperwork had proved a godsend. She had been able to accomplish in three hours what had taken him countless evenings. He had already made a firm decision to never try to do it all himself again.

Tom also knew that he would never take Liz for granted again. He had been so close to losing her, and they were certainly not out of the woods yet.

After her week of intense chemo, Molly had been a mess. Worst of all had been her dramatic loss of weight, through being unable to eat. Her beautiful strawberry-blond hair had begun to fall out soon after starting the chemo and now she was wearing little woolly hats, most thoughtfully given by Kate who had managed to visit each day. But Tom was amazed at her spirit and followed her lead by always appearing cheerful when he was with her.

In another couple of weeks or so, she would be starting a second slightly shorter course of chemotherapy and if all went well, she might be able to come home for a little while before the third and last course. With these cautiously optimistic thoughts, Tom turned his attention to the boys who were racing around the house and through the front and back doors, playing cowboys and Indians, with a great deal of shooting and shouts of 'you're dead!'

Cathy and Mark were also playing in their back garden, though with slightly less noise, as they were testing the new swing-set, erected only half an hour before by Uncle James and Grandpa William from next door. The swings were a gift from their own grandma and had arrived a week ago. Despite their excited pleadings, Uncle James had said they must wait until Saturday morning, when Grandpa William could help. Molly had backed up her husband, but knew that he was actually out of his depth assembling anything, furniture or toy.

The last few weeks had been about the best in the whole of Molly's life. She had never realised how satisfied she would feel as a mother. The four of them had settled so well into a routine that it seemed they had always been together. The children's schoolwork had improved by leaps and bounds. One day Mark had been completely befuddled by reading and the next he was away, as though a light had suddenly switched on. Joy was thrilled, and even Miss Browning had sailed across one afternoon in the playground and told Molly how pleased she was with their efforts.

The only cloud on the Standings' horizon was the health of the children's grandmother, whose heart problems had resulted in a short hospital stay a couple of weeks before. As Molly's own parents were living in the Lake District and James' were even further north, she enjoyed the weekly visits to Grandma and greatly respected her gentle support and non-interference. She hoped she herself would become a wise old woman, but rather doubted it.

★ ★ ★ ★ ★

Peace had descended on the Blackett household, with the departure, for a couple of days, of Dan, Joel and Sam. Scrappy seemed quite deflated and lay in his basket, head on paws, deep in thought. Tomorrow, after church, Isabella and William were invited to the christening of their youngest grandchild and had no duties to perform, except catching up with their extensive family and enjoying themselves. It was to be held in a very modern, and very ugly, church on the outskirts of Mansford, and Isabella thanked her lucky stars that they lived in Fairmead, with its beautiful church.

This morning, however, there was much to be done. Isabella planned to do a huge wash, followed by a mini spring-clean, before preparing a sit-down lunch when William returned with his guest. Scrappy was banished outside. By eight o'clock, the first load of washing was being hung out.

William was planning a slightly less hectic morning. After helping James to assemble the swing-set, being an expert with such a large family, he was to drive into Mansford to meet

Anthony Hawton at his hotel. The younger man had arrived from Australia only the day before and driven straight up in a hire car, which he would keep for the two weeks of his holiday. William had contacted him before his departure and invited him to lunch on the Saturday. On Monday Anthony would meet Timothy Miller and William to discuss the Hall, but the weekend was for re-visiting the village. Isabella was consumed with speculation as to what he would be like. Would he be tanned and have a strong Australian twang, like the characters in one of the soaps she loved? Would he be easy to talk to, being such a high-powered lawyer? Would he be interested in village affairs after so long away?

Many of the older residents remembered him as a boy, but there was no consensus as to why he had left. Some said he had quarrelled fiercely with his father, but others said that could not have been possible as Farmer Hawton was such an even-tempered man, so the youngster must have just gone for the adventure. Whatever the reason, all agreed that Farmer Hawton had never said a word against his son, and indeed had been extremely proud when he had learned that the boy was studying law at university. Unlike Isabella, William had decided to wait and see, and judge for himself when they met. He refused to listen to gossip, much to his wife's frustration.

Only one person in Fairfield Gardens was feeling less than one hundred percent on this Saturday morning. Emily Whitehead had woken with a very sore throat and a throbbing head. All through the winter and early spring, she had soldiered on through all weathers without a sniffle and now, on this beautiful, warm day, she was struck down.

Today, of all days! Tomorrow was Whit Sunday and the choir had been practising hard for the last few weeks. They were going to attempt a couple of tricky pieces and really needed Emily to guide them through. But she wondered if she would even be able to play the organ, let alone sing, as her energy seemed to be ebbing away with every passing minute. This would be the first time Emily Whitehead had let anybody down since arriving in Fairmead. She was always the one to support and help and encourage. The last thing she wanted was to disturb dear Dr Miles, but something had to be done quickly so she could fulfil her duties on Sunday morning.

Emily was made of stern stuff, having learned early in life not to give in easily, so she struggled out of bed and downstairs to the phone in the hall. All necessary phone numbers were written neatly in alphabetical order in a little notebook, so the doctor's number was soon located. When he heard Emily's voice sounding so croaky, he was kindness itself and said he would be there within the hour.

News of Emily's misfortune spread through Fairfield Gardens like wildfire. Sophia and Joy had seen Dr Miles arrive, as they were stretching their backs after completing the tidy-up of Hawton's. Isabella saw him as she was hanging out her third load of washing and Kate saw him as she was preparing to clean the windows in the sitting room. All the ladies were alarmed at this unexpected visit, but relieved when they saw him emerge in a few minutes looking quite relaxed. Kate hurried to waylay him before he could reach his car and promised to make sure that Emily followed his advice to the letter.

Kate found the patient, still in her dressing gown, resting in front of her fire, despite the warm day. Slightly overcome by the heat, she made her friend a cup of warm lemon drink, moved telephone and books close to hand and listened as Emily told how sad she felt at not being able to lead the choir tomorrow. Kate said she must not give it a thought. She would sort it all out and return at lunchtime with some soup.

When Paul was told what had happened, he promised to visit dear Emily later in the afternoon but was at a loss as to how the situation could be remedied and the Whit Sunday service saved. Sophia, however, had a plan. She hurried to her friend Joy's house, finding her, duster in hand, finishing a hasty house-clean, before spending the rest of the beautiful morning in the garden. After hearing about poor Emily and the Vicar's concerns, Joy's plans changed and she led Sophia across to the school, where she retrieved a small keyboard and stand from a locked cupboard in her classroom. These were then transported to the church, together with several books of music. As they were searching for a convenient socket for the keyboard, Paul arrived and found the answer to his prayer. Joy laughed at his look of surprise, telling him that she had taught herself, more or less, to play for her children and often accompanied the hymns at assembly. She was fairly proficient with the right hand but only able to produce simple chords with the left. If nobody else could be found, she was more than willing to provide music at the morning service.

Over the next hour or so, Paul, Sophia and Joy worked out a revised list of hymns, every one of which was well known to all the schoolchildren and most of their parents. Paul thought it was all splendid and would be most enjoyable for everyone. Joy and Sophia then offered to contact the choir members, though he did not feel there would be any need for a practice as the hymns were so well known.

Sophia caught Isabella just before her guest was due to arrive and she in turn promised to inform Molly and James. She then set off to locate other members, while Joy found Elsie Summerton tidying books in the library van, which was parked in its usual spot near the village green. It came on Saturdays between eleven-thirty and twelve-thirty and was very well patronised. There was a large and comprehensive library in Mansford, but most Fairmead people used the van for convenience and Elsie Summerton was most obliging. She would take careful note of any requested books and, without fail, produce them the following week.

She and her sister Jessie had worked for the Mansford Library Service for many years, Jessie in the Central Library and Elsie on the van which serviced outlying villages and small towns. As Fairmead residents of long standing, they were staunch church members and knew Emily Whitehead well. They had seen her only last week at the Prayer Circle meeting and at choir practice and had thought then that she didn't seem quite herself. Elsie promised that she and her sister would call round to check on their friend that evening and reassure her that all would be well on Sunday morning, though, obviously, the choir would not be able to attain the same high standard it always did under Emily's gentle hand.

As Joy was returning home, plans for gardening still in her head, she saw William's car draw up and his visitor emerge, laughing at something William had said. She knew, of course, as all Fairmead did, who it was, but was mildly surprised to see that he looked almost exactly as she had imagined him, tall and sporty-looking, with dark brown slightly curly hair, rather like her own, and a tanned, healthy skin. She knew Anthony Hawton was in his mid to late thirties but he seemed athletic and younger. She hoped he would enjoy revisiting the village and formed the impression that he would be easy to talk to.

This proved to be the case over lunch with Isabella and William. Anthony was in high good spirits. Having flown business class and slept for a great part of the journey, jet lag was not an issue. He admitted that when he left his high-profile job in Sydney it was as if a weight had been lifted from his shoulders. He was full of details about his life and questions about Fairmead, and the lunch passed quickly and pleasantly. Isabella thought him a charming young man and William felt he would make an interesting friend.

After lunch, the two men set off with Scrappy to explore the village and examine work at the Hall, which was well underway. Anthony was particularly interested in and impressed by Fairfield Gardens, as he had sold the land to the developer, almost without a thought, needing the money at the time. This had weighed on his conscience in recent years. Although he had seen photos, he was relieved to see for himself how well the houses fitted into the village as a whole.

Joy was just thinking of a late lunch and considering what to wear that evening for a party at a fellow teacher's house in Mansford when William and Anthony passed her delightful garden, stopping to admire her display. William introduced his companion to Joy, leaving them to chat for a moment while he hurried back home to collect his key, having just remembered that Isabella was proposing to drive into Mansford to buy a christening present for the next day.

Though he was about ten years older than her, Joy liked Anthony within the first thirty seconds of talking to him and knew that the feeling was mutual. However, before much could be said, William returned and the two men set off again, barely keeping up with Scrappy, who was thrilled beyond belief that he was getting an extra walk.

★ ★ ★ ★ ★

The walk around Fairmead was a great success and, to Anthony's great satisfaction, it was all much as he remembered it. Some things had even improved, notably the Village Stores, which was now a thriving and well-cared-for establishment. The addition of Louisa's Café was a great innovation. On this lovely May Saturday, it was full to overflowing with people enjoying lunch. Cars were parked up and down the High Street and Louisa had placed three tiny round tables and chairs on the footpath outside to cater for the overflow. This had been done without council permission and Louisa hoped their spies were not out this weekend, as she planned to do the same tomorrow.

The weather was due to hold and Whit Sunday was always popular with day-trippers. The café was running efficiently, as always, in the more than capable hands of Louisa's two ladies, Flo and Marjorie, helped today by Isabella and William's student daughter, Susie. Louisa herself was in the Stores, having a wonderfully busy day but not so busy that she didn't have time for a friendly word with all. Visitors from the city were always left thinking how wonderful it would be to live in the country, where people were so friendly.

Louisa greeted Anthony as if he were a long-lost friend and told him that Bessie, the previous owner, whom he had known as a boy, was fit and well and living at St Mary's Home, which had been the former vicarage.

After a brief hello to Susie, who was far too busy to have a chat with her father, William and Anthony set off for St Mary's Home to pay their regards to Bessie. This took quite a long time, as they were frequently stopped by young and old, all of whom were eager to meet this prodigal son. Those who had known him declared that he hadn't changed a bit, except for his accent and the healthy glow of his skin, not to wonder since he hadn't had to put up with the English winter. When they finally arrived at the home, all the residents were gathered in the common room, having already been informed of their arrival, and afternoon tea was set ready.

It was four o'clock by the time they left. They strolled along to the church and eventually the Hall, still warm in the late afternoon sun. William let them into the Hall and Anthony viewed the renovations his father's legacy was paying for. Tom had made a start a few days ago and was also involved in a couple of other projects.

By the time the two of them arrived home, Isabella was already back from her shopping expedition to Mansford, quite exhausted by her busy day and slumped in an armchair with a steaming cup of tea. When Anthony suggested that he should take them out to dinner at a top-notch restaurant in Mansford, Isabella visibly revived and happily mounted the stairs to find the new shoes she had bought at Christmas, which had never been worn and would go marvellously with her favourite pink dress.

During the evening it was mentioned that the choir, of which Isabella was an enthusiastic member, would not have poor Emily Whitehead with them tomorrow, Whit Sunday, and that Joy Taylor from number two had valiantly volunteered to play some hymns on her keyboard. On hearing this, Anthony felt he might like to come to the service, as he had nothing planned and it would bring back childhood memories. William took him at his word, but Isabella's antennae were raised and she wondered if by chance... but then she stopped herself briskly and returned to discussing the present vicar and all he had done for St Mary's Church and the village as a whole.

CHAPTER 11

The following morning dawned warm and windy, as befitted Pentecost Sunday. By nine o'clock the sun was shining in a windy, cloudless sky and the flag of St George above the Church fluttered madly. Joy went over well before the service to practise the hymns one more time before anyone arrived, except the Vicar, of course, who would be saying his prayers in the vestry.

Bill Hughes arrived not long after Joy, stumping down the aisle with his stick, and Sophia followed soon after in a much quieter fashion. Joy grinned to herself, remembering that she had been the substitute verger at Easter and was now the substitute organist. When would she take a leading role at church in her own right?

Isabella bustled in at that moment, accompanied by Elsie and Jessie Summerton, all looking resplendent in new outfits, Isabella in honour of the christening that afternoon and the sisters because they had always bought new clothes for Whit. Molly and James arrived soon after, having left Cathy and Mark with Megan for a few minutes. She and Jack would bring them with their own children, as they did every Sunday. They felt that as their Angie would be christened in St Mary's in a few weeks it was incumbent on them to attend regularly, at least for a while. Taking Cathy and Mark not only helped Molly and James with their choir duties but tended to encourage Sally, Jenny and Amy to be reasonably quiet and still. They were such good children. Molly and James were very lucky to have them.

As the last members of the choir were arriving, the congregation started to file in. The church was almost as full as at Easter, though Joy had a suspicion that several people were there mainly to see how she and the choir would manage without Emily. She ran her eyes, in the way of an experienced teacher, over the people settling into their places and with a little pleasurable shock, saw the tall figure of Anthony Hawton squeezing in next to Louisa and Kate, Louisa having delayed the opening of the Stores and Café until eleven o'clock.

Anthony had spied Joy as soon as he had entered the church and felt the same thrill of recognition as yesterday, when he had seen her among her flowers in the garden. It was a strange feeling and one he had never experienced before. He had always been a popular young man, having a wide circle of friends, both male and female. Several times he had thought he might be in love and had almost popped the question, but each time a slight doubt had held him back. Indeed, he was beginning to feel that he might never marry and must be content with his many interests. But he felt towards Joy, a girl he had met for the briefest time, an overwhelming sense that he knew her deeply already. For the next hour, his mind was hardly on the service, as he stole covert views of her albeit only her back as she played the keyboard. He was as entranced as any pimply adolescent and not at all the high-flying lawyer.

In the churchyard afterwards, everybody from the vicar down wanted to meet and greet Farmer Hawton's returned son. Joy was also a centre of attention, with all wanting to congratulate her on her playing and choice of hymns. Despite all the fuss, both Anthony and Joy were acutely aware of each other. Seemingly unconsciously, they edged closer to each other until they were finally able to exchange a word, though what they said were polite platitudes and not their true thoughts.

Anthony was returning to Mansford for lunch with old friends of his father's and Joy had promised to visit Emily and tell her how everything had gone. By chance, or so it seemed, both departed at the same time. As Anthony reached his car, he decided that action was needed. Apropos of nothing, he suddenly asked if she would like to go to the cinema that evening. He wasn't at all sure what was on, but could pick her up about five and they could have a bite to eat first.

Being a straightforward person, Joy said she would be most pleased to accept the invitation and the two went their ways in the best of good humour.

Naturally, this little exchange had not gone unnoticed and tongues were wagging almost before Anthony had started his engine. Most of the ladies and, it must be admitted, some of the older men, added this titbit of gossip to their agenda and made the most of it over the coming days and weeks.

CHAPTER 12

As luck would have it, Whit Sunday was the last and almost the only day of summer. From that day on, the weather deteriorated, remaining grey and damp over the next three months.

After many wet playtimes spent cooped up in stuffy classrooms, Miss Browning was seriously contemplating early retirement. Her dissatisfaction with school life was aggravated by the non-appearance of a suitable cleaner. Several people had come and gone, disliking the lack of much pay and the tie involved. Liz had always brought the boys with her about an hour before school and let them play as she worked, keeping them back with her for a little while in the afternoon. But although Miss Browning dropped many hints, no other mother seemed willing to commit to the job. Miss Taylor and Mrs Evans had both insisted on helping Miss Browning during the long periods with no cleaner, but they all sincerely hoped that somebody would be found before the new school year started in September.

Her little job as school cleaner was not uppermost in Liz's mind during that time. She had been down in the depths after the initial chemo, at least physically, though, surprisingly, she had never felt so peaceful and relaxed. It was as though she was floating along, being carried by life rather than trying to control or change it.

After the second session of chemo which, thankfully, had not caused such a severe reaction, she had been able to come home to gather her strength for the third and last session. She was released from hospital under strict instructions to return the moment her temperature started to rise or if she felt unwell in any way, as the risk of infection was very strong. Having three children, it was impossible to keep them at arm's length, even when Dan started coughing and had a runny nose after taking off his boots and paddling barefoot in a muddy puddle at the bottom of the garden on a particularly chilly day. The boys had come back to their own house when Liz's mother had come to stay for a few days. It was difficult for her to get away for more than a few days at a time, but she came as often as possible. Tom's mother, though not too well herself, also came as often as she could. At other times, her many friends and neighbours organised to call in regularly, for which Liz was extremely grateful, as she had never felt so weak in her life. Even making a cup of tea was beyond her at first.

She was much comforted by the thought of the Prayer Circle and attributed to their intercessions the fact that she remained home the whole month without succumbing to any infection.

During Liz's month at home, Sophia had driven her in two or three times a week for her outpatients' checkups. Sometimes these coincided with her own checkups, though mostly they didn't. While waiting for Liz, she spent the time peacefully by herself in Mansford, not in the busy shopping centre but walking in Central Park or sitting in the serene surroundings of the Buddhist Centre or in St John's Cathedral, particularly on Tuesday mornings when the organist would be practising.

Jim and Anita at Fantastic Flowers had been marvellous. They had agreed that Sophia could change her times to suit herself each week. So highly did they think of Sophia that they also said she could keep her job after the baby was born, bringing it with her to work if she wished. Sophia couldn't have been happier with the proposal. She was feeling extremely well, though tired by evening. She had suffered only minor nausea for a short time and had been able to continue all her duties as the vicar's wife.

She and Paul had been awestruck when they had seen their little one for the first time through the ultrasound scan. Paul had had tears in his eyes and, afterwards, gone straight to the church to give heartfelt thanks. Sophia had bought a beautiful baby album and put the grainy photo in pride of place on the first page. Neither of them wanted to know if it was a boy or girl and they had many happy conversations suggesting names for either.

★ ★ ★ ★ ★

Emily was also looking forward to an autumnal change in her life. After her Whitsun flu, she had never seemed to fully recover and she had been plagued with bronchitis all through the dismal summer. A pragmatist, and never one to feel sorry for herself, she had come to the conclusion that it would be best to apply for a place at St Mary's Home, where she would be among friends, be independent and yet within reach of assistance, should she need it. Relieved of the concerns of owning and running a house, she could concentrate on helping others and pursuing her spiritual life.

She would not, of course sell her house until she was assured of a place, there never being more than ten residents, though Fairmead people always got first choice. Without more ado, Emily put in her application and left it in the hands of God.

Towards the middle of August, she was informed that Ada Higgins would be leaving in a month's time to go and live with her widowed sister somewhere in the south and that there would be a place vacant. Used to making her own decisions, Emily said she would be most pleased to accept and set about putting her house on the market.

All Fairfield Gardens had been sad to see the 'For Sale' sign go up, especially Isabella, but no one had been surprised. Of course Emily would not be far away and, God willing, would be around the village for many years to come. It was also fervently hoped that she would feel able to continue playing the organ and leading the choir far into the future. Paul added a particularly heartfelt amen to this wish, as he knew how difficult it was these days to find an organist, let alone one who was so amenable and well loved.

Molly and James had had a roller-coaster summer. Since Molly had first started village hairdressing her business had grown tremendously, not only in Fairmead but in the villages around. Her willingness to have a chat and her reasonable prices were a godsend to many housebound women. She worked strictly school hours only, but Wednesday mornings she devoted three hours to Tom's paperwork and enjoyed the change of pace. In the school holidays she did no hairdressing at all and her ladies knew not to ask her. The children's school work was improving by the week and they had started making friends other than the Fairfield Gardens children, even being invited to one or two birthday parties.

As soon as school broke up, they had gone off for a week to visit Molly's and James' families, first to the Lake District and then to Scotland. Both visits had been a disaster as far as weather was concerned, but a great success otherwise. Nanny and Grampy in the windy Lakes and Nan and Pop in the rainy North were entranced by the children, telling Molly and James that getting them was the best thing they had ever done.

With some misgivings they had left Scotland and driven to an east coast resort for the second week of their holiday. This had lived up to expectations, being windy and wet, with a little sun peeping through occasionally towards the end of the week. However, a good time was had by all, the highlights being several hazardous walks along the beach, almost getting blown into the sea.

They had been home barely a week before news reached them of the sudden death of Grandma from a massive heart attack. A neighbour had called an ambulance after calling in to see her friend, as she did every morning. Sadly, Grandma had died before reaching the hospital. Molly and James had told the children, as gently as they could, and the foster service had been informed.

At first Cathy and Mark had seemed unchanged and they had gone to the funeral quite cheerfully. They were the only family present, but there were many friends and acquaintances, as Grandma had been well regarded in the neighbourhood. Once they returned home, however, Molly noticed a change. The children became more withdrawn and even quieter than usual, sticking together more than was usual for brother and sister. The foster service had sent round a pleasant young social worker who stayed for afternoon tea and quietly observed the children. She said they were feeling that everyone they loved had died and they must cling to each other, but she could see the affection between them and their foster parents and felt they were in the best possible environment.

Not two weeks after the funeral, they received a letter from Grandma's solicitor, informing them that the will had been read and she had left the children a small sum of money, to be held until they were eighteen, and some bits and pieces to remember her by. She had also left them a photograph album, with pictures of their mother and father and themselves as babies. The will had been written only a few weeks previously and included a few words at the bottom, saying how happy she was with the children being cared for by Molly and James and expressing her hope that they could remain there permanently.

This thought had indeed been uppermost in their minds for the last few days, though they knew there were other grandparents in New Zealand and their wishes must be taken into account. Several letters had been exchanged with them since Easter and they had been most pleased to receive some of the children's pictures and writing. They had, however, never met Cathy and Mark and neither were in the best of health. As Molly and James talked things over, staying up late several evenings, they decided to make an appointment to see Timothy Miller in Mansford for his opinion on the possibility of their adopting the children.

CHAPTER TWELVE

★ ★ ★ ★ ★

Meanwhile, Timothy Miller had had his own concerns during the summer. As senior partner at Miller Smythe Hitchin he had the final word in matters concerning the firm, though he always preferred to obtain the approval of Edward and George. The present matter was the question of asking another solicitor to join the firm. A couple of chaps in Mansford had recently retired and many of their clients had moved their business to Miller Smythe Hitchin, so many, in fact, that the three partners were rather overwhelmed. George Hitchin himself was nearing sixty-five and already planning his retirement, so a replacement was needed quite urgently.

That was not the problem. The vexing question was whether to ask the person Timothy had in mind, the high-flying lawyer Anthony Hawton. On the surface, it hardly seemed likely that such a man would want to leave London, and indeed his home in Australia, to become a relatively humble solicitor in a provincial city. However, in his conversations with Anthony concerning Fairmead Village Hall and other matters, it had become increasingly obvious that Anthony was feeling burned out in his high-profile life and was seriously considering a change of career. It was also obvious to Timothy, and many other people, that the younger man's thoughts had been overtaken by the late onset of love, the young lady in question living not far from Mansford.

Having weighed up the pros and cons and consulted his partners, Timothy had contacted Anthony at the beginning of August and was pleased to hear that serious consideration would be given to his proposal.

During the summer, Anthony had much on his mind and major decisions needed to be made. He had taken up the position in London as a welcome change to his hectic life in Sydney, but had soon discovered that work was every bit as stressful on the other side of the world. He did not want to suffer the ravages of stress in early middle age which had happened to numerous colleagues over the years and was rather attracted to the idea of downgrading his career and taking up Timothy Miller's offer of a partnership in his firm of solicitors. Naturally, the financial rewards would be considerably less and the work more prosaic, but the joy of being able to work reasonably regular hours and have a life other than the law was most attractive.

Overriding all these thoughts, however, was his growing love for Joy Taylor, infants school teacher and resident of the lovely village of Fairmead. More and more frequently he found his thoughts wandering in her direction, as he became more and more certain that this was indeed love. On the first day of September, Anthony made his decision. Without further procrastination he set wheels in motion that would change the course of his life.

Joy had been oblivious to the dreadful weather and had enjoyed the best summer of her life. While others had complained endlessly, she had been cocooned in the delightful sensation of love. All was well with the world, and, although she continued performing her everyday tasks, her mind was often far away. After two magical weeks, during which she and Anthony had managed to see each other every day, he had departed for London. Sometimes he had returned to

Mansford for the weekend and was so often to be seen around Fairmead that he was soon accepted as a local. Other weekends, when the pressure of work was too great, Joy journeyed to the capital, staying in unheard-of luxury at a boutique hotel, paid for by Anthony. He himself had rented a delightful, modern flat overlooking the river and close to all transport. If he had to work, she spent happy hours rediscovering London's many attractions. Any sunny spells were spent in a park, if at all possible, but museums and galleries were usually the safest bet. In the evenings, there was always a new restaurant to visit or theatre to enjoy. With no sense of surprise, they soon became aware of how similar their tastes were and revelled in the companionship.

On the last weekend in August, a few days before school was due to resume, Joy travelled up to London with the prospect of seeing not only Anthony but also her father, who had just arrived on business from his home in Nice. Though he still travelled extensively, in the last year he had decided to create a permanent base. As he had always loved the South of France, he had acquired a large house on the outskirts of his favourite city. This suited him so well that he had begun to curtail his forays abroad and to understand why Joy so appreciated her house and position in the small village of Fairmead.

Rather to her surprise, Anthony was not working as she had thought but was waiting when the train arrived. He told her his client had cancelled and they sauntered off, hand in hand, to a cosy café for coffee and shelter from the drizzle. Despite the Saturday morning rush, the two young people occupied their table in a far corner for more than two hours, remaining undisturbed and oblivious to the hubbub around them.

After the first warming sips of coffee, Anthony took hold of her hand and the coffees went cold. During that two hours, he told her how much he loved her, that he would be the happiest man in the world if she would marry him, and that if she said yes, he would contact Timothy Miller concerning his proposition and other matters.

Joy, for her part, was surprised only by the timing. She had known with a beautiful certainty that the two were absolutely right for each other since the very first brief meeting over the garden fence, and the certainty had only deepened through the summer. She had no hesitation in accepting her dear Anthony's proposal and the two became engaged in plans for the future, the first of which was to acquaint Joy's father with the momentous news. Anthony was determined to do the thing properly and ask her father's permission to marry his daughter when they all met that evening for dinner at his hotel. Joy giggled, but was secretly pleased that the proprieties were being adhered to.

Somehow the news of Joy and Anthony's engagement seemed to reach Fairmead even before Joy's return on Sunday evening, a mystery no one could explain. The news was greeted with universal approval, both being well liked and, very importantly, involved in the village. At first there was some dismay as to whether Joy would move to London or even Australia, but their minds were soon put to rest when it was revealed that Anthony would be leaving the London job and moving to Mansford in a few weeks to take up a position with Miller Smythe Hitchin. What they didn't know for at least two weeks was that the old firm would have a new partner and be renamed Miller Smythe Hitchin and Hawton. Quite a mouthful, but most pleasing to have dear Farmer Hawton's name remembered in Mansford.

On the same day Anthony had met Joy in London, Miss Browning's worries concerning a cleaner had been solved, or so she fervently hoped. All through the summer holidays, and even during her two weeks in Malta, she had been plagued by the thought of a cleanerless new school year. She knew that this was a relatively minor irritation compared with some people's worries, but nevertheless it was never far from the surface of her mind. Then, on the last Saturday of the holidays, she had bumped into Jane Simmons, wife of the Farmer's Arms landlord, in the Village Stores and the two ladies had chatted amicably with Louisa for ten minutes during a lull in customers. Miss Browning was about to visit the school to attend to a little paperwork, preparatory to the new term commencing in a few days time, and had mentioned her inability to find a suitable school cleaner. As if having a brainwave, Jane suddenly thumped the counter and declared she had the very person. Her mother-in-law, recently widowed, had come to live with them. She sometimes helped out in the bar on busy evenings but was an active lady for her age and was looking for a few hours of work, preferably somewhere local, as she didn't drive. At one stage of her career, she had cleaned houses and she loved children, so, in Jane's opinion, she would be ideal.

Miss Browning's face lit up and Jane suggested she should come back to the Farmer's Arms now and speak to Doris herself. This was exactly what had happened, with a very positive result. Miss Browning had liked Doris immediately and that lady had been thrilled with the job offer, promising to turn up at eight o'clock on Wednesday morning. Without a doubt Miss Browning knew that she would keep her promise and prove to be the answer to her prayer.

CHAPTER 13

September brought an Indian summer. On the first day of the month, the grey clouds had rolled away to be replaced by days of sunshine and perfect autumn weather. As the month progressed, trees began to turn glorious colours. Mansford Forest was a kaleidoscope of vivid reds, oranges and yellows and Fairmead itself was not far behind in autumn splendour.

Although nearing the end of her long wait, Sophia had hardly slowed down, during the days at least. Apart from her many parish duties and her welcome hours at Fantastic Flowers, she continued to drive Liz into Mansford for her regular checks. On top of all that, she was on the committee responsible for organising the grand reopening of the village hall. This was scheduled for the same weekend as the Harvest Festival and entailed much work, though Sophia, in her calm, gentle way, had managed to delegate many of the responsibilities. Several people had found themselves agreeing to tasks they had never before undertaken. Those living in Fairfield Gardens were particularly susceptible to Sophia's requests.

Liz was the only one excused duties, for which she was rather thankful. She had been home a couple of months now, after having to return to hospital for two weeks in early July with a mystery infection which had caused her temperature to skyrocket. Since then, however, she had remained well and gone from strength to strength. Initially, it had taken all her reserves of energy to have a shower and get dressed, but gradually she was able to make a cup of tea and perform small tasks. Her mother and mother-in-law had been wonderful, taking it in turns to come and stay for a few days. The neighbours, too, had been exceptionally helpful. Dear Emily had been unwell herself and didn't come round for a long time, for fear of passing on any infection, though she rang every day to assure Liz of her continuing prayers and those of the Prayer Circle.

Isabella and William were always there to help and sometimes the boys stayed overnight with them and went round to play with Scrappy. Though Isabella was considerably less tired than when the young ones had been there all the time, she missed having them around and was always pleased to welcome them for a few hours. Cathy and Mark from next door were also welcome to visit Scrappy anytime. He was the most popular and spoilt dog in the village.

Sally, Jenny and Amy also went round to Granny Isabella's now and again. They loved their own dog, Bonnie, but she wasn't as playful as Scrappy and was too heavy to lift into their prams or bicycle baskets. During the damp school holidays, Megan had been relieved when they went round for an hour knowing that Isabella was always happy to have the children.

Once school started again, she began to turn her attention to Angie's christening. Jack was far too busy to give it much thought so, on the first Friday of September, on her way home after dropping the girls at school, she called next door at the

Vicarage. Sophia and Paul were both home and welcomed her in. While Sophia cuddled Angie, Paul searched for his diary and a date was fixed for the middle of October, a week after the Hall opening and Harvest Festival. After a welcome cup of tea, Megan left, as it was almost time for Angie's feed and she was beginning to grizzle, but as she went next door she realised that the gate to the back garden was open and Bonnie was not to be seen. She had been in a rush to get the children to school and had forgotten to close it. For the moment, there was nothing to be done, as Angie was now crying steadily. Once the baby had been satisfied and nappy changed, Megan popped her back into the pram and went off to search round the village.

Louisa was rearranging the Village Stores window when Megan arrived, looking slightly worried. She promised to ask all her customers if they had seen Bonnie and Megan promised to let her know when the dog was found. By the time she had to return to the school, Bonnie was still missing and Megan had to tell the girls. Sally immediately burst into tears and Miss Taylor hurried over to see what was the matter. The girls insisted on going round the village again and asking everybody if they had seen their dog.

Just as Jack arrived home, they received a phone call from Jim Turner at Hawton's Farm, informing them of the sad news that Bonnie had been found on the grass verge about a mile out on Bridge Road, obviously hit by a car which had not stopped. Jack had the upsetting job of retrieving the dog and digging a deep hole in the back garden so a funeral could be held. News had spread round Fairfield Gardens and many of the neighbours came round. William had to go out on Cubs business, but Isabella came, as did Louise and Kate, though they were just about to eat their tea. Molly brought Cathy and Mark, and Joy left some books she was marking. Sophia came round, though longing to put her feet up after a busy day, and Paul conducted a little service before attending a meeting in Mansford.

Tom had taken the boys to kick a ball around on the green and arrived home only as people were leaving number eight. Joel and Sam insisted on going round to visit the grave, but Dan sucked his thumb and sat on Liz's knee. The girls cheered up visibly when the boys appeared and proudly showed them the cross made out of twigs and the bunch of flowers hastily picked from the garden.

The next morning, just as the sun was peeping over the horizon, Louisa was startled by the phone. It was too early for a business call and she hoped it wasn't Chloe with bad news. Kate was still asleep and Louisa didn't want to have to wake her. But ten minutes later, Louisa couldn't help herself rushing into her friend's bedroom and shaking her hard.

It was the best possible news from her son Andrew in America. He and Margaret had been thinking long and hard over the last few months and had finally decided that they wanted their children to grow up in an English village, rather than the suburbs of Los Angeles. They had not mentioned this to Louisa or Margaret's parents, in case their plans came to nothing. But miraculously, everything had fallen into place; a transfer to his firm's brand new premises in a new business park recently opened with much fanfare by the Mayor and the MP for Mansford, and an eager buyer for their house. It had all happened in the nick of time, as the baby was due around the third week of October and there was no time to be lost. Though the new position wouldn't commence for a month, they had booked to fly immediately and would be arriving at Heathrow on Wednesday morning. They were planning a week in London being tourists and then would drive a hire car to Mansford, stay in a hotel there and start house-hunting.

★ ★ ★ ★ ★

For the first time ever, Louisa was late opening the Village Stores and three people were already standing around waiting for their papers. Louisa was beaming even more brightly than usual all through the day and nothing seemed to trouble her, neither the late arrival of the bread van nor the child who spilled a full glass of sticky soft drink all over the table, floor and several people in the café. Every customer, local or visitor, in both establishments was told the glad tidings and the day passed in a haze of goodwill.

Kate was almost as pleased as Louisa herself. She had always been very fond of Andrew and Margaret and was thrilled that they would be able to reacquaint themselves with the children and the new baby too. As soon as Louisa returned home, the two ladies started plotting and planning, while eating a hasty meal, balancing plates on their knees and sitting companionably in front of the recently-lit fire, the evening having turned chilly. Both had had the same marvellous idea, Kate when sweeping the front path and Louisa when rummaging to find a frozen pie for a customer. What about

Emily's house, which was still for sale? The previous prospective buyers had failed to secure the finance. It was perfect! The children would grow up in the best village in England, Andrew would be close to work, Margaret would have Megan and Sophia with young babies, and the two ladies would have their family close. Without further ado and without any care for the time difference, Louisa rang Andrew. The ensuing long conversation was most satisfactory.

In no time at all, plans were afoot. Emily was filled with quiet pleasure at the prospect of such a lovely family in her house. She had already arranged to move into St Mary's Home in two weeks' time and was going to Ada Higgins' farewell afternoon tea tomorrow. It was an answer to her prayers, and she had no doubt at all that all would go according to plan. She would speak to Andrew on the phone later in the day and consult dear George Hitchin, who had been her solicitor for thirty years, on Monday morning. Thankfully, he had not yet retired but, when he did, she would have no hesitation placing her affairs in the hands of dear Farmer Hawton's son Anthony. With these thoughts, she collected a jacket to counteract the chill of the church and set off to offer prayers of thanks and then to practise a Mozart sonata to be played before tomorrow's service.

Joy was up almost as early as Louisa on the Saturday morning. In fact, she had hardly slept all night. She was to meet Anthony in Mansford about midday and after lunch at their favourite French restaurant they were going to look for an engagement ring. All morning she couldn't settle to anything, flitting from vacuuming to picking flowers for her many vases to putting washing in the machine and forgetting to hang it out. By nine thirty, she had decided to go next door and visit Liz for half an hour, but her mother had just arrived, so Joy said she would call again and proceeded to Sophia's. On such a pleasant morning, Sophia had abandoned any thoughts of indoor tasks and was sunning herself in the back garden, deep in a yellow and white striped deckchair, from which it was difficult to arise. After some minutes attempting to arrange the contraption, Joy sank into a similar deckchair and the two friends chatted amicably. Feeling much more relaxed, Joy finally drove off to Mansford, allowing herself plenty of time to negotiate the Saturday morning crowds. Not only the sun was causing the world to shine that morning.

CHAPTER 14

By the end of September, the school holidays were well and truly forgotten. Miss Browning was now able to focus all her considerable concentration on being a teacher and headmistress. All domestic duties were now being magnificently performed by Doris Simmons. Her skill with cleaning implements and the motherly way she treated the children had made her absolutely indispensable. The lady herself was as pleased as punch to have a job that suited her so well and she had even been asked a couple of times by mothers to babysit their little ones for an hour or so while they slipped into Mansford. It had been the best decision to move in with her son and daughter-in-law at the Farmer's Arms, where there was plenty of company in the evenings and now plenty to keep her occupied during the day.

Emily Whitehead was also settling into her new home. She had taken a few bits and pieces with her to St Mary's, but everything else had been donated to a charity for the homeless. Despite seeming outwardly cheerful, she had been inwardly quite nervous. Having lived on her own for so long, she wondered how she would cope with community living. After the first week, however, her fears were set to rest. She knew all the residents and staff well and they made her feel more than welcome, while at the same time respecting her need for privacy. She had a delightful room at the back of the house, overlooking the extensive and well kept garden. Being the original Victorian Vicarage, the rooms were large and Emily's had a fireplace, no longer working but with a modern gas heater and its realistic flames. Two of Emily's comfortable armchairs stood on either side, and her own familiar bed was pushed against the far wall. Under the window was a tiny round table, covered with a delicate cloth, embroidered by her mother many years ago, and two chairs were on either side. The small table had been purchased in Mansford and delivered three days after her move, but the chairs were her own. On the table was an old cut-glass vase filled with flowers brought by Louisa and Kate, who had been among her first visitors. In a corner of the room was a small wooden cabinet containing an electric kettle and several pieces of china, together with tea, sugar and a small amount of milk, donated by Betty in the kitchen. There was also a packet of Emily's favourite ginger biscuits. Her books were neatly arranged on a shelf above her bed and a small wardrobe, opposite the door, contained her modest collection of clothes and other necessities. On the little mantelpiece and windowsill, a few well-loved ornaments completed Emily's domain.

By the end of the week, she had already spent happy hours with a cup of tea, reading in front of her fire or sitting at her little table looking out at the autumn garden and fields beyond. When she felt like company, she could go down to the common room and chat with others or watch television. She was also being taught how to play whist by Bill Hughes and, wonder of wonders, was even being initiated into the complexities of the computer by Jan Fletcher, another recent arrival, who had kindly installed her own computer in a corner of the common room so all could enjoy it. As Jan was the only one proficient in using it, she was in high demand as a teacher and revelled in the role.

The sale of Emily's house to Andrew Ward and family was proceeding swiftly and smoothly. George Hitchin had been efficiency itself and settlement was expected in the not-too-distant future. In the meantime the family were staying in a modest hotel near Mansford Central Park and enjoying being tourists. Louisa and Kate had offered to have them but been secretly relieved when their offer had been refused with thanks.

Andrew said the children could start at the village school at the same time as he was due to commence his new job. In the meantime they would enjoy their holiday and letting the children see some of their new country. George Hitchin knew that speed was of the essence and was doing all in his power to get them into their new home before the baby arrived. Margaret had already been to Mansford Royal and felt secure in the knowledge that such a good hospital was only a stone's throw away.

* * * * *

Sophia was also looking forward to becoming a mother. For many weeks now, all her spare time had been spent making tiny baby clothes and knitting miniature jackets. She had learned these skills at an early age from her mother, who had been a dressmaker before moving to Spain. Although this was no longer her career, her mother still made almost all her own clothes and several for Sophia when she visited. Monica Newson loved her life in the warmth of Spain and welcomed all visitors from cold northern climes. But once a year, she made the ultimate sacrifice and flew over to visit friends and relations for two weeks in July. She had been overjoyed when she was told Sophia, her only daughter, was expecting a baby at long last. She was very fond of her son-in-law too and thought they would make a lovely family. Having paid the usual visit in summer, she informed everyone that she would be returning at the beginning of October and staying until Sophia and the baby were settled or until they threw her out.

She was due to arrive two days before the Hall reopening party and Harvest Festival service the following day. Despite Paul's misgivings, Sophia was adamant she would drive to Heathrow and pick up her mother. She said she was feeling wonderful, had lots of energy and Paul was not to fuss. The baby was not due for another couple of weeks and all would be well. Paul admitted that she knew best and indeed she had been cleaning and washing for the last few days with an intensity most unlike her usual self, so she must be feeling very well. So, early on the Thursday morning, as mist was clearing and the sun shining orange on the horizon, Sophia set off, with the heat turned up and soothing music playing, heading for Mansford and the London road.

Paul would also be heading for Mansford after lunch, as he had a meeting in the Cathedral. He always enjoyed visiting Henry Procter, his friend and bishop. The two had studied together and had much in common. Timothy Miller was also due to attend the meeting and was to be accompanied by Anthony Hawton, who had begun his new duties on the Monday.

After that weekend a few weeks ago when Anthony had popped the vital question, his life had changed with startling rapidity. His plans for a year's break in London changed in the twinkling of an eye. He had now switched careers and was living in a provincial English city, and was soon to be living back in his boyhood village. His house in Sydney was being rented out on a short-term lease, pending a future decision.

Yet these events, important as they were, were as nothing to the anticipation of his life with Joy. They had carefully weighed the pros and cons and found themselves in complete agreement. Each felt they had found their soulmate and saw no reason to delay the wedding. Both had confessed to their deep attachment to Fairmead after years of travelling, in Joy's case, and living on the other side of the world, in Anthony's. Joy knew she would have moved anywhere to be with Anthony, but was filled with gratitude that not only did he want to live in the village but that he was more than happy to live in Fairfield Gardens. So with almost complete accord, they agreed to be married as close to Christmas as possible, and had been more than pleased when Paul had said they could have the seventeenth of December. This date seemed to be common knowledge in the Village before they themselves knew, but to Anthony, that was part of the pleasure of living in Fairmead after many, too many, years of living in huge cities where one could remain anonymous, unknown and uncared for.

With his life settling in its new direction, Anthony prepared for the meeting later that afternoon with Bishop Procter. He was pleased to see that the Rev. Adamson was also to be present. He and Paul had become firm friends and had even been persuaded by William Blackett to take up golf. Anthony was a natural, having pursued several sports during his years in Australia, but Paul, being of a more scholarly disposition, was never going to be a pro. For the last month the three friends had tried to meet once a week, not an easy task, given that Anthony was still working in London. However, now he was established in Mansford, they had agreed to a couple of hours on Saturday mornings. Anthony had also been asked by Timothy Miller to join him at his club on Wednesday evening, and as this was Joy's evening for her gardening group, he gladly accepted.

An hour or so before their meeting with the solicitors, Henry Procter and his friend, Paul Adamson, settled themselves into ancient leather armchairs in the Bishop's study with strong, hot coffee, and immediately launched themselves into an erudite conversation concerning divergent views on the Apocrypha. Ten minutes into this deeply satisfying subject, the ringing phone suddenly returned them to the present. Henry answered and passed the receiver straight to Paul, who listened for five seconds then shot up, looking like a ghost. Babbling something about Sophia and the Royal, and most unlike his usual calm, thoughtful self, Paul hastily excused himself and dashed out of the door.

Having parked in a ten-minute drop-off zone, Paul almost ran through the main hospital entrance and was met by his mother-in-law, Monica, who reassured him that everything was fine and nothing would happen for several hours. Sophia was seeing a doctor, so he should park in a long-stay area, meet at the café and she would explain all.

By mid-afternoon, Paul was acquainted with all the facts and feeling much calmer, though he still blamed himself for allowing Sophia to drive all that way. It transpired that she had met her mother with no problem at all, then the two had retired to a restaurant for an early lunch, prepared to pay the exorbitant airport prices in honour of this extra visit. Monica had noticed that her daughter didn't seem to eat much, but nothing was said until they were negotiating the exit from Heathrow, when Sophia confided that she had a rather bad stomach ache and maybe her mother could drive once they found a suitable stopping place. As they had driven home, both had realised that it was more than stomach ache and decided to call in at the Royal when they reached Mansford. To their surprise they were told that things were happening rather quickly and it would be a good idea to stay rather than go home and return in a short time.

When Paul finally saw Sophia, she was propped up in bed, wearing a hideous hospital gown. He was dispatched home post-haste to collect her hospital-bag, packed a couple of weeks before in case of sudden departure.

Isabella and Molly saw Paul looking rather distracted as he jumped from his car in a distinctly unclerical manner and fumbled with the door key, emerging two minutes later with a small suitcase. That could only mean one thing. Both ladies hastened into the road, waving and calling good luck. They then returned to Molly's kitchen and brewed a fresh pot of tea.

Isabella had come round to congratulate Molly on having

their application for adoption approved in such a short time. It would not be actually finalised for another few weeks, as the legal aspect was always long drawn out, but to all intents and purposes, Cathy and Mark were now their own children. Isabella made no secret of the fact that Molly and James had done a wonderful job. In a relatively short time Cathy and Mark had changed from being reserved, quiet and shy, to being, in Isabella's words, 'normal children'. They ran and played and made a noise with the best of them. They were often to be seen with Liz's boys and Megan's girls playing at each others house, up and down Fairfield Gardens and rushing about on the green. Isabella said it was a sight for sore eyes.

To tell the truth, she missed having Sam, Joel and Dan around on a permanent basis and was extremely pleased that Louisa's family would be moving in next door very soon. She had already met them and knew they would get on like a house on fire. Of course she would miss Emily's quiet presence tremendously, but she would still see her almost every day around the village, not to mention at choir practice and other church affairs. In fact she had promised to pop over to Emily's that afternoon to collect a pile of copies of *St Mary's Matters* for distribution around Fairfield Gardens and nearby streets. If she didn't hurry, it would be dropping dark, so she bid a hasty goodbye to Molly, kissed Cathy and Mark, and emerged into the chill mistiness of late afternoon.

CHAPTER 15

It was early the next morning, as a pale sun was appearing through the mist, when Maria Adamson was born. An hour or so later, Paul stood in awe as he gazed down on the sleeping mother and child. Nothing in his whole life had prepared him for the wonder of last night. It was engraved on his heart, and he felt his whole being to be one huge Te Deum.

His dear mother-in-law had been a steady rock in a sea of emotion. As he looked round he saw the dark rings under her eyes and knew that he must get her home. While Sophia and Maria were resting, he and Monica would return to Fairmead, she to sleep and he to make numerous phone calls. Parish business could be put on hold for one day. The Hall reopening party and Harvest Festival Service were well under control and a meeting with William concerning various financial matters could easily be postponed.

His own parents must be the first to be told the wonderful news. His father had been vicar of an ancient church in north-east Yorkshire for many years but was retired now and living in a tiny cottage almost as ancient as the church and as inconvenient, with very few mod cons. The old couple were, however, serenely happy, spending their days pottering in the garden and drinking innumerable cups of tea with their village friends. They had three sons, all vicars, and five grandsons. Maria would be their first granddaughter and Paul knew she would be the apple of their eye.

To Paul's immense surprise, three baby cards were already reposing in his letterbox. How anybody knew that the baby was born and was a girl was a complete mystery. But before these thoughts could be pursued, visitors started arriving. Nobody stayed long, just wanting to offer their congratulations, but it was ten-thirty before he was able to make the first phone call. By eleven-thirty he was heading back to Mansford, having left Monica sound asleep. He himself had never been so wide awake. He felt on top of the world, singing the song of that name in his best church voice as he drove along.

Megan's thoughts were also directed towards her infant but were of a more perplexing nature. With just over two weeks to go before Angie's christening, the prospective Godparents had, with great regret, pulled out. Milly and Jake were old friends of her parents whose children had grown and left many years ago. They had been so pleased to be asked that Megan had felt slightly guilty that she had not thought of them for Sally, Jenny or Amy. But this morning, Milly had rung to say that Jake had been asked to fly out to New York for his company, at very short notice. Milly was to accompany him and they would visit their daughter near Chicago once his business was completed.

Megan had, of course, wished them all the best and promised to see them around Christmas time. Now she was hastily running through the names of other possible Godparents. It wasn't that she couldn't think of people, the problem was that they would know they were not the first choice. She doubted that Jack would be any help at all and had just decided to walk over to Emily Whitehead's before picking up the girls from school when Angie woke with a sudden scream, quite unlike her usual placid self. Pleased with the prospect of Emily's wise advice, Megan picked up the baby and resumed her morning routine.

Emily's old home, usually the quietest in Fairfield Gardens, was full of life on this slightly misty morning. George Hitchin had worked miracles and managed to push through the legal aspects of the sale of number ten. If the truth were to be told, he wanted the matter out of the way as speedily as possible, as he had decided to bring forward his retirement by a couple of months. Anthony Hawton was now living in Mansford and had commenced work at the beginning of the week. After only the first day, all the partners of Miller Smythe Hitchin had agreed that he was an inspired choice. His pleasant manner and razor-sharp mind were exactly what the old-established firm needed. They were also heartened by the news that he intended marrying a local girl and settling down in the nearby village of Fairmead.

★ ★ ★ ★ ★

Andrew and Margaret Ward and their children felt at home in Fairmead even before they moved into number ten. They had visited Louisa and Kate several times in the last few years and felt they knew every nook and cranny of the village. Adam and Hannah had been ambivalent about moving from Los Angeles with all their friends and many activities, but once they knew they would be almost next door to Gran and Auntie Kate they became much more enthusiastic and cooperative. They already knew the other children in Fairfield Gardens and had been told that Mr and Mrs Standing at number fourteen now had two children, so there would be plenty of friends to play with. They even remembered nice Miss Taylor who would be their new teacher at the village school.

Margaret was simply thankful that the family would be in their new home before the arrival of the baby. There really was no time to lose. They had collected the keys that morning at nine o'clock and driven straight to Fairmead, armed with brushes and cloths and various cleaning detergents, but very little needed doing as they knew Miss Whitehead had left the place spotless. Even the garden had been attended to each week since she had left by Jim Turner's teenage son from up the Farm. He had been trying to persuade his dad to let him leave school and work for a small gardening company, so he was determined to do a wonderful job on Miss Whitehead's garden.

Though the decorations were slightly more subdued than the Wards were used to, they were perfectly adequate and there would be plenty of time in the future to change them. Some of their belongings were in storage and would arrive on Monday, but most of their furniture had been sold, their thinking being that they were unlikely to find such a large house in England. This had certainly been the case with their purchase of the Fairfield Gardens house and they had spent the last few days touring furniture shops in and around Mansford, much to Adam and Hannah's disgust. Most of these new purchases would be delivered on Monday or Tuesday, if all went to plan. So, crossing fingers and toes, they hoped to move into their new home in a week's time.

Kate was looking forward to the arrival of Andrew's family almost as much as Louisa was. Her disposition was definitely motherly, having been the eldest child in a large family, and she had been saddened to be left with only one child when her darling husband had died so many years before. There had never been anyone to replace him in her affections and she had been immensely grateful to have Chloe and her nursing. The last few years, sharing her home with Louisa in this lovely village were probably the best in her whole life. She and her friend were the best of companions and Chloe had exceeded all expectations at University.

Two days before, however, she had rung her mother with the news that she had been approached to join a UN team in some African country Kate had never heard of. She would be gone a year at least and would be earning virtually nothing. Although Kate had been expecting something of the sort and put on a cheerful, excited voice, she still felt a pang of disappointment. Of course it was totally selfish, but she wished Chloe could settle down and give her grandchildren. However, through the years she had learnt to stand on her own two feet and knew that her daughter was doing just that, so, discounting all negative thoughts, she invited Chloe to come at the weekend and discuss the exciting proposition. She would be arriving mid-morning on Saturday and would be able to join in the frivolity of the grand Hall reopening party. To Kate's great pleasure, she said she would also stay overnight and attend the Harvest Festival service on Sunday morning. The pleasure of the forthcoming weekend gave Kate unaccustomed tingles of delight as she went about her duties on the children's ward.

In a different department of the Hospital, Liz was also feeling the warm glow of pleasure at hearing good news. Isabella had kindly driven her in, after the boys had been dropped at school, and had waited while she queued up for a blood test. The two had then gone to a quiet café where they remained undisturbed for three hours, drinking several cups of tea and nibbling delicate sandwiches, which Isabella said wouldn't fill a mouse. But she had been tact itself, offering to drive Liz, in the absence of dear Sophia, and respecting her fragile condition by unobtrusively offering her arm and walking slowly, and by curbing her robust conversation and allowing friendly silences at frequent intervals.

This was Liz's first major outing. Previously she had rested in outpatients before seeing the doctor and then being driven home by Sophia. Though more tired than she had thought possible, Liz had thoroughly enjoyed getting out. After what seemed like aeons in hospital and at home, the outside world seemed like a foreign country and she felt like an alien, registering slight surprise that everyone didn't stare at her. But in this chilly weather, wearing a warm, woolly hat seemed in no way strange. Tom said he loved her short, punk hairstyle, though Liz knew he was so relieved she was still alive that he loved everything about her, even her pale, thin face and old woman's walk.

Today, however, the doctor had been very pleased with her. She had seen Dr Miles striding through the main entrance as she and Isabella were leaving. He said she was doing wonderfully and told her to keep on doing whatever she was doing, because it was obviously working.

While Liz had been waiting to see her specialist, Isabella had taken the opportunity to visit Sophia in maternity. She was not at all surprised to find mother looking calmly radiant and baby sleeping soundly by her side. Sophia said she felt a fraud occupying a bed but she would, of course, follow advice and remain until Monday. Isabella's advice was to have as much rest as possible, and she should know, having herself had many children and acquired many grandchildren, the latest of whom would be born in the New Year. Sophia laughed, enquired after Liz and said she was looking forward to bringing Maria home. Sadly, she would miss the party and Sunday Service, but Isabella thought she didn't seem too sad and her mouth twitched in a barely-concealed grin.

★ ★ ★ ★ ★

Friday was a much more stressful day for Joy and her fellow teachers. All week one class or the other had been practising the folk dances they would be performing at the Hall reopening party, and the constant sound of jolly music, clapping hands and stamping feet had rendered schoolwork almost impossible and given everyone a permanent headache. In addition every child had been invited to bring in some interesting natural object to add to the display around the baptismal font in church, ready for the Harvest Festival service on Sunday. Skeletal leaves and squashed berries found every nook and cranny, despite Doris' best efforts to keep them under control. Grasses, twigs and pot plants borrowed from dad's greenhouse or mum's window sill covered every available surface and walls were decorated with drawings and paintings of harvest bounty. All this was to be transported over to the church just before home time and excitement was building throughout the morning, reaching fever-pitch by two o'clock.

On her way to visit Emily Whitehead, Megan saw three harassed-looking teachers assembling their classes in the school playground. Each child had an armfull of objects, and several disputes seemed to be in progress. Two older boys were severely annoying the girls in front of them by dropping berries in their hair, two little ones were arguing fiercely about who should be leader in the line and one tiny girl was sobbing loudly because she had picked up the wrong bunch of grass. Megan smiled, feeling relieved that her three weren't involved in these dramas and, indeed, appeared to be standing still, waiting in angelic innocence. However, she had the distinct impression that the moment she was out of sight, they would revert to normal. She greatly admired the three teachers and felt she couldn't do their job for the world. It was hard enough with four children and she didn't know what she would have done without Jack's help.

As she had hoped, Emily was home, having a little after-lunch rest. She was more than pleased to welcome Megan and Angie into her simple home. She made a fresh pot of tea, sat Angie on her knee and talked gently of this and that, while Megan collected her thoughts.

When the problem of the Godparents was finally mentioned, Emily gave it her full attention. Her gentle suggestions filled Megan with pleasure and she relaxed. Even Angie behaved herself, making them laugh by shuffling around the floor on her bottom in a most comical fashion. As the afternoon grew dimmer and a misty drizzle began to wet the pavements, the two ladies reluctantly turned off the cosy heater, wrapped up warmly and emerged into the world outside, one to collect her children from school and the other to visit Clarissa Jones, who was confined to the house with a broken arm - the first time she had broken anything in eighty-eight years, or so she said.

Trying to get home quickly, out of the misty damp, was no easy matter. Even Molly, with five children, was more successful. She had promised to pick up Dan, Joel and Sam, as Isabella was taking their mum to the hospital in Mansford and the traffic would be bad, especially in this weather. They were already taking off raincoats and shaking umbrellas before Megan had even turned the corner. The problem was that Amy wanted to play with her friend Alison, who lived near the Village Stores, and they had promised each other that they would swap Barbie clothes. Unknown to Megan, she had taken some in her schoolbag that morning. Neither mother knew anything about it, and Alison was going to visit her Grandma. Amy was most upset, dragged her feet and wouldn't hurry. Jenny was also feeling put out because her raincoat had lost a button and she couldn't find it. Only Sally was in a good mood, walking smugly, holding on to the pram handle.

So absorbed were they all that they almost bumped into Mrs Newson coming out of the Vicar's gate, clinging tightly to Lady's lead and hanging on to a huge multi-coloured umbrella. After laughing apologies and assurances that Sophia and baby Maria were fine, they hurried off in opposite directions. As Monica tramped through muddy fields, wearing two pairs of socks in Sophia's old wellington boots, she realised why she lived in Spain. Only the thought of darling Maria kept her from booking the next flight out.

As soon as Jack returned and was acquainted with the new christening plan, Megan hurried across the road, leaving him warming in front of the fire, bouncing Angie up and down on his leg, listening to Amy's tale of woe and attempting to watch the news on television. Kate was home, but Louisa was staying later at the Stores to do a little stocktaking. Megan said Kate was just the person she wanted to see and, without preamble, launched straight into her request, explaining why it was made at such short notice. As Emily had expected, Kate was thrilled and honoured to be asked to be Angie's Godmother. She quite understood that family friends had had to be asked first.

After Megan had left, she sat and pondered her good fortune and many blessings. Though it didn't seem she would have grandchildren of her own for quite a while, she would soon have Andrew's children to love and now little Angie to be her Godchild, not to mention the dear girls and boys at the Royal.

CHAPTER 16

Saturday morning was blessedly fine, though grey and rather uninspiring. Fairmead was bustling, earlier than usual, as there was much to be done. Household tasks were completed as soon as possible and washing hung out in the still air, with little hope of its drying any time soon. Paul and William escaped as soon as the coast was clear to have a quick game of golf with Anthony, and other husbands around the village suddenly found reasons why they had to leave the house.

At ten o'clock, a group of ladies and far too many children, laden with boxes and bags overflowing with fruit, vegetables and flowers were standing chatting near the church door, waiting for Bill Hughes to come and unlock it. That gentleman had never been known to hurry in his life and no one was unduly concerned when he had not appeared at ten-fifteen. However, by ten-thirty, people were beginning to feel slightly annoyed and Isabella, as honorary leader of the Harvest Festival Church Decoration Contingent, sent two of the children in search of him. Enjoying the freedom, they made a slight detour around the Green before arriving at St Mary's Home, only to be told that Mr Hughes was ill in bed with a bad dose of flu.

Dr Miles was just leaving, but he quickly returned to his

patient's room to request the church key. Bill was sure it was in his coat pocket but, as this was not the case, a long search began. Eventually, it was located in an ancient tea caddy, sporting a faded picture of Queen Victoria's Diamond Jubilee, which had been his dear mother's pride and joy.

At this point, Emily Whitehead knocked diffidently on the door, an old wicker basket on her arm, and asked if Bill would like anything from the Stores, as she would be calling in after helping in the church. Bill requested a newspaper and bottle of orange squash, then settled back to watch a repeat football match on his portable television set, thoughtfully provided by his daughter.

The children returned, accompanied by Miss Whitehead, at a much more sedate pace, but filled with excitement at their adventure. When they finally arrived back, the church door was wide open and decoration was in full swing. The Vicar had appeared about two minutes after the children had sped off and was now busy up a ladder attaching an unwieldy arrangement of flowers to the top of an old picture. When he heard about Bill, he came down immediately and went off to visit his old friend, thoughts already whirling around his head as to who could be asked to perform Bill's duties at such short notice. Joy, he knew, would gladly fill in temporarily but someone permanent would need to be found, as Bill would have to retire sooner or later.

Bill was thinking the same thought at the same time. He loved his little job at the church, but the previous winter the old building had chilled his bones and had definitely not improved his rheumatism. Even before he had come down with flu, he had more or less decided to pass on his duties to a younger and fitter person before this winter well and truly started. His daughter thoroughly agreed, having been urging him to do so for the last five years. So when the Vicar arrived, just as his team were scoring their second goal, he switched off, rather reluctantly it must be said, and told him of his decision.

The church key had been left in Emily Whitehead's capable hands. When the decoration was finally completed to everyone's satisfaction and the whole place had been swept and tidied, she locked the door and all returned home for a well-deserved bite to eat. Elsie Summerton had just arrived with the library van and was pleasantly surprised at the large number of borrowers on this still, grey day. As she stamped books, she chatted about the week's news, expressing delight at little Maria's birth and the imminent arrival of the Ward family and nodding sadly at the news of Bill's flu. She and Jessie were stalwart Fairmeaders who had long been associated with the Village. They were looking forward to the Harvest Festival Service and were certainly coming to the Hall reopening party, being cheerful souls who loved a good get-together.

★ ★ ★ ★ ★

About one-thirty, William, James and Tom drove up to the school together to collect the tables, still stored in the sports shed and which after today's party would be returned to their usual home in the Hall. Miss Browning had kindly agreed to supervise their exit and she would then proceed to Miss Whitehead's for a convivial hour, drinking tea and chatting kindly about village affairs. The older lady never spoke of anyone in less than a generous way and never disclosed any secrets she was privy to. After their pleasant hour, the two would stroll up to the Hall and offer their services before the party commenced at four o'clock.

Once the tables had been erected, the waiting ladies spread colourful red and white check tablecloths, freshly washed and ironed for the occasion. They then opened the many bags and boxes dropped in during the morning, containing every type of food imaginable, from the usual sausage rolls to more exotic curry and rice dishes. Louisa had sent up a beautiful selection of cream buns, specially ordered in this morning's delivery. She had also sent a container full of soft drink bottles and these now filled the little fridge in the Hall's tiny kitchen. Anthony Hawton had been the bearer of these gifts, after returning from his foreshortened game of golf. He was now totally part of the Fairmead scene and his high-pressure job on the other side of the world was a fading memory. He had never realised how much he had missed feeling part of a small community and was looking forward with real pleasure to marrying his darling Joy and settling in Fairmead once again.

For the first time, Molly had agreed to attend to several ladies' hair requirements on a Saturday morning. These were people who had not previously been clients of hers as they worked during the week. However, Molly's skill, pleasant manner and reasonable rates were now well known in the Village and surrounding areas, and four ladies had begged her to make an exception and do their hair ready for the party, as they had no time to travel into Mansford. James had been perfectly happy to have the children all to himself, and the three of them had spent a happy morning tidying up the garden and having a little bonfire of all the leaves and twigs produced by the morning's work. When Molly returned, they were standing next to its remains, drinking hot soup from cracked mugs that should have been thrown away years ago. They were streaked with mud, liberally decorated with garden debris and smelled strongly of smoke. But they looked so contented that Molly felt her heart would burst and laughingly chivvied them into the bathroom for a thorough clean-up before the party.

Liz was taking the opportunity to rest after her excursion the previous day and before the exertion of the party. She had decided to go up for a couple of hours. The party was scheduled to end about nine o'clock, but Tom would run her back about six before she felt too tired and the evening got colder. Since the chemo she had lost a lot of weight and felt the cold tremendously. Tom grumbled that the house was like a sauna when he came in after work, but he always smiled as he said it and went to change into T-shirt and shorts.

This morning he had taken the boys to football, as usual. The team was an unofficial gathering of small boys who met about ten o'clock on Saturdays in Mansford's Central Park and kicked a ball around for an hour or so, encouraged by their fathers. If there were enough to make two reasonably-sized teams, they attempted a match, amid considerable squabbling and sometimes a few tears. Sam was one of the oldest and had recently begun pestering his dad to let him join a proper team. Tom had said he could when mummy was better, probably next year.

Also in Mansford that morning was Kate, who had arranged to meet Chloe's train. The two were planning to have lunch at the King's Head before indulging in a couple of hours of clothes shopping. Neither was particularly fashion conscious but they knew they would enjoy this rare mother and daughter time.

Kate was determined to be nothing if not totally supportive of Chloe's plans and was looking forward to telling her of her own forthcoming role as Angie's Godmother, not to mention the imminent arrival of Andrew's family. Seeing her mother so positive pleased Chloe tremendously, as she felt quite protective towards her and knew of her desire to have children to love, but Chloe also knew that she must follow her own dreams and pursue her path through life.

About three o'clock, Kate looked at her watch and said they should think about getting home, as she had promised to be at the Hall around four when the party was due to begin, having committed herself to taking charge of the soft drinks table. However, locating the car in the huge, new multi-storey car park was easier said than done. She had completely forgotten the level and could only remember that it was next to a blue Mini. After fifteen minutes of searching high and low, giggling like school girls, they spied the errant vehicle next to a white van bearing the legend 'Steve's Steam Cleaning Service'. Still laughing, they wove their way out and merged into Mansford's busy Saturday afternoon traffic. It was a relief to leave the city behind and drive along country roads to Fairmead.

About halfway home, Chloe suddenly stopped talking about Professor Bradley, newly appointed and causing quite a stir in his department, to exclaim that she had had a blinding flash of revelation concerning Megan's problem as to who should be Godfather to little Angie. Why shouldn't it be Andrew Ward? He was almost related to Kate, being Louisa's son, and was an exceptionally nice person. He would also be living next door to the Todds and could keep a Godfatherly eye on Angie as she was growing up. Kate thought it was a wonderful idea and promised to speak to Megan that very afternoon.

By three-thirty Megan was threatening the girls with missing the party altogether, so exasperated was she by their racing around and general excitement, which had disturbed Angie and resulted in a very grumpy baby. Jack had escaped most of the upset by darting off to the Hall as soon as he saw William and James squeezing into Tom's van. He had looked after the children until about twelve while Megan was out shopping and felt he had done more than his fair share of child minding. The possibility of not seeing all their friends at the party quietened the girls considerably and Megan's good-temper also returned. With little further fuss, Sally, Jenny and Amy put on their party dresses and Angie was attired in a sweet pink outfit which Megan had purchased that morning in the Baby Shoppe sale. All pulled on warm coats and hats for the short walk to the Hall and were the first to arrive.

Isabella and a cohort of helpers were already there, having arranged the food tables to their satisfaction, and were just about to organise the soft drinks when Kate arrived, accompanied by Chloe, full of apologies. The hot water urn was switched on and the party was under way. Balloons of all shapes and colours hung around the walls, having been heroically blown up by Jim Turner's son who had been sent down from the farm with milk for the tea and coffee. The Vicar had volunteered for this onerous duty but been excused on the grounds that he had to visit his wife and daughter in Mansfield Royal. This he had done. So besotted was he by his darling wife and baby that, for the first time in living memory, he had forgotten the time and was late for an appointment. Fifty-five minutes late, he gave his little speech of thanks to Tom Norris for the wonderful renovation work he had so speedily completed and to all who had helped in any way towards this great celebration. He also thanked the people of Fairmead for their patience and good humour during the last few months when meetings and gatherings had had to be relocated or postponed. He hoped everyone would have a marvellous evening. He blushed as the whole Hall reverberated with clapping, stamping and cheering.

The party was indeed a wonderful success. Music was provided by a trio of senior citizens from St Mary's Home, playing mouth organ, banjo and snare drum. They had volunteered their services several weeks before when the party was being discussed at a Village Affairs Meeting, and had practised every day since then, much to the amusement and occasional irritation of other residents. They were received with great enthusiasm by all the party goers and every twenty minutes, when they took a well-earned break, a couple of the younger generation of Fairmead played considerably more modern music on a portable CD Player. Dancing ranged from the *Dashing White Sergeant* to jive to hip hop, depending on the ages of the participants, though everybody from Dan Norris to old Bessie Crabtree joined in the Progressive Barn Dance, causing great hilarity. So popular was this dance that it was requested at least half a dozen times. Kate was kept busy handing out drinks to perspiring dancers and Louisa, Flo and Marjorie were kept on their toes making endless cups of tea and coffee, so much so that they felt they were still busy in the café.

After an hour or so Jane Simmons from the Farmer's Arms and Elsie and Jessie Summerton from the library took control of the drinks, allowing the other ladies to relax and enjoy the party. All through the evening, various people offered to man the food and drink tables, so no one felt overburdened. Fortunately, enough food had been donated to feed an army and it lasted until about eight-fifteen, by which time everyone was full and felt certain they would not eat again for a week.

At five to nine, the band played *The Last Waltz*, and were driven off home by the Vicar, exhausted but completely content to be greeted by Emily Whitehead with a welcome cup of cocoa in the Common Room. She and Bessie had been given a lift home a few minutes earlier by that nice young man, Anthony Hawton. He had then returned to assist some of the other men with the clearing up. Since the ladies had prepared the party, they had felt obliged to tidy-up and leave the Hall spick and span, ready for the next day. By ten o'clock the Hall was once again in darkness and most people were cosily sitting beside warm fires, drinking yet another cup of tea and switching on the telly. Only a handful of hardy youngsters was preparing for a night out in Mansford, the village party having been only the entrée before the night's real entertainment.

CHAPTER 17

On the Sunday morning most people were late up, children were fractious and there was a general feeling of the morning after. However, this was no day to sit around reading the paper, as most people in Fairmead, even non-churchgoers, were going to the Harvest Festival Service. It was a tradition in the village which nobody wanted to see die out, so it was always extremely well supported. All the village school children had contributed to the decoration of the church, and almost every Fairmead family had sent something, however small.

Joy was awake particularly early on this hazy, autumn-smelling morning, as she had promised Paul that once again she would take over Bill Hughes' duties until a permanent replacement could be found. But her thoughts were far from church affairs as she pottered about in her warm red dressing gown, drawing back the curtains and switching on the electric jug. She and Anthony had begun discussing the details of their wedding and her mind was whirring with delightful conundrums. Guests, bridesmaids, colours, flowers and The Dress all floated around with tingling pleasure. Though she sternly forbade such thoughts while at school, they rushed in, unchecked, at other times. Even during the party, she had been assessing the suitability of the Hall for their reception and had found in its favour. Anthony had decided to leave all the planning to Joy, who seemed to have been born for the job and knew he would be in complete agreement with anything she decided. He would have been happy to marry her in a registry office with two strangers as witnesses, but knew she longed for a traditional village wedding and wanted nothing to spoil her big day. Accordingly, he was in complete agreement concerning the Hall and said he would mention it to William who could then put it to the next Village Affairs Committee meeting.

Paul was up even earlier than Joy, having been jerked out of a deep and dreamless sleep by his alarm. Quietly passing his mother-in-law's room, soon to be baby Maria's, he entered the third small bedroom which served as his office, den and prayer room, switched on the electric heater, pulled on an ancient tracksuit and settled down to his morning prayer. This was his blissful, uninterrupted hour of union with his Maker and was the foundation on which the whole day was built. It was still early when he emerged and went downstairs to be greeted by Lady's licks and wagging tail. She had spent the night curled tightly in her warm basket in the kitchen and was more than ready for her morning constitutional. She never went upstairs, having been discouraged as a small puppy. Joy was the only one to see the Vicar and his dog striding up the Gardens as she drew back her curtains. All the others, even Angie Todd, were still warmly tucked up in bed.

Sophia's mother was woken by the sound of the closing front door and she lay for a few minutes reliving the last exciting few days. She could hardly believe it had only been Thursday when she had taken a taxi to the airport for her flight from Spain, which she had almost missed due to the driver misunderstanding the pick-up time. Then she had met Sophia, only to rush to the hospital and support Paul, as well as her daughter, through the next few hours until the birth of that darling little scrap, her first grandchild. She had visited several times and was going this afternoon after the service and a hasty lunch. She had not been to a Harvest Festival since she had been a girl, and she was looking forward to it, but the thought of getting up was not attractive after her exertions at the party.

She knew many people from the village, as she was a sociable person, and had managed to dance and chat almost the whole time, barely stopping for a cup of tea and sausage roll. But after ten minutes of reviewing the past three days, she dragged herself out of bed and went down to make breakfast for herself and Paul, pleasantly surprised that her ever-thoughtful son-in-law had already put on the fire and warmth was spreading.

Isabella was having a well-earned lie-in. After her efforts preparing the church and at the party, it was wonderful to be pampered by William, who brought her an unexpected cup of tea at about eight-thirty before setting off with an impatient Scrappy. He too felt tired after his busy Saturday but the morning was so inviting that he felt like getting out. Somehow, the clearing mist evoked a feeling of nostalgia for the days of his youth, playing with his numerous brothers and sisters in the fields around their home before he was overtaken by the responsibilities of career and family. This feeling was so unusual in the normally competent and practical William that it caused him to stop and lean on an ancient gate and stare into the middle distance. Poor Scrappy's whines and tugs went unheard for at least ten minutes, until his master suddenly realised the time and set off again at a hearty pace.

★ ★ ★ ★ ★

For the first time in many months, there were to be refreshments in the Hall after Morning Service and they were to be presided over by Isabella's good friend Jane Simmons from the Farmer's Arms, ably assisted by her mother-in-law, Doris, and Betty Cummings from St Mary's Home kitchen. This had always been Isabella's responsibility, but today she had gladly delegated her duties and was looking forward to a nice hot bath before William's return and the necessary cooking of the extra large Sunday breakfast.

Liz was extremely tired after the last couple of days but had enjoyed them thoroughly and was looking forward with pleasure to the Harvest Festival Service, after which she would enjoy a traditional Sunday lunch, cooked by her mother, who was staying for the weekend. Her appetite had returned wonderfully, though the strange thing was that she felt neither hungry nor full but could eat as though she had holes in her feet, as a result of which she had recovered some of her lost weight. This, together with her rosy cheeks, now made her appear to be the picture of health, but she still tired easily and had learned to let go and expect much less of herself.

During the past few months, Tom and the boys had come up trumps. Between them, they made their beds and picked up toys. Their clothes were put in the basket, awaiting the attention of dear Joy, who still did the washing, folding and ironing when Liz's mother or mother-in-law were not there. Sophia had also helped at first but had been persuaded to stop a month or so ago. Such good friends! Isabella, too, still had the boys over often, to give Liz a break. How she could ever thank them enough, she didn't know.

Kate's visitor was also planning lunch, but her intention was to treat her mother to an expensive meal at a riverside restaurant some miles away. Looking out of the window at the clearing mist, Chloe hoped that by lunchtime the sun would be out and the temperature would have risen sufficiently to let her sit out on the terrace overlooking the quiet river with its swans and overhanging willow trees. She knew she would miss her mother, but felt only excitement and satisfaction at the thought of her new job in Africa. Plans for her move were progressing well and last week she had had all the necessary jabs, not pleasant but thankfully she had suffered very little adverse reaction. Some of her friends were organising a night out for her and even that nice Professor Bradley had wished her well as they passed on the library steps. All in all, she was very happy with her life at present.

Louisa was also preparing for guests. Once Chloe emerged from the spare room, she would quickly change the sheets and set up the two folding beds, borrowed from Isabella and William. Andrew, Margaret and the children were leaving their Mansford hotel this morning and arriving in time for the Harvest Festival Service. They would then stay with Louisa and Kate until their new home was ready at the end of the week, if all went well. Andrew was starting work the next day and the children would be starting at the Village School. Margaret would be at number ten to supervise the arrival of new furniture. There was also to be a delivery of various crates from storage. Louisa had insisted on being there to help and Margaret was most grateful, with her time almost due. The café was closed on Mondays and Tuesdays in winter, so Flo and Marjorie had cheerfully volunteered to come in and look after the shop. Doris Simmons had also said she would help between school cleaning duties, if it was necessary any day. So, with all problems solved, Louisa busied herself preparing the room and Sunday lunch for her family.

Molly and James had arranged with Megan and Jack to take all the children to Mansford Central Park, where there was a circus. After church, they would drive there and attempt to park as close as possible. Then they would meet up near the large lake for a picnic and walk around the Nature Track before the circus started at two-thirty. James and Jack got on well and would have plenty to talk about. She and Megan were now also good friends since she had been home with the children. They had much in common. Both were interested in hair and fashion and all that went on in the Village. Megan tried to take Angie out for a walk everyday and spoke to everyone she met. Molly also spoke to many people in her role as village hairdresser, though she was careful never to disclose confidences or gossip unkindly. She regarded her position as akin to that of the vicar, doctor or teacher. Mark and Cathy were highly excited at the prospect of going to the circus, as they had never been before, just seen one at Christmas on the television. Molly hoped they would settle down somewhat in church.

At that moment, Emily Whitehead was slipping quietly into

St Mary's through the back door, kindly unlocked by the Vicar, on his way home after an invigorating walk with Lady. The Prayer Circle started for Liz Norris had continued, much to Emily's delight, and now included many other intentions. Some were people from the village who needed prayers, while others were more distant friends and relations. Of late, national and even international events had been included.

Emily had implicit trust in the power of love and prayer and conscientiously included all in her prayers. Throughout the wet summer, when she had been unwell, she had not always been able to come to the church and had had to content herself with saying her prayers in front of her own fire, but she loved the ambience of the old building and the sense of tranquillity it inspired. Now she had moved to the Home her health had improved, and once again she wrapped up warmly for her morning hour in the church.

This Sunday it had lost its sense of mystery and was transformed into the outdoors. Sheaves of corn, vegetables, fruit, berries, flowers and plants of all kinds filled every available space and the air was sweet with autumn scents. Emily glanced around with real pleasure, adding her own prayer of thanks for the Earth's wonderful bounty, before settling in her favourite spot and bowing her head.

Later she returned to the church, entering this time though the heavy main door, to sit at the organ and prepare herself for the joyful service. Paul had been there for an hour already, as was his custom on a Sunday, praying quietly in the vestry, and Joy had arrived a short time later to make sure all was in readiness. The last of the mist was clearing and the sun had a touch of warmth. It seemed everybody in Fairmead had made an effort to be there, even Bill Hughes, who was determined to attend despite Dr Miles' strict instructions to stay in his warm room, and Clarissa Jones, with her arm in a sling, who had likewise been requested to rest. Old and young sang the traditional Harvest Festival hymns with gusto, almost drowning out the choir and organ and competing with the birds outside, who were celebrating a feast of berries on this lovely autumn day.

CHAPTER 18

Monday morning came as rather a shock to many after the weekend's celebrations. Jack Todd and James Standing both had to depart at what seemed to be the crack of dawn to attend early meetings, leaving their wives to cope with the children. Andrew Ward was also off bright and early to tackle his new responsibilities. Margaret, however, had the help of her mother-in-law, and relished the prospect of an extra hour in bed before facing various delivery men.

Louisa was in her element helping Adam and Hannah find their clothes and bags, all of which had been laid out the night before but had mysteriously disappeared again. She noted with amusement that their delicious American accent was already being tempered by the local burr, and they no longer spoke of Los Angeles as home. Children adapt so quickly, she thought. Maybe we adults should take a leaf out of their book and stop clinging to the past.

With this thought, she poured milk on to their cereal and popped two slices of bread into the toaster, hoping to tempt them with a little scrambled egg. She was a great believer in the sustaining power of a good breakfast, having herself always partaken of fruit, porridge and something on toast, however early the hour.

Margaret rose about eight o'clock and was ready to walk the children up to school by half past. They had arranged to meet up with Cathy and Mark and the four children skipped ahead as Molly and Margaret chatted. Cathy and Mark had forgotten what it was like to be new at a school and prattled on about their teachers and the other children in their class. Adam would be in Mrs Evans' and Hannah in Miss Taylor's. Sam Norris was also in the Juniors and had organised to meet Adam near the school gate. Whoever came first had to stay put until the other arrived. Already the two of them were firm friends with interests in shiny sports cars, pulling apart anything to see how it worked, swapping football cards and playing marbles. Sam was hoping that Adam's dad would let him come to the Saturday morning football in Mansford and maybe next year they could join a proper team. But before that, he wanted to introduce his new friend, with his strange way of talking, to the joys of conkers. Sam was really glad to have another boy his own age living in Fairfield Gardens.

Having delivered the children to their respective teachers and introduced herself to those mothers and grandparents who were able to stay for a while after the bell, Margaret walked home with Megan, while Molly set off for her first hair appointment. Louisa was already established in the new house, perched on a kitchen stool brought from her own home. A fold-up camping chair was set up for Margaret, with a small cushion for her back. Louisa had resisted the temptation to stroll over to the Village Stores, telling herself firmly that Flo and Marjorie could manage perfectly well and would be in touch if there was any problem. As Margaret walked in through the door, she turned her thoughts resolutely to her daughter-in-law and the imminent arrival of the first furniture.

Monica Newson was already up and the first load of washing on before Paul returned from his early morning walk with Lady. She was always grateful for his quiet, pleasant manner early in the day, as she was rarely her best in the mornings. This morning, however, she was feeling wide awake and excited at the prospect of Sophia and Maria's homecoming. This wouldn't happen until mid-afternoon, but she wanted to give the house a thorough spring clean, so she didn't have to do much for the next week or so and could concentrate on her daughter and darling granddaughter. Also, at the weekend, Paul's parents would be travelling down to see their brand new grandchild. They had insisted on staying overnight in Mansford, not wishing to cause Monica any extra work, but she still wanted the house to be clean. Over breakfast, she and Paul spoke now and again, reverting to their own thoughts at frequent intervals, and she reflected again what a dear man Paul was and how lucky Sophia was to have found him. Paul's thoughts were all of his wife and baby, and the amazing fact that he was now a family man, when for years he had resigned himself to remaining single. God certainly worked in wondrous ways!

★ ★ ★ ★ ★

Up at the school, Miss Browning's thoughts were not quite as sanguine as the Vicar's. Her class were working fairly quietly, attempting a maths test on all they had learned so far this term.

Out of the corner of her eye, she spied two boys surreptitiously extracting calculators from their desks, but with one stern word from their teacher, these were hastily replaced. Miss Browning then resumed her perusal of the morning's post from the office, sighing at the number of rules, regulations and directives emanating from that centre of bureaucracy, not to mention new items to be slotted, somehow, into the curriculum and new methods of teaching. It was all getting too much and she was seriously thinking that this might be her last year. It would mean taking early retirement but she had spent almost forty years in the profession, to all intents and purposes giving her life to it and suddenly there seemed so little time to do everything she had always meant to do. Liz Norris' serious illness, coming on so suddenly, had shaken her more than she cared to admit and the trite phrase 'you never know' kept repeating itself in her mind. As fast-finishers began rustling their papers and clicking their pens, Miss Browning made the decision to make a decision by Christmas and with this thought, she turned her attention to the next lesson.

Miss Taylor's class were also grappling with maths, but with considerably more noise and enthusiasm. Equipment of all shapes and sizes was spread around the classroom. Some children were weighing objects, ranging from pencils to books, while others were arranging coloured counters in patterns. Yet others were measuring water, pouring it into different-sized containers, within the confines of an old baby bath donated by Mrs Evans' daughter. A final group were rolling plasticine into lengthy snakes, then squashing it back into balls. All were supposed to be recording their results in large books, but most were far too involved in the practical aspects of their experiments. Joy remained quite calm amid this seeming chaos. She had placed the new little girl, Hannah, with her friend Cathy and the two were deeply involved with the counters. Sally Todd was also in their group, though her sisters were elsewhere. Joy felt strongly that it was important for the triplets to form their own friendships and pursue their own interests, but this was difficult in a small village and small school. Nevertheless, she did her best to treat the girls as separate identities with different needs.

As the bustling activity continued in the infants' classroom, Emily Whitehead popped into the Village Stores for a packet of ginger biscuits and was greeted by the wide smiles of Flo and Marjorie. These ladies were often mistaken for sisters but were in fact old friends and neighbours of thirty years. They had both arrived in Fairmead as brides and lived across the road from each other. Now both widows, they were inseparable and had been very pleased to be asked to help in Louisa's café when it opened a few years ago. They were both small and wiry, with steely-grey hair, kept in position by Molly's perms, and had the uncanny knack of finishing each other's sentences, as if they were identical twins. Always smiling, their smiles widened as they saw dear Miss Whitehead and she was welcomed as a honoured guest.

It was twenty minutes later when Emily finally emerged, clutching her biscuits, having gently refused the offer of a plastic bag. As she entered the garden of St Mary's Home, she caught a flash of white near the old holly bush and when she turned to look more closely, gasped as she saw a tiny kitten curled in a pile of fallen leaves. It woke as she approached but stayed resolutely where it was, allowing Emily to reach down and almost imperceptibly stroke its thin back with one finger. She could almost see its ribs and its white fur was a dirty shade of grey.

Her kind heart was touched. Ever since her beautiful old cat, Fluffy, had died peacefully in her basket, just before the move from Fairfield Gardens, she had wondered if it would be the right thing to do at her age to get another cat and had considered visiting the Animal Rescue Shelter in Mansford. Now this little scrap had found its way to her and she knew she had found the answer. There seemed no possibility of finding its owner, it was so obviously abandoned, so, picking it up carefully, she made her way into the house.

Small animals were allowed at the Home. Jan Fletcher had a budgie and Bessie Crabtree had a fish, but no one had a cat, so, to be on the safe side, she tapped on the office door and had a word with Mrs Campbell. One look at the tiny ball of bedraggled fur was enough to put that lady under its spell. She knew Emily would be the best of owners and gladly gave her consent. Having no family of her own, she loved all the residents and wished for nothing more than their contentment. So with a purring kitten and packet of biscuits impeding her somewhat, Emily Whitehead found her key and opened the door to her little domain.

By Friday evening, Fairfield Gardens had its full complement of residents. On Monday afternoon Sophia and the baby had been driven home by Paul, who had spent much of the morning attempting to fix in the baby carrier on the back seat of the car. Being of a scholarly, rather than practical nature, he had finally swallowed his pride and called round to enlist William's help. As the father and grandfather of many, all things baby were second nature to him and he had the contraption installed satisfactorily in no time, after which the two men disappeared into the den for a restoring cup of strong coffee, well out of the way of Monica's vacuum cleaner.

Sophia, meanwhile, was enjoying her last few hours of rest, sitting in a sunny corner reading and waiting for Maria to wake for her next feed. She had bathed and changed her earlier and was amazed at how quickly these skills had come to her, with a little help from the wonderful nurses. Other mothers she had spoken to would be thrown in the deep end, once they left hospital, but she was blessed to have her mother staying for a while and a husband who more or less worked from home. So, with no worries in the world, she enjoyed the sun, her book and the anticipation of a joyful homecoming.

The Ward family moved into number ten officially on Friday afternoon. All the stored crates and new furniture had arrived during the week. There had been a slight mix-up with the beds, an extra double bed having arrived instead of two singles for the children, much to the embarrassment of the department store which assured them this had never happened before. But by late Thursday evening, Andrew had returned spanners and screwdrivers to Louisa and Kate's tool box, making a mental note to buy his own tool box during his lunch break the next day, and sunk gratefully into his mother's armchair to watch the late news on television. On Friday morning, Andrew and the children had left from number sixteen and returned to number ten where boxes and crates were still piled outside the back door but all necessary items were in place. Megan had called round during the morning and helped Margaret locate the new sheets and bedding. With much good humour, they made the beds and sorted out kitchen utensils, these having been delivered only that morning. Angie played on a blanket nearby, still content to sit but already moving into the shuffling-on-the-bottom stage, when, Megan sighed, all her peace would be gone. Margaret laughed and said the street would have to be renamed Babyfield Gardens now Sophia had Maria and her own was due very soon. Megan sincerely hoped she would be able to attend Angie's christening. Andrew had generously agreed to be her Godfather and, of course, Kate was to be her Godmother.

CHAPTER 19

On Saturday morning Adam was up early, far too early. Sam Norris had said his dad would take him to play football in Mansford Central Park. Adam had never actually played football before, but he and Sam and a group of other boys had been kicking a ball around the playground all week. Granted, it was a tennis ball, but it was better than nothing and Miss Browning wouldn't allow footballs at school. Hannah was glad she didn't have to go with them. Her plans were much more exciting. She was going to play with Sally, Jenny and Amy and was going to show them the beautiful Barbie she had brought from America with her box full of sparkly dresses and accessories. Hannah thought it must be wonderful to have sisters and really hoped the new baby would be a girl.

Meanwhile, her teacher was having similar thoughts of sparkly dresses. Joy was planning a trip to Mansford to look in a wedding dress shop. To her great pleasure, her two friends, Sophia and Megan, had insisted on coming, saying she couldn't look at wedding dresses on her own. Sophia was leaving Maria in the capable hands of her mother and Jack would have the girls, plus their friend, Hannah, as usual on a Saturday morning. Megan said she would do her usual grocery shopping first and meet the other two at Beautiful Brides. Over the last week or so, Joy had been thinking long and hard about who to have as bridesmaids. Neither she nor Anthony had sisters or even cousins. Anthony had three cousins, all male, and she had never even met her only cousin, as she had moved to Canada as a baby. It would have been nice to ask a couple of the little girls in her class but this was completely out of the question, as she would be accused of favouritism and this was something she had strenuously tried to avoid at all times. So the solution seemed to be friends and Joy had made up her mind to ask Sophia and Megan to be her Matrons of Honour. She was planning to ask them this morning while perusing the dresses.

Anthony was hoping to have a good game of golf with William and Paul, after which he would meet her for lunch in a delightful old riverside pub several miles west of Mansford. This old inn was a favourite of theirs and they had enjoyed many weekend lunches on the lawn leading down to the river, but now the weather was becoming cooler, they looked forward to the scented log fire and hoped to find a table close to the deep set fireplace.

Louisa's fire was much smaller but equally cosy and welcoming. As her café had once been the parlour of a typical Fairmead cottage, a tiny Victorian fireplace took pride of place on the wall. In summer, Louisa placed a vase of flowers from her garden or an arrangement of twigs or grasses there. But towards the middle of September, she had the chimney cleaned, ready for the cold months ahead, and this was the first lighting of the season.

With some ceremony and much good humour, Louisa, Flo and Marjorie attempted to coax the flames into life, before the arrival of their first customers for morning coffee. A shiny old coal-scuttle stood at one side, filled with thick branches and small logs, delivered by Farmer Turner's son on his way to meet a mate, whose father was driving them to the football ground to watch Mansford Monsters slaughter Branton Bears.

Margaret had meant to sleep in this morning after the exhausting week organising their move, but the children were eager to be off to their respective friends, and once they had gone, she didn't feel inclined to return to bed. Surprisingly, she had quite a lot of energy today, so, after breakfast and a hasty glance at the paper, she set to work unpacking one of the crates, still sealed after its long voyage across the Atlantic.

Vast relief was the best way to describe how she felt. Now they were established in their own home, the baby could arrive whenever it chose. Hannah and Adam had taken to life in Fairmead like ducks to water. It was marvellous how adaptable children were. They liked their new school and Margaret felt they would thrive in the family atmosphere, so different from the huge school they had attended in Los Angeles. They had also made friends instantly with the other Fairfield Gardens children and she herself had been made to feel totally accepted by everyone on the street. Sophia, Megan and Molly she knew would be particularly her friends, and Liz too, when she had completely recovered.

Liz was feeling the same way and beginning to want the company of others, though only for short periods, as it still tired her to talk a lot and be sociable. Intuitively, her friends knew this and stayed for a few minutes only. Megan and Joy put their heads round the door most days and Sophia had called to show her little Maria. Emily Whitehead often called after visiting the Church and dear Isabella still had the boys on a regular basis, often keeping them until Tom got home. Kate and Dr Miles called round when they could and Molly came one morning a week to catch up on Tom's paperwork. She had been a godsend, freeing Tom for other duties, and had refused payment for months until Tom declared that he would have to sack her unless she agreed to accept something. With a laugh, she named a ridiculously low figure, saying that she enjoyed the few hours away from hairdressing. Liz's own hair was coming back in short, tight curls, making her look like Shirley Temple, prompting Molly to say she would go out of business if everyone had lovely hair like that.

On this cool, crisp Saturday morning, Molly was preparing to catch up on neglected housework, after a busy week of hairdressing, bookkeeping for Tom and helping with the Infants' Reading Groups. This latest activity took place from nine till ten two days a week and was a revelation to Molly, who hadn't set foot inside a school during lesson time in many years. She loved helping the little ones with their reading activities, trying hard not to give too much attention to Cathy, and she saw Joy in a new light, keeping order and teaching in a way that was kind and patient but firm and controlled. By Saturday, the house was in dire need of a once-over and Molly usually enjoyed her couple of hours restoring order while James took the children out, sometimes to play on the Green and sometimes for a muddy walk through the nearby fields and woods. When they returned, boisterous and dirty, she would give them a snack, wash their hands and faces, collect their library books and set off for the mobile library, while James settled down for a peaceful hour with the paper and, if time permitted, the crossword.

On this particular morning, the phone rang while Molly was plugging in the vacuum cleaner. To her surprise, it was their social worker, apologizing for the weekend call but wondering if they would be able to call into the office sometime next week to complete some requirement necessary for the adoption to proceed. Molly said she would speak to James and ring back shortly. With a singing heart she replaced the receiver and stood for several minutes with the vacuum cord in her hand, imagining what it would be like to have Mark and Cathy as their very own children. The thought of it was delightful, causing her to put on some music and dance around the room with the vacuum as her partner.

CHAPTER 20

By the following weekend the weather had turned decidedly chilly and a blustery east wind made it feel even colder. Hats and scarves were hunted out and leaves were swept from paths, only to return within five minutes. Those of a tidy frame of mind were almost driven to distraction, while those of a more poetic nature delighted in crunching through them.

At school, Miss Browning was attempting to teach her class to recite 'Season of Mists and Mellow Fruitfulness' for Open Day in a couple of weeks, but Keats' beautiful language was lost on most of the children and only a small group of girls were even slightly interested. Nevertheless, Miss Browning was determined to expose them to Real Culture, whether they appreciated it or not.

On Saturday morning the library van arrived under the control of a quiet, middle-aged man called Malcolm previously seen only at the main desk of Mansford Central Library. Elsie Summerton had been struck down by a particularly bad cold and had completely lost her voice, so Malcolm had been recruited at the last minute to take out the Saturday van. Fortunately, he had taken it now and again during the week and was only too pleased to escape the confines of Central Library. Though by no means as chatty and full of local information as Elsie, his encyclopaedic knowledge of books was amazing to behold and those from Fairmead who made use of this Saturday service left well-pleased with their borrowings. Even one or two who rarely read a book were encouraged to step into the van, just to see what the new man was like.

Megan was late home after her shopping and hoped Jack had remembered to take the girls to change their books, one of which had proved elusive on Friday evening. After much searching and threats of no television until it was found, *Florrie the Flower Fairy* was located under Jenny's bed. The girls were very much into fairies at the moment and were insistent on wearing their fairy wings to tomorrow's Christening. It was hard when the three acted as one and Megan had almost capitulated, as she had other things to think about, preparing for the event. There was to be quite a large gathering of family and friends, who would be returning to the house after the Christening and would need warm food after the chill of the Church. Her shopping had been extra large and her car was filled almost to overflowing with bags. The cost had rather shocked her but it was on Jack's credit card and she certainly wasn't going to stint on her darling Angie's big day. What a good baby she was and how easy to care for. One child at a time was easy after the chaos of three at once. How she had coped with three babies, she couldn't imagine, but they were turning into beautiful little girls and she knew she loved all her children equally.

Today was the due date for Margaret's baby, but she didn't feel it was anywhere near arriving and had every intention of attending Angie's christening. More and more she felt part of village life and was looking forward to the afternoon. All the Gardens children would be there and it was to be hoped the weather would remain fine so they could play outside. Adam was turning into a football fanatic, under the influence of his new best friend, Sam, and this morning Andrew had accompanied Tom taking the boys to Mansford. He was taking his responsibility as Angie's Godfather seriously and had asked her to buy a little gift. This she had done yesterday when she and Sophia had spent a couple of hours in Mansford. In a little gift shop, just off Queen Anne Parade, she had found a sweet cup and saucer, delicately painted with tiny animals and flowers, and, mindful of the religious significance of the occasion, had found a picture of Jesus with the children in the Cathedral Bookshop. When they were walking back to the car Anthony Hawton was emerging into the street, intent on obtaining a cup of coffee from his favourite café. They waved and had a quick word before resuming their trek to the car park. Sophia had promised her mother that she would be back before midday as Monica had a lunch date with Isabella. She would be returning to Spain in two weeks and was making the most of her time in Fairmead, at least until next summer. Much as she loved Sophia, Maria and Paul, she was suffering from the cold and looking forward with pleasure to warmer climes. Her small apartment was almost on the beach and she had many friends, both English and Spanish.

Sophia would miss having her mother around, but both were great letter writers, preferring their own handwriting to the impersonal type of an email. Every week one would ring the other. It would also be nice to settle down to being their own little family and establishing their own routines. Sophia simply couldn't imagine the time when Maria had not been a part of their life and was awestruck at how much love she felt for this tiny human being. She knew, too, that Paul felt exactly the same and she felt her heart melt to see him trying to change a nappy or get the baby's wind up. Once, she caught him sitting on their bed, humming Rock-a-bye-Baby to Maria, peacefully sleeping in her cot. Going to Mansford with Margaret had reminded her of their own christening, which would probably happen sooner rather than later, and she decided to speak to Paul that evening.

Emily Whitehead, too, was enchanted by a small creature which had recently appeared in her life. The bedraggled sadness of the previous weekend had been transformed, as if by a fairy godmother, into plump, silky whiteness. Snowball was now completely at home, her every need taken care of by a willing slave. But while the kitten thought she had the better part of the bargain, Emily knew that Snowball had made her life complete and finally allayed the small doubts still lingering about her move. Within five minutes of arriving, Snowball had decided to stay permanently. The bowl of milk, a warm fire and Emily's lap sent the little kitten into a delicious trance and having landed in heaven, she never wanted to leave.

On the first afternoon, she scrambled from the chair, to the table, to the windowsill and sat staring out. With some trepidation, Emily opened the window a crack, wondering if Snowball would return if she once went out. But that determined little cat simply wanted to perform her private duties outdoors. Aided by a bench placed conveniently under the window, she was soon sitting delicately on the window ledge, waiting to be let in. On Sunday evening, Emily had carried her down to the Common Room, much to the delight of all. Snowball had bestowed her favours on everyone, rubbing against legs and royally receiving loving strokes and cuddles, but when Emily rose to leave, she followed behind, her miniature tail held high in the air.

At the Village Stores, Louisa was enjoying a five-minute break between customers. As the weather cooled, fewer visitors passed through the village and the shop and café were quieter. Though the Stores stayed open until late afternoon, the café's hours were reduced, catering only for morning coffee and lunch. Marjorie and Flo were more than happy to work the few weekend hours, in addition to those on Wednesday, Thursday and Friday, producing mouth-watering vegetable soup and toasted sandwiches.

The shop was causing Louisa some thought. Though she had kept well over the last few years, she was mindful of keeping a watchful eye on her health and not allowing work to become all-consuming, as it had done during her fashion-buying years. She was also determined to enjoy her grandchildren, now they had been miraculously restored to her. She had come to the conclusion that she must delegate, and employ somebody to take over the shop at weekends. The person she had in mind was Doris Simmons, who had, in fact, offered several times to relieve Louisa and had proved extremely competent. As the bell jangled and Bessie Crabtree hobbled in, accompanied by a sprightly Jan Fletcher, she made up her mind to call in at the

Farmer's Arms when the shop closed and ask Doris if she would be interested in a permanent position.

In the stiff wind, Kate was having considerable trouble hanging sheets on the line. Having spent years in hospitals, she was rather fanatical about clean bed linen and towels and prided herself on their snowy whiteness. As the last sheet was finally being subdued, the phone began to ring and she hurried indoors, with a smile on her face. It was indeed Chloe, making her weekly call, and the two chatted for ten minutes.

After saying goodbye, Kate replaced the receiver thoughtfully. Probably without realizing it, Chloe had mentioned Professor Bradley at least half-a-dozen times and her mother felt a slight stirring of hope that at last she had met someone she cared for. Of course, Kate knew very little about the man and Chloe would be travelling abroad shortly, but still… she pulled herself up sharply, chided herself for acting like a schoolgirl and started on the next load of washing, turning her thoughts to what she should wear for tomorrow's christening.

Fortunately the wind had lessened to a breeze by the next morning, though it was still quite cold. Sophia decided not to attend the service but she would definitely come across for the christening at midday. Monica said she would be perfectly happy to look after Maria and bring her to the gathering afterwards, for a short time at least.

When Paul had returned home late the previous afternoon after a meeting at the Cathedral, he had barely got through the door before spilling his exciting news. While chatting over tea and biscuits with his friend Henry Procter, the Bishop had congratulated him on the arrival of little Maria and offered

174

himself as Godfather, unless they had a better person in mind. Knowing that Sophia thought the world of Henry, he accepted the offer with the greatest of pleasure. The only slight drawback was the fact that the Bishop's only free Sunday until well into the New Year was the coming week but, if Sophia could work around the very short notice, he would be most happy to fulfil the role, indeed he would regard it as a privilege. As Paul had known, Sophia was delighted, not least because her mother would still be in the country and the inspired idea came to her that Monica could be both grandmother and Godmother, the Bishop being a confirmed bachelor. So by bedtime on Saturday, it had all been arranged and Maria was to be baptised in Mansford Cathedral at two o'clock the following Sunday, with the Bishop inviting all back to his home for afternoon tea, insisting that it would be his great pleasure to provide the spread and all Sophia and Paul needed to bring was the cake.

With two christenings imminent, Margaret felt it was high time she produced the third baby, but no amount of thinking would make it appear before it was ready. She was feeling fine, if a little unwieldy, as she strolled to church with Andrew and the children. Her husband was looking very smart in his new suit and was even wearing the blue and white striped tie bought for him by his mother several Christmases ago. Gallantly, he had called for Kate and was now walking with his wife on one arm and his fellow Godparent on the other. Hannah and Adam were lagging behind, waiting for Cathy and Mark to catch them up.

As stalwart members of the choir, Molly and James always

turned up, but since having the children, they were often only just on time. This morning, Mark had been ready in good time for a change, as he wanted to sit near Adam Ward and bathe in the reflected glory of a friend who was both slightly older and, most importantly, American. His other friends would be envious and his own status within the group would surely rise from that of lowly newcomer. It was Cathy who had held them up by fussing with her dolls when she should have been cleaning her teeth and changing her shoes ready for church. But Auntie Molly and Uncle James were never really cross with them and, as a result, they were hardly ever deliberately naughty. Hopefully they would belong to them for always and nobody could move them ever again.

Mark gave a secret little smile and crossed his fingers behind his back as they turned the corner from Fairfield Gardens into Bridge Road. He would never completely forget his own mummy and daddy and Grandma, but he was very happy with Auntie Molly and Uncle James and all his new friends. He just wished they didn't have to go to church every Sunday.

CHAPTER 21

On a dull, damp and rather dismal day, Monica Newson boarded her plane, along with a hundred or so others, bound for sunshine and blue skies. She was both pleased and sad to be leaving. She had greatly enjoyed being with her little family and felt she had been of help. Sophia was proving to be a lovely mother, calm and unflustered, and darling Maria was responding likewise. Her cries were soon soothed and even the night feeds were never prolonged.

Maria's Cathedral christening was something Monica would never forget. Maria had been dressed in an old lace gown which had been brought by Paul's parents and which had been in the family a hundred years or more. The sun had come out by early afternoon on that Sunday and a beautiful stained-glass window near the ancient font had scattered coloured beams on all those gathered around. Miss Whitehead had come, and at the Bishop's request, she had played quiet organ music as the ceremony was taking place. And afterwards they had been made to feel so welcome in the Bishop's Residence. It was wonderful and William Blackett had taken lots of photos on his new digital camera, which he had printed out himself. She had placed a set in her hand luggage, with every intention of putting them in an album as soon as she got home.

Paul had done the airport trip today, joking that he didn't know what would happen this time if Sophia went. On his way back, he made a few parish visits, calling in to see his old friend, Bill Hughes, first. On this dark day, Bill had wisely listened to everybody's well-meaning advice and stayed indoors rather than braving the elements to occupy his favourite seat on the green. However he was not forgoing his customary pleasure for reasons of his own health, but rather because his companion Bessie Crabtree had been persuaded to spend two days with her great niece and family near Birmingham. Bill rather suspected it was because they wanted her to babysit while they attended an important business function, but had managed to hold his tongue. Paul found him sitting in front of the heater, engrossed in the sports section of yesterday's paper. Though obviously pleased to see the Vicar, Paul was quite shocked to see how much older he looked after his recent illness and made a mental note to call in for five minutes each day, if at all possible.

His next visit was to Clarissa Jones, who had made a remarkable recovery from her broken arm. She had resumed doing her own housework, such as it was, Clarissa always having had too many other interests to waste time being houseproud. She insisted on making the Vicar a nice, strong cup of tea to keep out the cold. It was certainly strong. Not wanting to offend, Paul allowed the old lady to chatter on and when she jumped up to find some suddenly-remembered chocolate biscuits from the depths of the crowded sideboard, he swiftly poured most of it on to a sad-looking pot plant which was clinging to life on the table next to him. Feeling guilty that he had probably finally killed it, he was, nevertheless, relieved that it wasn't himself succumbing to the deadly drink.

Paul's final call was to Liz Norris. He usually popped in for a couple of minutes most days and, in recent weeks, he had been heartened by her gradual return to health. He could only pray that if anything serious should befall Sophia or himself, they would cope as magnificently as Tom and Liz had done. They seemed to him to have matured and learned lessons often not mastered in the longest life and, for them, it was no longer an intellectual truism that, just as a seed needs to die to bring forth new life, so we need adversity in order to grow.

As he was opening his own gate and mulling over these reflections, wondering if he could incorporate them in Sunday's sermon, he heard the phone ringing. He struggled with his key, but just as he managed to turn it in the lock, it stopped. Hoping it had been nothing urgent, he went through the house and out of the back door, to be met by an ecstatic Lady. Sophia had declared that it was time to resume parish duties and promised her husband that she would bundle Maria up within an inch of her life. She was only going to the Hall for a quick meeting of the Bonfire Food Sub-committee, actually three ladies who were coordinating the food for Bonfire Night, and the meeting had to be quick because it was sandwiched between the Tiny Tots' Playgroup and the Seniors' Craft Club.

After reporting on her plans to have several sacks of potatoes delivered directly to the bonfire at about three o'clock by Jim Turner, in whose field the celebrations were to be held,

Sophia was delighted to taste a sample of Plot Toffee brought by Jane Simmons, who was widely regarded as the World's Best Toffee Maker. Other village ladies had also volunteered to provide toffee, but none could produce such a dark, sweet, sticky concoction. The recipe was a closely-guarded secret and competition was fierce in the bid to try and reproduce it. Isabella was providing gallons of mushy peas and was responsible for organizing the setting up of the Hall's trestle tables and urn, essential on a cold evening. As plans seemed well in hand there didn't seem to be any need of a further meeting before the big night. All three ladies were highly experienced in organising events, even Sophia, who had had to learn this skill on becoming the Vicar's wife.

When they emerged into the late morning gloom, Jane hurried back to the Farmer's Arms to make ready for lunchtime business, Isabella dashed off to the Stores to get a birthday card for one of her many children and Sophia tucked Maria into her pram and set off for Margaret's. The baby was just waking and she hoped to reach her destination before it was time for a feed.

Margaret had just finished feeding her own baby when she saw her friend coming up the garden path. Within half an hour both were sipping hot soup from huge mugs, while their offspring were peacefully sleeping once more. To her great satisfaction, Margaret had attended both Angie's and Maria's christenings, her own little one having been born between the two occasions. So neatly had it all happened that Hannah and Adam had hardly noticed anything unusual happening. On the Monday following the first christening she had felt something was probably starting, but had waited until nine in the evening. Louisa had come to babysit and, in the event, stay the night. Andrew had driven his wife to Mansford in very quick time, there being little traffic, which was just as well as the baby had decided to linger no longer and was born within a short time of arriving at the hospital.

Joey was a fine, healthy boy with fine, healthy lungs. His cries were ear-piercing on his arrival in the world, much to Andrew's pride. But in no time at all, once fed, he snuggled up to his mummy and fell into a blissful sleep. And indeed, from that time on food and his mummy were his priorities.

At school, Miss Browning was rather wishing Open Day had come and gone. It was scheduled for the afternoon before Bonfire Night, as was customary, the thinking being that very little work would be done before such an exciting evening. Each class would be putting on a short performance, parents would be free to admire their children's work and the afternoon would end with tea and biscuits. It was usually a happy, relatively stress-free occasion, regarded by Fairmead as the prelude to the main event, which was the lighting of the bonfire at six o'clock. All villagers, whether parents or not, were most welcome to the Open Day and many availed themselves of the chance to revisit their old school.

Yet this year, Miss Browning was looking forward to it with little enthusiasm. The pent-up excitement in her class and indeed the whole school, was quite trying. The atmosphere felt like a violin string being tightened a little more each day. Goodness knows what it would be like by the morning of November the fifth. More children had had to be reprimanded in the last week than in the whole of the past term and Miss Browning was beginning to think of herself as a dragon.

Still, the classrooms looked very presentable and most of the work had been done on the little class concerts. Her own class were reciting a poem, singing a couple of songs, one of which involved a folk dance, and presenting a very short play about Guy Fawkes and the Gunpowder Plot. This had been written and produced by the children with very little input from their teacher, and they were immensely proud of it. Even the quiet children who never pushed themselves forward had been included. The classroom was awash with costumes, cloaks made from old curtains and hats from rolled black card, thoughtfully ordered in specially by Mrs Ward at the Stores. Some had even been into Mansford and bought fake beards and moustaches, even the girls, who had to be conspirators or soldiers, as there were no female parts. Reflecting on all the effort and enthusiasm of the children, Miss Browning felt a softening of her heart and knew that, despite all the trials and tribulations of being a teacher, she still had the best job in the world.

In the infants' room, an extra activity was taking place during reading groups. A long piece of paper was reposing on several small tables, destined to be a mural depicting the seasons, and children were taking it in turns to paint part of it. Each child had been given a particular item to paint and two mothers stood guard ensuring it all went to plan. John Fyne had already spilled blue paint on the floor and Dan Norris had accidentally started painting a snowman in the summer section. Joy felt her mind was split into half-a-dozen different pieces and wondered if that was how schizophrenia started.

She was attempting to hear a small group of readers, marking the stories of another group, helping a particularly slow child match words and pictures, keeping an eye on the group playing Word Bingo, and watching the painters.

Thoughts of the weekend had faded but not quite disappeared. She and Anthony had gone up to London on Saturday morning. Fortunately, Anthony had been able to stay in his usual hotel, having recently given up his city apartment. Her father had rung early on Friday morning to say he would be unexpectedly in London on Saturday and would love to see them. Joy could stay at his flat and he himself would be willing to sleep on the sofa. The three of them had had a lovely time discussing the wedding and catching up on news.

Wonderfully, all the wedding arrangements seemed to be going very smoothly indeed. Joy had heard horror stories of endless complications from friends and was keeping her fingers and toes crossed that everything would work out well. Megan and Sophia had been delighted to be asked to be Matrons of Honour and had spent several happy evenings discussing colours and styles of dresses. Joy had seen a delectable dress in Beautiful Brides and had put a deposit on it. It didn't even need altering and seemed to have been made for her. In a couple of weeks, the three would again have a trip to Mansford to buy shoes and the veil and all being well, dresses for Sophia and Megan.

Jim and Anita from Fantastic Flowers were only too glad to provide all the flowers, including those for the Church and table settings for the reception in the Hall. William had insisted on doing the photography as a wedding present, and a firm of caterers, recommended by Isabella, was to provide the food and drink. Invitations had been sent out two weeks ago and already some replies had been received, including two from Anthony's friends in Australia. As neither of them had a great deal of family, the majority of the guests would be friends and of these they had plenty.

$$\star \quad \star \quad \star \quad \star \quad \star$$

Choir practice that week was a rather sorry affair. Only Emily and James were in robust health, the others having tottered along out of a sense of duty rather than enthusiasm. Elsie and Jessie Summerton had more or less recovered their voices, but their singing had suffered a setback and both were unable to reach high or even middle notes. Molly had started coughing the moment she entered the chill church, and others were shivering noticeably. The reason for this misery was that the little heater which was normally plugged in near the organ and provided a modicum of heat, at least for the feet, had failed. It had sparked alarmingly as James was switching it on and immediately thereafter had died. He had offered to return home and hunt out a small heater from somewhere under the stairs, but this had taken quite a while and the choir were turning blue in the meantime.

Fortunately, Bonfire Night was considerably milder and the sun shone most of the day, making it feel almost springlike and warming the bones of Bill, Bessie and a couple of their friends sitting on the Green in the late morning and putting the world to rights. For the last two weeks, all the village youngsters had been busily chumping, and not a branch or twig remained on the ground in the whole of Fairmead and surrounding areas. The bonfire had grown most satisfactorily and some of the older children had begged and borrowed clothes for the magnificent guy which now rested peacefully on top. Farmer Turner had donated bundles of straw for its body, as he did every year, and as it was his field in which the evening was held, he was regarded as an essential part of Bonfire Night and was Chairman of the Bonfire Committee. Not that there was too much to do, as it all followed a strict routine laid down over the years.

This year, however, he had weightier matters on his mind. His family was growing fast. He now had six children and his own farmhouse was old and cramped. Since he had started renting Hawton's Farm and moved into its much larger farmhouse, everyone had been happier. But with more land to farm, he had had to employ two more men and the yearly rent for Hawton's was becoming an increasing burden. He knew he must speak to Anthony Hawton and wanted the discussion out of the way as soon as possible. Accordingly, he decided to take the opportunity of having a word during the evening.

The school's Open Day was enjoyed by all. It seemed as though every Fairmeader who was not at work had come along for the afternoon and the old building bulged. No one, except the teachers, noticed when Tony Pearson turned left instead of right in the Infant's dance or that Hannah Ward, completely overcome by the occasion, sang not one word, simply staring at the audience with an open mouth. Miss Browning's children were a huge success with their play and had to return for three encores. Doris had kindly volunteered to make the tea and coffee and very little was spilt in the crush, though biscuit crumbs were found in most unlikely places for a week afterwards.

When it was home time, children, parents and friends poured out, expressing sincere thanks to the teachers, who sat for half an hour with their feet on children's chairs drinking a final cup of tea. Miss Browning took a couple of aspirins and began to feel more relaxed. Doris, full of life as ever, started vacuuming, singing well known songs from musicals in a rather tuneless voice.

In most Fairmead homes that afternoon, tea was a rushed and meagre event, if it happened at all. Those returning from work made an extra effort to be home early. Six o'clock was bonfire lighting time, and the Vicar always had the honour. All the village children, including the tiniest babies, were wrapped in layers of clothes and assembled round the huge pile of wood a few minutes before the official time. When the Vicar arrived at the scene, a countdown began and on zero, he lit a large match and set alight some newspaper soaked in a little kerosene which had been carefully pushed into the bonfire. The guy sat looking unconcerned as the flames took hold, much to everybody's satisfaction. Potatoes had already been positioned around the perimeter by two of Farmer Turner's boys and several fathers were delegated to keep an eye on them and were under strict instructions from their wives to not allow them to become charred.

Isabella did a roaring trade with the hot tea and coffee. Joel Norris burnt his mouth on hot potato and mushy peas, but a slab of Mrs Simmons' plot toffee soon stopped the tears and the firework display put it right out of his mind. William Blackett, Tom Norris and Anthony Hawton were in charge of the fireworks, which had been ordered in by Louisa at a discount price. Behind a rope barrier, beyond which children were not allowed, the three men had a wonderful time lighting fireworks and reliving their boyhoods. Towards the end of the evening, as the fire was dying, everybody lit a sparkler and sang *When the Saints Come Marching In* with great gusto. All agreed it had been a perfect Bonfire Night and the bucket for donations was filled to overflowing.

At school the next day, the whole occasion was relived in detail. Stories and poems were composed, with much pencil-sucking and many furrowed brows. Drawings and paintings were centred on huge fires, lighting the faces of all gathered around, and enormous multi-coloured stars decorated the black sky. Everyone had a tale to tell, from John Fyne, who had seen Miss Jones take out her false teeth which were stuck together with plot toffee, to Amy Todd, who had burnt a little hole in her glove from holding the sparkler too near its sparkles. Amid the chatter were many yawns and the teachers were looking forward to returning to relative normality, at least until preparations for Christmas began.

Isabella was not having a good morning. For many weeks she had resisted William's pleas to take poor Scrappy to the vet to be 'done'. It didn't seem right to diminish such a joyful creature, but finally she had caved in to all those family and friends who were constantly enquiring as to when the deed would be done. William had taken Scrappy into Mansford, after their walk and breakfast, and now she felt a guilty traitor.

The poor darling had jumped into the car with tail madly wagging oblivious to the cruel plan. She was trying to keep busy by rushing round the house, skipping from one job to another and completing none of them. Every five minutes she glanced out of the window when she felt they had been gone long enough. Eventually, about midday, William returned with a much sadder Scrappy who slunk into his basket and turned huge, sorrowful eyes up to Isabella. She could hardly bear it, but heartless William was whistling as he washed his hands for lunch. It was just as well she had arranged to go to an important meeting of the Christmas Bazaar Committee this afternoon, or she would have murdered him.

Dogs were also on Megan's mind at this time. The girls had been heartbroken when Bonnie had so suddenly left them. She had been there since their earliest memories and they had thought she was a permanent fixture. Megan and Jack had discussed the possibility of getting another dog and had decided to wait until the girls' birthday, and that celebration was only a week away. Megan was adamant that she didn't want a puppy, not with Angie being so young, so a compromise had been reached and the whole family would be going into Mansford on Saturday morning. Jack had promised to take the children into the park while Mummy did the shopping. Then they would visit the dog shelter and see if they could find a suitable pet.

Megan only hoped they would find one or the girls would be devastated. They had talked of nothing else for days; even Bonfire Night had taken second place. Bonnie's old basket had been hunted out and cleaned and a fresh blanket lovingly installed. With their pocket money, they had bought new food bowls and a red collar and lead, which would be taken on Saturday.

Louisa had no misgivings about the weekend. Doris had been thrilled to be asked to take over the Village Stores on Saturdays and Sundays, on the understanding that if anything came up Louisa would take her place. She was a competent woman, brimming with energy, who was already indispensible at school and a great help at the Farmer's Arms. She regarded coming to live with her daughter and son-in-law in Fairmead as one of the best moves of her life. She loved nothing better than to feel needed and an important part of the community.

In a short time she had become Isabella's right-hand-woman on numerous Committees. So the idea of serving just about everyone in the village, plus numerous visitors at weekends, pleased her immensely. The work was not hard and Louisa would be only a short distance away if any problem arose. Louisa herself was most relieved to have found someone trustworthy so easily and felt a burden had been removed from her shoulders. On Friday afternoon at closing time she actually burst into song, relishing the prospect of a lie-in followed by a trip to Mansford with Kate, for lunch and a little shopping for new boots and handbag.

CHAPTER 22

Over the following week, the weather deteriorated miserably and the season of mellow fruitfulness became the season of mud and fog. Classes were depleted at school, thanks to an outbreak of coughs and colds. Dr Miles was run off his feet with full surgeries and numerous house calls, particularly to the elderly. Jan Fletcher and Emily Whitehead were the only two unaffected at St Mary's Home. Even Mrs Campbell, in the office, was laid low for several days. Emily thought it was something of a miracle that she remained well, after a summer of poor health.

Little Snowball was thriving, and no longer very little. Like the Ugly Duckling, she was turning into a beautiful, pure white creature, and her placid nature exactly complemented Emily's. Not only was she now beloved by all at St Mary's but also by all Emily's visitors, of whom there were many. There was hardly a family in Fairmead untouched by Miss Whitehead's kindness over the years and a visit to her neat little room was always a pleasure. Children often called in on their way home from school and people popped in on their way to the Stores or after whist or craft in the Hall. If she wasn't in, as was often the case, they would leave a hastily-scribbled note or tiny bunch of wilting wild flowers outside her door. Emily thought she must be the most blessed person in the world and continued unobtrusively helping and praying for all her friends in the village.

That Saturday morning golf was cancelled, as William had been awake half the night coughing and sneezing and Isabella had put her foot down, insisting that he visit the doctor. This entailed driving into Mansford to Dr Miles' surgery and could possibly take most of the morning. Paul was also occupied in Mansford, at a meeting in the Bishop's house, which would take at least three hours, once elevenses were taken into consideration, Henry Procter's hospitality being legendary.

Anthony was therefore free to drive in the opposite direction to see Joy in Fairmead. As he was carefully negotiating the traffic, slowed considerably by the fog and wet road, he reflected that he was happier now than he had been since he had been a small boy. Though his present job was not as stimulating as his high-powered career in Sydney, he knew he wouldn't miss that life at all. He felt fitter and more relaxed. He had quietly visited Dr Miles one day for a check up. To his great satisfaction, his blood pressure had returned to a normal reading and all other bits and pieces seemed to be functioning well. His love for Joy only seemed to be growing stronger and he found himself impatient to be married to her and living in Fairfield Gardens. His hotel room was pleasant but far from homely, and he was ticking the days off until he could say goodbye to it.

Anthony arrived about ten o'clock, and as it was not actually raining, they decided to have a quick cup of coffee and then go for a walk through the fields around Hawton's Farm.

Anthony thought it would be a good opportunity to acquaint Joy with the outcome of his conversations with Jim Turner. Jim had approached him on Bonfire Night and the two had chatted amicably. Anthony was sympathetic to Jim's difficulties and by no means wanted to lose him, as he was an excellent farmer and the farm was prospering. After a little thought he suggested that he should call round one evening and the matter could be discussed at greater length.

Anthony had returned with a briefcase full of papers. To Jim and Dora Turner's intense relief, he had suggested that their status be changed from tenants to employees. In effect, they would still farm Hawton's in addition to their own smallholding in whatever way they deemed best, but would receive a wage instead of paying rent. After a little friendly discussion, a fair split of the profits was agreed on, several papers were signed, a hearty supper was eaten and both parties waved goodbye, equally satisfied.

The morning's walk was magical. Bushes and trees faded in and out of the clearing fog, spiders' webs glittered with moist beads and boots made a sucking noise as they trod along the paths. It was impossible to walk side by side on many of the narrower footpaths, so Anthony led, moving aside stray brambles, like the Prince in Sleeping Beauty. Joy had never felt so invigorated or so happy. Every thought of school and wedding preparations completely disappeared, to be replaced only by the moment. Sounds were deadened, as were sights, only the smell of wet leaves and a distant bonfire were sharp.

As they came in sight of Hawton's Farm, they made out the figures of two of Jim Turner's boys attempting to coax a fire in a pile of leaves and small twigs. There was plenty of smoke but no visible flames. The fuel was far too damp to be consumed easily, but the boys continued hopefully poking it with large sticks.

At that moment, Jim came out of a nearby shed, saw Anthony and Joy and invited them into the house, with his usual huge smile. Dora was just about to make a late elevenses and was soon setting out freshly-baked scones to go with the steaming strong tea. While waiting for it to cool, Jim said once again how happy he and Dora were with the new arrangements and explained that they had decided to rent out their own little house to bring in some extra income. This plan had been unsuccessful previously, as no one seemed to want to live in a slightly run-down place in the middle of a farm. However, last week at Salston Market Jim had happened to meet an acquaintance from round there, who had happened to mention that his daughter and son-in-law were looking for a place. The outcome was that they had agreed on the modest rent and would be moving in shortly. As he imparted this news, Jim sat back in his chair, looking like the cat with the cream. Hands were shaken all round and a toast to the future drunk in cooling tea.

On their way back to the village, Anthony and Joy met Jack and the girls near the Hall. Angie was fast asleep in a kind of haversack on her father's back, but the triplets were racing along ahead, trying to keep up with a mud-spattered small dog which was leading the whole procession, straining on a bright red lead. Calling a greeting as he sped by, Jack vainly tried to keep his family under control. It wasn't until they reached the old stile leading into the copse which marked the beginning of

Hawton's farm that the dog suddenly stopped and sat, panting happily. With rosy cheeks and equally mud-spattered legs, the girls almost fell over each other, laughing and screaming in delight at the fun. Their father soon caught up and helped everyone over the style and the walk continued in a slightly more sedate manner. He wondered what Megan would say about the mud but didn't think she would be too upset.

Rusty had brought so much pleasure into all their lives and was proving to be the perfect pet. It hardly seemed believable that he had been with them only a week. About this time last Saturday, they had met Mummy after shopping and trooped off to the Dog Rescue Centre. Though there were lots of dogs, Rusty stood out at once, a small brown bundle of long hair with an enormously long feathered tail and huge ears like a startled bat. He had been found wandering on a country lane some miles from Mansford, shiveringly thin and with a severely matted coat. Having been taken by a kind motorist to the shelter, bereft of any identification, he was soon fed and washed and introduced to his temporary home. When the Todds met him, he had been a happy resident for almost a week but was perfectly pleased to abandon the shelter for the home comforts of family life.

In no time at all he had adapted to life in Fairfield Gardens, sleeping peacefully in his basket or, if possible, close enough to the heater to singe his now clean coat. As soon as the girls came home from school, they took him for a walk up and down the street, often accompanied by several of their friends, all wanting to hold the dazzling new lead. Megan took him with her and Angie when they went to the Stores or for morning coffee or even to the Tiny Tots Playgroup, to which she had just started going. Rusty enjoyed his outings with the pram and waited patiently while his humans disappeared inside. Sometimes, if the wait was to be long, he was provided with an old baby blanket and bowl of water and he soon learnt to curl up and make himself comfortable.

This walk through the fields and woods was, however, by far the best since his arrival and Rusty could hardly contain himself for sheer joy. So many interesting smells and sounds and sights! He was in seventh heaven and his exuberance was catching. By the time they arrived home, the girls were glowing and chattering ten to the dozen. Jack, too, felt as though all his workaday worries had vanished into nothingness and were totally unimportant. Even Angie, who had woken as her daddy was scrambling over the stile, had enjoyed the exciting outing and forgotten that she normally had lunch at that time.

Megan was already home and putting away the shopping in unaccustomed peace, her favourite music playing quietly in the background. She was glad of a little time to herself as soon enough chaos would reign. This afternoon the girls were having their party, although their actual birthdays had been during the week. Jack had wisely taken them out to channel their feverish excitement and being late back, allowed Megan to begin preparations in peace.

All the girls in their class were invited - boys were not even considered. It was to be a Barbie Party. Everyone had been asked to bring their favourite doll and accessories. Megan was very much hoping everyone actually had a Barbie to bring and that all would return home with their own dolls and dresses. Since the girls were still very keen on fairies, they were going to wear their wings and fairy costumes and several mothers had indicated to Megan that their daughters would be doing the same. She knew, however, that one or two families were in no position to buy outfits or Barbies, so she had stressed to all that there would be plenty of spare wings and dolls. This morning, in addition to the party food and balloons, she had purchased several wings and wands from the Discount Superstore. Barbies, she knew, were plentiful, as her girls had several and were only too willing to share with their friends.

Next door, Hannah Ward was counting the minutes until the start of the party at two thirty. This was her first party in her new country and she couldn't wait. Sally, Jenny and Amy were her heroes, looked up to with something akin to adoration. Hannah could think of nothing more wonderful in the whole world than to have three sisters, two of whom even looked like her. Adam was all right, as big brothers went, but he was always going over to play with Sam Norris and didn't have much time for her. Joey was a nice baby, when he wasn't crying or making disgusting nappies, but she had really wanted a sister. For the umpteenth time, she asked her mother if it was time to go. She had been washed and changed hours ago. Her wings and favourite Barbie were in a plastic bag ready to take and the clock wouldn't move.

Two doors away, there was similar excitement. Uncle James had taken Mark into Mansford on 'men's business', but she knew it was to buy a Cubs uniform from the Scout Shop. Grandpa William had asked if he would like to go to the Cubs meeting next week to see if he liked it. Strictly speaking, he didn't have to wear a uniform, but Mark wanted to be like the others and Uncle James said he could have one. Cathy thought the triplets' party would be much more fun. She had two Barbies and had changed her mind a dozen times, deciding which to take. The chosen one was now sitting on the table guarding a Barbie lunchbox containing her very best clothes. Next to her was a pair of sparkling fairy wings bought during the week by Auntie Molly, who had gone into Mansford specially. Cathy couldn't be happier if she had been given a million pounds and Molly felt her heart swell to see the child's pleasure.

Just before the designated time, a crowd of little girls and their mothers appeared through the gloom and headed for the lights of number eight Fairfield Gardens. Outer garments and boots were cast aside and fairy wings attached. Megan took some photos of the charming group, then left them with their Barbies. Pass the Parcel and Pin the Tail on the Donkey were to be played after the food at three-thirty, but for an hour the girls were totally absorbed in their dolls and not one argument erupted. Megan thought it was bliss and even had time to chat with a couple of mums who had stayed.

Jack had conveniently taken Rusty to William's to meet Scrappy. William was feeling considerably more himself, after taking the pills and potions prescribed by Dr Miles, and the two men settled down to watch football on television, while Isabella baked something delicious and the dogs stretched in front of the fire.

CHAPTER 23

By Monday the fog had cleared somewhat, but there was still a general mistiness and everything remained damp. Paul was enclosed in his office, opening the morning's post, and Sophia was settling Maria after her feed and bath, when the phone rang. The office door opened and Paul called down to tell his wife that Anita from Fantastic Flowers was on the line. Expertly cradling the drowsy baby, Sophia picked up the downstairs phone, pleased to hear from her good friend.

After the small talk, Anita came to the main reason for her call. Jim was confined to bed with a bad dose of flu and was proving a rather crotchety patient. Anita was finding it very hard being constantly at his beck and call and running the Garden Centre. Would Sophia be able to do her a huge favour and come in a couple of hours each morning, possibly more at the weekend? It wasn't busy at this time of year, but help seeing to the plants and doing a little paperwork would be wonderful and she could certainly bring Maria with her.

With no hesitation, Sophia assured Anita that she would be delighted and would come that very morning, though she would have to leave just before midday, as she had promised to attend a charity lunch organised by Jane and Doris Simmons, which was being held in the Hall in aid of the children's ward at Mansford Royal. All donations of money or toys would be taken to the hospital later in the week by Doris who, among all her other activities, had volunteered to be a 'Grandma' to the children and was determined that they should have plenty to occupy their minds. To this end, she was on a campaign to amass a large and varied collection of toys and games.

The charity lunch had actually been Jane's idea. Both she and Doris enjoyed cooking, and they had united to provide a deliciously tasty stew. On hearing of the good cause, Louisa had offered to provide bread rolls and the Craft Club had allowed their store of tea and coffee to be used. Apart from the usual small donation to the Village Affairs Committee for use of the Hall, all proceeds would go towards toys for the children.

Monday was probably not the best day for the lunch, but so popular was the Hall since its renovation that it was fully booked for the remainder of the week and, indeed, until well after Christmas. Jane had placed an ad in the Church Newsletter and Doris had put a notice in the Stores window, so all in the village were aware of the lunch and about a dozen had said they would definitely attend, mainly older residents who always enjoyed a good lunch and chat with their friends. Several younger mothers had said they would wait and see how the children were on the day but most of them hoped to get there at some point, as they were also looking forward to Jane and Doris' delicious lunch and a chance to get out of the house in this miserable weather. Naturally they all supported the cause, especially those who had had children of their own in the hospital at one time or another, and the thought of giving a generous donation was very pleasant, as is the case with all good deeds.

This latter thought was on Emily Whitehead's mind as she braved the dampness for the third time that morning. Much earlier, she had left her warm room for the bone-chilling dark of the church. The Vicar and many well-wishers had tried many times to dissuade her from her morning prayers during the colder months, but she always smiled kindly, assuring them that she was so well wrapped up that she never felt the cold.

This was certainly the case. It took her ten minutes to don the layers of cardigans, scarves, hats, gloves, socks, boots and, of course, her long black overcoat, with its belt and huge collar. Most days she also took her umbrella, just in case. She was determined to follow Dr Miles' advice and keep warm at all times. By this means, she hoped and prayed to avoid the summer's ill-health.

Having returned home about an hour later for a cup of tea and slice of toast with butter (never margarine) and strawberry jam, she had departed once again to visit a very old friend who lived in a tiny house near the green and who was quietly fading away. Her husband was in not much better condition. Their children and grandchildren were supporting them wonderfully and Emily tried to help in any little way she could. This morning she had read the old lady a favourite passage from the Bible for about fifteen minutes, before she had drifted off to sleep. Emily had then read various articles from the morning's newspaper to the husband, who had similarly dozed off, though his snores were considerably louder than his wife's.

Just as she was preparing to leave, one of the daughters

arrived to stay with her parents for a few hours. Emily then returned home for the second time, rescued Snowball from the outside ledge, wrote a letter on tissue-thin writing paper to one of her many friends and managed a few rows of the pullover she was knitting for little John Fyne, youngest of five and the recipient of his four brothers' hand-me-downs. At twelve exactly, she ceased her morning activities, closed her eyes and spent five minutes quietly praying for all who had asked for her help and offering thanks for her own many blessings. She then dressed for the outside world once more and took her leave of her warm haven.

The weather had neither improved nor worsened since first light. Several others were making their way to the Hall, having had to struggle with their consciences over whether to turn out at all. Bessie Crabtree and Clarissa Jones wouldn't have missed this lunch for the world. Both loved nothing better than a good meal and a good natter and they arrived almost at the same time, ten minutes early, to find Jane and her mother busily unpacking the food.

The two older ladies set to and soon had the tables organised. The urn was turned on, rather late in Clarissa's view, as she was dying for a cup of tea. Jane's husband, who had brought up the food in his van, now left to attend to his own duties at the Farmer's Arms, and, as more ladies arrived, the Hall soon buzzed with conversation. For a long time, coats were kept firmly on and some even refused to part with their hats and gloves, as the heaters bravely attempted to dispel the damp cold.

However, once the stew was released from its huge sealed

containers, warmth seemed to spread like magic and everyone enjoyed themselves tremendously. Sophia, Megan and Margaret from Fairfield Gardens had brought their babies and were joined by several other young mothers, more or less the same ones who formed the core of the Fairmead Village Playgroup and who had agreed at last Thursday's gathering to try and increase their membership. Megan had already indicated that Angie was almost old enough to start attending, so Margaret and Sophia were targeted, despite the tender ages of their babies. So friendly were the other mothers and so persuasive in their appeals that both, by the end of lunch, felt it would be a privilege to join.

Sophia had, of course, promised Anita to help her at Fantastic Flowers, assuring them that she would definitely start in the new year. Margaret, having no valid reason for delay, said she would accompany Megan that very Thursday, all being well.

By three o'clock Doris was locking the Hall door, hoping to slip home for fifteen minutes with her feet up before setting out for her school duties. Jane had already departed with some of the stew containers. Everyone had given a hand with the clearing up and some now set off for home, via the Farmer's Arms, laden with the remainder of the large containers and enough toys to stock Santa's Workshop. The lunch had been a huge success. Doris was more than happy with the donations and had promised to list in the parish newsletter all the toys and games she hoped to be able to buy when she went into Mansford in a couple of days.

Molly had thoroughly enjoyed herself, having postponed a

haircut until the following day in order to be able to attend. Now she hurried with Isabella to the Stores, both ladies having almost run out of milk.

Louisa greeted them cheerfully. She was feeling so much better now dear Doris had taken over so competently at weekends. There had been only the most minor of problems, understandable as Doris was still new to the business, but that organized woman always left everything in apple-pie order for Louisa on Mondays. Where she got all her energy from goodness knows, but she was certainly a treasure and Louisa knew Miss Browning felt the same because she had said just that earlier when she had called in to renew stocks for the playtime break.

The head teacher didn't believe in plastic bags and always brought her own canvas one, neatly folded in her briefcase. This morning had required a particularly large shop, tea, coffee, sugar, milk and various packets of biscuits. Everything seemed to have run out at once. Miss Browning had staggered to school, wondering if her back would hold out. Fortunately, Joy was just approaching and hurried to relieve her of her burden. Each term, one of the teachers had staff room duties, and after Christmas it would be hers.

With barely a month to go before the wedding, Joy had no sense of panic. She hadn't the slightest doubt that she wanted to marry Anthony and every plan seemed to have fallen into place. The last major item was a veil. Her dress was due for collection next Saturday and Anthony's suit was already safely in his wardrobe. Sophia and Megan had chosen their outfits, with the minimum of fuss. They had elected to wear a matching dress and jacket in different shades of creamy-pink, Megan's being a little darker than Sophia's. The skirts were elegantly slightly below the knee and would be ideal for later use on special occasions. In their hair, each would wear a Christmas rose and Joy herself would have a coronet made from the same living flowers. Anita had seen this in a florists' trade brochure and was eagerly looking forward to making it.

Many replies had been received to the invitations and most had been in the affirmative. The catering people had requested final numbers a week before the wedding, sooner if possible, and their menus were propped on Joy's mantelpiece, awaiting a final decision. As far as Anthony was concerned they could have beans on toast, so Joy knew the final choice would in reality be hers. Naturally they would be having a warm meal, given the time of year, but it all looked so delicious that she knew it would be hard to finally decide.

The Hall was well and truly booked for the reception. She and Anthony and a crowd of friends would decorate it with flowers and balloons the evening before, to the delight of the Whist Club, which would be holding its Annual General Meeting about seven pm. As there was very little to discuss and no new office-holders to be elected, the prospect of a contingent of young people arriving to decorate for a wedding was most welcome.

Liz was also looking forward to her neighbour's wedding and was pleased to note that she now had the energy to concentrate for a while on things other than herself. For several months, her focus had been solely on herself and managing each day. All other considerations had faded into insignificance. Even the daily concerns of Tom and the boys had seemed beyond her capacity to deal with. But over the recent weeks as her strength had slowly returned, she had begun to appreciate their little problems; Tom's with the business and the boys' issues at school.

Even so, she was aware of a subtle change in her awareness. No longer did she worry about things, taking them on as personal burdens. Nothing seemed important enough to disturb her peace of mind. Amazingly, she now seemed able to stand apart and observe her own feelings and reactions, rather than being totally absorbed in them. As a result, she was happier than she had ever been in her life.

On that damp Monday, Liz had wrapped up warmly and been whisked up to the Hall in William and Isabella's car. Once there, she had been ceremoniously led to the chair closest to the struggling heater and had been the first to receive a steaming cup of tea. It was wonderful to have her appetite back, and she thoroughly enjoyed the spicy stew. As she sat, surrounded by chatter and activity, she thought, with a smile, that the trauma of the last few months had been worth every uncomfortable minute, to have reached this point, when nothing was taken for granted. Everything happening right now was appreciated as perfect.

Later that afternoon, Joy dropped the boys home and sat for ten minutes happily telling her friend all the exciting wedding plans. In the middle of a detailed description of the proposed Hall decorations, Liz suddenly interrupted, declaring that she had just the thing. Hastily explaining that she meant the veil, she wondered if Joy would like to look at the one she had worn. It was beautiful French lace and had been her mother's, passed down through several generations. Of course, if Joy preferred to buy one, that would be perfectly understandable but, if she would care to borrow it, it would be the 'something borrowed' that she must have.

With a sense of absolute rightness, Joy followed Liz as she made her slow way upstairs, past the boys' room where sounds of a struggle over racing cars were beginning to emerge, subsiding as their teacher passed the open door. They entered the spare room, which was overflowing with Tom's papers and tools. The files and journals were neatly arranged on a desk, left in good order by Molly, as was the newly-installed computer, but various tools were taking up valuable floor space and competing with a large wardrobe and several huge plastic containers on wheels.

From inside the wardrobe, Liz extracted a small cardboard box, well-protected inside a strong plastic bag. When the box was opened and the tissue paper gently folded back, a delicate lavender scent wafted out and the veil was carefully removed. It was the most gorgeous thing Joy thought she had ever seen and she knew immediately that it would be perfect with her dress. With no hesitation, she said she would be delighted to wear it and, to seal the deal, hugged Liz and gave her a resounding kiss. A few minutes later, she emerged from number four and made a quick dash to her own front door, the precious veil safely enclosed once more.

CHAPTER 24

Preparations for the Christmas Bazaar had been underway for months, since the New Year in some cases, and in many Fairmead homes a special box or bag was to be found into which a steadily increasing number of items had been carefully placed. Clarissa Jones insisted on making old-fashioned pinafores. She had done this for sixty years and saw no reason to stop now. Not that she herself ever wore one, but her mother had and it was the only article of sewing the young Clarissa had ever managed to complete satisfactorily.

Emily Whitehead always presented a pile of beautifully-knitted jackets for babies, together with bootees and bonnets. These were so exquisite that any young woman who was even considering having a baby in the near future would make a beeline for the baby stall and feel the day was worthwhile if she had managed to acquire one of Miss Whitehead's offerings. Indeed, on one memorable occasion two young mothers had almost come to blows, one holding one sleeve and the other the opposite one of a tiny blue jacket. The matter was only resolved by the Vicar.

The bazaar was, of course, the main reason for the Craft Club's existence. Every week they would meet under the leadership of Isabella Blackett, surrounded by overflowing boxes of material scraps, coat-hangers, bobbins of lace, glue, toilet roll centres and bits and bobs of all descriptions, collected mainly via tubs left in the church porch and just inside the door of the Village Stores, into which people could pop anything they felt might be of use. Though some items could not be used, despite the inventiveness of the club members, rarely a week went by without some useful material appearing.

It was so much more convenient now they could use the Hall again. During its closure they had been obliged to meet in each other's homes with the boxes distributed between them. For several weeks they had been fortunate enough to be able to gather in the common room of St Mary's Home, but just as they were becoming used to their new premises it had become unavailable due to re-decoration, and they had had to revert to their nomadic existence. The Hall was, therefore, much appreciated. On this mid-November day every member of the Craft Club was present, working fast and furiously. There would be three more meetings only before the big day.

Isabella was happily attempting to stick glitter on Christmas baubles. A box of the plain glass balls had been thoughtfully left in Louisa's care yesterday by a lady driving through the village. She often passed through and sometimes stopped at the Stores. On the odd occasion she had left something in the craft tub, but the balls which had been bought the previous year and never used were too delicate to be thrown in with everything else.

Isabella now had glitter on her face and in her hair, as well as on her fingers. She had no delicacy as far as craft was concerned, but gained such an obvious sense of satisfaction from her efforts that no one ever complained. She was also a born leader and organiser and had a knack of getting things done. Never bullying or overbearing, somehow she managed to make people feel that everything had been their idea. She had taken over the organizing of the bazaar almost as soon as she had moved into Fairfield Gardens, having been asked by the Committee, on the death of their long time chairwoman, if she would lead their rather dispirited group. Recently, she had been greatly helped in this and other duties by Doris Simmons, whose energy was becoming legendary.

As the Craft Club ladies were busily knitting, sewing and sticking, the infants' class at Fairmead School were also deeply engrossed in preparations for the bazaar. Earlier in the morning they had written about their families, illustrating their stories with wobbly pictures of stick-thin people sporting spiky hair and huge toothy smiles. These efforts were to be laminated and sold to doting parents at the bazaar. Now the class had progressed to craft and were working on various projects, started two weeks ago, some of which would be never completed, as Miss Taylor well knew.

The parents didn't seem to mind at all, and would pay good money for anything produced by their children. Clay models of houses and animals, coiled snakes being particularly popular, were lined up on a high cupboard top, out of reach of small hands wishing to alter the original attempt. These were to be placed very carefully in a large box whenever Joy had a few spare minutes. Anthony had promised to take them in his car up to the Hall, where they would remain, hopefully untouched, until the bazaar.

Now the children were engaged in making a large mural,

depicting Fairmead Village and environs, to be raffled at the end of the bazaar. Miss Taylor had drawn the streets, by no means to scale, on a large piece of card and Amy Todd, the best handwriter in the class, had written their names. Everybody had drawn and cut out a representation of their own house and stuck it on in approximately the correct spot, though their sizes differed quite considerably. The older ones were given the tasks of providing the church, Hall, Village Stores and other landmarks, while the rest made trees and plenty of grass from fringed green coloured paper. Those who had finished their part in the mural were industriously working on 'surprises' for their parents. Joy was hoping that one more craft session would see most items completed but rather feared this would not be the case. However, the children were enjoying themselves. Mrs Evans had assured her, slightly untruthfully, that she couldn't hear a thing, so teacher and pupils settled down to enjoy this unexpected morning treat.

As with most village occasions, the Church Bazaar was a thing of tradition, and its particular unbroken rule was that all items for sale were to be handmade. Several years ago, an enthusiastic young mother had suggested that her toy stall would make more money by buying in wholesale and selling for a profit. After a long, shocked silence from the other stallholders, the young woman had withdrawn her suggestion in blushing confusion. The bazaar had proceeded on its untroubled way from year to year, with woolly soft toys, embroidered hankies, painted wooden alphabet blocks, craft articles galore, and of course pinafores.

The proceeds were divided in an equally traditional way.

From the time of its beginnings, in the early days of Victoria's reign, all monies made were to be equally divided between three worthy causes: Christmas flowers for the Church, the Children's Christmas Party and 'a deserving poor villager'. As a concession to modern times, this last requirement had been modified to become a donation to the Hall fund. The Rev. Adamson had suggested this arrangement, as it was causing great discomfort to those chosen as the recipients, and he felt that all in the village would benefit from donating to the Hall's running costs, resulting in a slight lowering of its hiring costs.

Louisa's contribution, as to most Fairmead events, was food and drink, usually consisting of bread rolls and soft drinks. For the bazaar, she also included some cheese, tomatoes and ham. November and January were her two slowest months, both in the shop and café. Marjorie had been off with a bad cold for two weeks, but Flo had been able to manage without help over the weekend, despite Louisa's offering to come. Until about three weeks before Christmas, the café would be closed on weekdays. Once it reopened, various groups from the village and surrounding areas would start having Christmas lunches. Marjorie was certain she would be completely recovered and assured Louisa that she and Flo were looking forward to the seasonal rush. Louisa was also anticipating the hectic weeks ahead with optimism. Last year, she had taken only Christmas Day off. Even New Year's Day was spent in the closed shop, arranging sale items for the next day. But this year, she had Doris, whose enthusiasm was infectious. She had ideas about everything, several of which had been successfully implemented. Her ideas for the forthcoming Christmas decorations were innovative, for a person no longer in the first flush of youth, and Louisa was imbued with her excitement.

In addition, free weekends were doing Louisa the world of good. She and Kate could now share the housework more evenly, for one thing. Kate had never complained but Louisa had felt bad about it. Now they whisked through the necessary chores and most Saturday afternoons were able to shop contentedly in Mansford, always incorporating afternoon tea at Rigton's, the most prestigious establishment in town. Sundays were usually quieter but no less enjoyable: church, followed by roast beef and Yorkshire pudding, followed by reading, sewing or a walk through the fields.

Kate was also pleased to have company during the weekends and even more pleased with life on this dark November day. The previous evening, she had received a phone call from Chloe informing her that their departure for foreign parts had been delayed indefinitely due to civil unrest in the country they were going to. Though Kate's kind heart was saddened by the thought of so much suffering for so many people, she couldn't help rejoicing at the prospect of having her daughter relatively close for the foreseeable future.

Surprisingly, Chloe herself didn't seem too upset. Her role as a temporary lecturer at the university had been extended, the holder of that position still being unwell, and she was hoping to complete her PhD shortly. She was very busy with all her commitments but would try to get back for Joy and Anthony's wedding. After ringing her mother, she would contact Joy and let her know she could attend after all and would be bringing a partner.

Trying to make it sound like a casual aside, she then mentioned that Professor Bradley had agreed to accompany her. Kate's smile had been wide, but she had followed her daughter's cue and feigned unconcern. After chatting for twenty minutes, she had put the phone down and waltzed round the kitchen singing *I could have danced all night,* much to Louisa's enjoyment.

CHAPTER 25

As November wore on, the weather remained unchanged, not particularly cold but damp and miserable. Playtimes at school were often not wet enough to cause the children to stay inside, but moist enough to result in the teacher on duty feeling wet and chilled, despite a hot cup of coffee cradled in her hands. While the children ran around oblivious to the climatic conditions, Miss Browning's thoughts were drawn irresistibly to the vision of retirement, with its promise of warm heaters, good books and a painting class she had wanted to join for years. Mrs Evans, when on playground duty, tended to consider what she and Mr Evans would be having for tea. She was an excellent cook and, having no children of her own, all her culinary skills were directed at her husband. However, after years of rich living, Dr Miles had sternly commanded that it stop immediately or dire consequences could not be avoided. A dietician had been consulted and Mrs Evans was now obliged to curtail her excesses.

Joy's thoughts also tended to stray while patrolling the playground, attempting to keep warm. As far as plans for the wedding were concerned the last piece of the puzzle had fallen neatly into place when Liz had so kindly offered her antique veil. The only arrangement remaining uncertain was the honeymoon. Most places were out of the question at this time of the year and even the thought of a few days in Paris didn't seem to fill either of them with great enthusiasm. The question had been shelved, in favour of organising the wedding, but would have to be resolved in the next week or so. Of course, just being together would be wonderful but secretly both yearned for the sun.

In the Village Stores, one person after another declared that they had completely forgotten what the sun looked like. Bill Hughes said he was turning green with the damp and Clarissa Jones swore that her television was 'interfered with' by the weather. Louisa promised to ask William Blackett, when he called in for his paper, if he would pop round to have a look at it. Housewives gloomily predicted that their electricity bills would be astronomical, due to the constant use of driers. Anyone foolish enough to hang out washing would see it hanging limply for days, then bring it in wetter than it had been in the first place. Christmas still seemed unimaginably far away, only the bright posters for the bazaar, in the Stores window, the church porch and outside the Hall, held out a little hope that the festive season might be approaching. Sophia had produced these posters, as she had done for several years and they were always much admired for their colourful artwork. For the last couple of weeks, she had been extremely busy, looking after Maria, attending to parish duties and spending extra hours at Fantastic Flowers. Jim, however, was now back on his feet and Anita able to return to the business, so Sophia had a little more spare time, though she would still call in for a few hours on Saturdays.

On this last Tuesday in November, she decided to take the opportunity of visiting her aunt and uncle on the far side of Fairmead. They were actually her great-aunt and uncle on her father's side and had lived in the village for many years. Sophia had always felt a deep affection for them, but more so in the last few years, since it was while staying with them that she had met Paul.

Sarah Barnett was just switching on the electric jug for the first of many cups of tea when she saw Sophia opening the little white gate and expertly pushing the pram through. With a shout to her husband Phil, completely engrossed in a cryptic crossword, she flung open the door, letting in a blast of damp air. Once mother and baby were settled in front of the fire, with tea and biscuits on a little coffee table, and the usual comments about the weather had taken place, Sophia and Sarah began to discuss the forthcoming bazaar, while Phil's eyes strayed to the crossword and began to take on a faraway look. Sarah was to be on the preserves stall with Doris Simmons and had been busily chivvying all her friends and vague acquaintances to make numerous jars of jams and marmalades for the last few weeks. She herself saved every suitable jar throughout the year, filling every one of them with delectable contents, first for the garden party and then for the bazaar.

After exhausting that topic, Sophia came to the actual reason for her visit. Emily Whitehead had had a quiet word with Paul after the Sunday Service, asking him if he knew anybody who would be willing to join the choir for the Advent and Christmas season. He had, of course, offered to make an announcement next Sunday but Sophia had thought immediately of her aunt, who was always humming and loved musical films. Sarah was slightly startled by the unexpected request but her second reaction was of pleasure. She had never sung in a choir before in her life and had never thought of offering her services but this was, after all the church in which she felt completely at home, and, what was more, all the choir members were friends. It didn't take more than a couple of minutes wondering if her voice was good enough, before she smiled widely and said she would give it a go. Sophia promised to ask Isabella to pick her up for choir practice that very week and went away feeling well pleased with her morning's visit.

Choir practice that week had its full quota and more. For once, every regular member was present and two newcomers were also welcomed. Isabella had been more than happy to collect her friend Sarah Barnett, and that lady enjoyed the experience so much that she wondered why she hadn't joined years before. Her fears regarding her voice were quite unfounded. Nobody in St Mary's church choir had operatic talent, but they all made up for it in enthusiasm and comradeship.

Emily was a delightful choirmistress and organist, never criticizing anyone personally or letting anything ruffle her calm manner. As a result, she got the best out of people and choir practice was a highlight of the week for all concerned, rather than a penance to be endured, and this was despite the fact that, at certain times of the year, the church could be perishingly cold. In this last week of November, the damp was like a soggy blanket, even though the heater had kindly been switched on an hour earlier by the Vicar. Emily had taken precautions and was well wrapped-up, as usual, and the others arrived similarly protected. Isabella had advised Sarah to don more clothing and put on an extra pair of socks. As a result, most people were fairly warm after the hour, except for their noses.

The second newcomer was Louisa Ward from Fairfield Gardens, who had always had a hankering to join the choir but had always felt she was too busy. Now, with some of the burden removed by Doris, she was determined to extend her horizons and do things she had put off for years. This attitude of 'do it now' was encouraged also by the fact that an old friend of hers in London had recently been diagnosed with cancer and was in hospital receiving treatment. Louisa had been unwell herself a few years ago and she felt that her present good health should be celebrated and used for her own pleasure and the good of others. While singing in the choir could not actually be classed as a work of mercy, it might certainly help, in a small way, to raising people's spirits. So she went to her first choir practice with Molly and James and thoroughly enjoyed it, both for the music and for the friendly atmosphere.

Most of the hymns for Advent and Christmas were well-known and not difficult, though a couple of more tricky pieces were being attempted for the Christmas Service. Molly and James were the mainstay of these, as they had the best voices and could read music, but Louisa and Sarah did their best and were rewarded with smiles of encouragement from everyone, especially Emily who was the gentlest teacher imaginable.

★ ★ ★ ★ ★

At the same time as the choristers were gathering, Joy was cosily enclosed in her warm sitting room winding tangles of multi-coloured wool into bright balls. Next to her was a pile of over two dozen pairs of thick knitting needles, bought the previous Saturday in the Mansford Craft Shop. The wool had been a gift from the kindly owner, who had recently delved into the recesses of the storeroom and made up a bulky parcel of spare odds and ends of wool in readiness for Miss Taylor's visit. Being a father himself and very fond of children, he had also sold the needles at cost price. Joy had read recently in an educational magazine that knitting was a good skill for children to develop and had decided to attempt it with her class. Every year they made a gift for someone in their family and this year it should be a scarf or a little woolly mat. The project was scheduled to start the following afternoon and the children had been informed that day, amid huge excitement on the part of the girls and slightly less enthusiasm on the part of the older boys.

Joy had impressed on them that it was a great secret and they must not breathe a word to their parents. This would be somewhat hard for the more chatty children, particularly the Todd triplets, but all had assured their teacher that no hint of the surprise would pass their lips.

With impeccable timing, just as Joy was placing the last ball into a large bag ready for the trip to school the next morning, the phone rang. To her great pleasure, it was Anthony and, even as he greeted her lovingly, she could sense the excitement in his voice. He would give nothing away, however, merely saying that he would be finishing work fairly early tomorrow, all being well, and would come over for tea, as long as they could have his favourite casserole. Laughingly, Joy said she would see what she could do and they then passed a happy half-hour chatting of this and that. But as she put the phone down, she knew something exciting was afoot and looked forward to the next day when she would see Anthony and the first knitting lesson would be over.

Liz would have laughed if she'd known two of her rumbustious sons were about to become knitters. After a major argument over Lego pieces, the three boys were now sitting in front of the fire in their pyjamas, sipping hot cocoa and listening to a story read by their dad. Before his wife's illness, Tom would never have considered reading anything for pleasure, but he had mellowed in the last few months and become much more considerate of others. He had started reading the boys a bedtime story while they were at Granny Isabella's and had enjoyed it so much that he had continued the practice almost every day since. Though Liz's energy was slowly increasing and she could have resumed the bedtime reading, she was content to allow Tom the pleasure and gained as much pleasure herself from watching.

This morning, Sophia had kindly driven her into Mansford for her regular check up and the news had been good. So much so that the time between visits had been slightly increased and it would be just after Christmas when she had to go again. Her specialist had told her to enjoy the festive season and she intended to do just that. She had already made a list of possible presents for family and friends and her dear neighbours, Kate and Louisa, had bravely offered to get as many items as possible for her when they went into Mansford in a couple of weeks. This Saturday was the Christmas Bazaar, so they would forego their usual shopping trip. Liz had every intention of attending the bazaar for an hour or so and hoped to buy a few small gifts there but felt unequal to a major outing to Mansford. It was dear Kate who had known this instinctively and who had offered to take on the duty.

While peace reigned for a few minutes at number four, the same could not be said for number ten. Little Joey Ward was awake and the family knew all about it. He wanted something, but no one could discover what and his screams grew louder by the minute. Margaret had offered food and checked his nappy but these were not required. Hannah had sung a new song learned in class that day and Adam had dangled various toys and rattles, but these did not do the trick. Andrew had walked up and down with him, but this was not the answer either. All were at their wit's end. What would have happened in the end no one knew, but at that moment, Isabella arrived, seized the baby, hugged him to her ample breast and, with a shuddering sigh, the noise ceased.

In the unexpected silence, no one moved, frozen with shock. By the time they recovered themselves, Joey was fast asleep. Isabella placed him carefully in his cot and accepted a cup of tea from the very grateful Ward family. She had come to check on a Bazaar matter with Margaret who, to her pleasure, was now completely accepted as a local and was being slowly drawn in to several village organisations and events.

The day of the bazaar dawned as different as it could possibly be from the previous couple of weeks. The earliest risers found, on drawing their curtains, a clear sky and spring-like temperature. The clouds had disappeared as if by magic and a bright sun was peeping over the horizon just as Paul and William simultaneously opened their doors, accompanied by a wildly wagging tail each.

The two friends joined up and were soon briskly walking along Bridge Road, deep in conversation. Even Jack was out bright and early this morning with the rapidly growing Rusty. The previous three Saturdays had been so miserable that he had only gone, under protest, as far as the church and back as quickly as possible, but this morning was quite different and he set off with a willing step.

By ten o'clock, preparations for the bazaar were well under way. Tom Norris, James Standing, William Blackett and Anthony Hawton had erected the trestle tables in double quick time and were then excused until half an hour before the official opening time of two o'clock. For the rest of the morning, bazaar preparations were a female affair. About a dozen ladies descended on the Hall and had transformed it into Aladdin's Cave within an hour. People from Fairmead and beyond arrived in a steady stream, proudly delivering their articles for sale and competition was fierce regarding the positioning of their donations. Isabella and the other stall holders had to use all their diplomacy in these matters.

As soon as Anthony had performed his duty, he hurried over to Joy's and they left village activity for the frenetic bustle of Saturday morning Mansford. They were heading for Apex Travel, at the far end of Queen Anne Parade, and had little interest in the busy shops and supermarkets.

Anthony had enlightened Joy as to his news the previous evening, as they were drinking their coffee after completely demolishing the tasty casserole. No amount of pressing on Joy's part would prevail on him to disclose a word until the appointed time and she had soon decided to enjoy both the meal and the anticipation of good news. When all was cleared away and Anthony felt he had teased her long enough, he told her of his plan for their honeymoon, subject to her approval, of course. A couple of days before he had received an email from one of his friends in Sydney, who was soon to depart for London, first to attend the wedding and then to spend Christmas with family in Scotland, asking him to phone almost immediately, if at all possible. Being quiet at work, Anthony did as requested and was soon listening to Stuart's idea. In lieu of a wedding present, he wondered if the newly-weds would like to stay in his house and use it as a base to see a bit of Australia. A little bird had told him that they had not yet fixed up a honeymoon.

Naturally, it would have to be discussed with Joy but they would be most welcome, if they had no better idea, and could Anthony please bear in mind that he would be doing his friend a great favour, otherwise Stuart would have to think of a present.

Joy's immediate reaction to this plan was so obviously enthusiastic that Anthony was sure she was just as pleased as he was. All other possibilities faded into vague ideas for future holidays and the remainder of the evening had been spent in animated discussion. Anthony obviously knew much more about Australia than Joy and was much more aware of the great distances between places, compared with Europe. He had thoughtfully brought a large map and this had been spread on the floor, while Joy provided paper and pens for note taking, plus several more cups of coffee. As a result of the coffee and excitement neither of them could sleep very well that night but they woke up fresher than if they had had eight full hours. Anthony had emailed Stuart the minute Joy had given her unreserved approval and a reply had been received within the hour. Now all that remained was to book tickets and sort out summer clothes.

The library van was busier than it had been for several weeks. Elsie Summerton was run off her feet and hoped she wouldn't be too tired to make the most of the bazaar. She would have loved to have run a stall, but having to return the van and drive back to Fairmead meant that she would miss the first hour. From previous experience she knew that the best buys would have well and truly gone by that time but hoped enough would remain for her to start her Christmas shopping and buy dear Jessie's birthday present, her sister having the misfortune to be born three days before the twenty-fifth. This always involved a certain amount of subterfuge as that lady herself would be present but, having chosen the gift, Elsie usually asked a mutual friend to engage Jessie in conversation at the far end of the Hall, while she quickly made her purchase. Of course, Jessie knew exactly what was happening and, indeed, Elsie knew that she knew. But the fact was never mentioned and harmony prevailed.

Possibly due to the lovely weather, attendance at the bazaar was exceptional and by four o'clock hardly an item remained, the rest soon vanishing with the help of heavy discounts. At four-thirty the afternoon was declared a huge success. The hardworking stall-holders pulled chairs into a companionable circle, sipped hot tea and nibbled on wedges of dark fruit cake, thoughtfully provided by Doris Simmons who, sadly, had been unable to attend, as she was presiding over the Village Stores. The trestle tables were dismantled with practised ease by the same four gentlemen and returned to their dark home in the storeroom. William and James then proceeded to count the takings and cries of satisfaction greeted news of the total amount.

The raffle of the Fairmead Village mural produced by Miss Taylor's class had surpassed expectations. It had been won by Andrew Ward, who had immediately donated it back to the school, where Miss Browning had promised to display it in a prominent position. The clay models had also been snapped up by parents willing to spend inordinate amounts of hard-earned money on their offsprings' efforts. Emily Whitehead's baby outfits had, as usual, been sold within the first half hour. Clarissa Jones' pinafores had taken somewhat longer to disappear, the last two having been quietly purchased by Emily herself in order to save Clarissa any distress.

As a leading member of the Children's Christmas Party Committee, the Vicar being the chairman, Isabella was thrilled with the amount they would receive and, while helping to tidy the Hall, her thoughts ran happily to party foods and decorations. Sophia was also extremely pleased to think how much she and her ladies would have to spend at Fantastic Flowers and how beautiful the church would look for Christmas. William's thoughts were more practical, as it was he who kept the Hall's accounts in good order. The windfall from the bazaar would cover the next quarter's electricity and several other necessary expenses. With great satisfaction he accompanied his wife home, to be met by the mouth-watering smell of a stew, slowing simmering in the oven, and the anticipation of his favourite programme on television.

CHAPTER 26

By the time the bazaar had been held, the Christmas season was well under way. At the Village Stores on Monday morning, Doris kindly dropped in after her school duties to help Louisa decorate the shop and arrange the Christmas display in the window. Both ladies loved this time of year and with Louisa's experience and Doris' enthusiasm, the job was soon completed in the pleasantest way possible.

Those customers who were fortunate enough to arrive at that time, stayed as long as possible, offering unhelpful advice and generally getting in the way. Bessie Crabtree, the previous owner, was the only one whose sensible ideas Louisa and Doris heeded. She was always most welcome in the stores and she, in turn, was always amazed and cheered by the wonderful success Louisa had made of a business on the verge of collapse. Once the shop had been arranged to their satisfaction and Louisa had made Doris a cup of tea, accompanied by her favourite chocolate biscuits, the ladies bade each other farewell with a hug and a kiss, one to a well-earned rest for a couple of hours and the other to open up the café.

At about midday, Flo popped her cheerful head into the Stores to say a quick hello and then disappeared next door. Five minutes later, Marjorie appeared and disappeared in the same way. Soon the two ladies were happily unpacking several boxes of decorations provided by Louisa, who sailed in and out at frequent intervals between customers. The café was due to open tomorrow for the Christmas and New Year season. It would be open every day, except Christmas Day itself, and Marjorie and Flo were eagerly looking forward to the challenge. Louisa had offered to engage an extra person to help in the kitchen but they would not hear a word of it. Isabella and William's daughter, Susie, would come at the weekends and immediately before Christmas to help as a waitress but they insisted that was all the help they needed.

At about one-thirty Jim Turner arrived, bearing a miniature Christmas tree cut that morning from the woods near the farm. This was soon decorated and placed near the window. Flo draped the lights around its branches, Louisa ceremoniously switched them on and they were soon blinking on and off in a most satisfactory manner. At three o'clock she was standing outside, wrapped up against a rather chilly wind which had suddenly arrived, gazing with great satisfaction at her two windows, that of the Stores, with copious amounts of glitter and cotton wool, and that of the Café, with its twinkling tree and holly-bedecked sign announcing its Christmas opening times.

Children passing Louisa's Café and the Village Stores at home time were entranced, and a sizeable crowd soon gathered on the pavement to admire the two establishments. From that moment on, no parent in Fairmead was left in peace. During that week, Christmas trees began to pop up in the front windows of homes all around the Village. The first to be erected were found in boxes under stairs and in attics. Those who preferred the real thing had to wait until the weekend until the perfect tree could be found at Fantastic Flowers, Salston Market or one of the street vendors in Mansford. Some brought inside little live trees growing in pots at the far end of gardens. These had been purchased over the last couple of years from the Village Stores and Louisa had promised to have a new batch of potted trees by Saturday. It was Jim Turner's honour and privilege to provide a tree for the village green. He had a small area of fir trees on the edge of the woods and usually managed to find a tree of suitable dimensions.

On Wednesday morning, Scrappy was quite literally in the doghouse. The previous evening, Isabella had located their venerable tree, wrapped in a huge plastic bag, nestling amongst her summer clothes in the far recesses of the wardrobe. Why she had put it there last year, she couldn't imagine. It was like meeting an old friend after a long absence. The tree had been purchased many years ago when the eldest Blackett children had been young. It was now decidedly threadbare and showing its age, but the whole family would have been devastated if it had not occupied its central position on a little table near the window. Family traditions were sacred to the Blackett clan and Christmas required its presence.

Unfortunately, Scrappy had no such feelings. An hour after Isabella had lovingly decorated it with ancient dangling ornaments, he had joyfully attacked it, knocking it over, smashing two irreplaceable glass balls and bending three mangy branches. Fortunately, the lights had not yet been added but even so, the damage was considerable. William had arrived as soon as he heard the crash and found the dog cowering in a corner, waiting for retribution to descend, and descent it did. Scrappy was banished outside and had to find solace from the cold in his kennel. For the next couple of days, Isabella found tiny shards of coloured glass in impossibly distant parts of the room. Not being a person to harbour ill-feelings, however, she soon replaced the missing ornaments with two decorated by herself and purchased from the Bazaar. These were placed towards the back of the tree, in hopes that they would be hardly noticed.

★ ★ ★ ★ ★

While Isabella was vacuuming her carpet, Emily Whitehead was knocking at Liz's door. She had been calling faithfully since Liz had come home from hospital and was thankful to witness her friend's slow recovery to good health, though in no way surprised that her prayers had been answered. The Prayer Circle had grown since its beginning at Easter and now ten people met regularly to offer prayers of petition, thanks and praise. A further dozen or so had promised to remember the Prayer Circle's intentions everyday. Indeed several of the beneficiaries of these prayers had been among this number and Liz was one of them. Though formerly not particularly religious, since her illness her view of life and spiritual matters had changed significantly. She was now calmer and, being less concerned with trivial matters, had more time to enjoy her family.

This subtle change had resulted in a more peaceful and happier way of life for all of them. Tom found himself less stressed with work and more able to delegate. Molly had his book work totally under control and that was a huge blessing. Sam, Joel and Dan still had disagreements and the occasional fight but, on the whole, they were quieter and more obedient and, consequently, were doing better at school. Joy had commented to Liz at the bazaar that the boys were a pleasure to have in class and that Mrs Evans felt the same. She said that Joel had taken John Fyne under his wing and was showing that young man a good example.

In the Standing household excitement was growing as Christmas drew nearer, and the feeling was by no means confined to the children. Molly and James were revelling in their first Christmas as parents. Already little surprises had been secreted away, wrapped, beribboned and labelled, in the top of their wardrobe. A trip into Mansford on Saturday to see Father Christmas was eagerly awaited and much soul-searching had been occurring on Cathy's part as to whether to ask for another Barbie or a baby doll which was being heavily advertised on television. Mark had no such problem. He wanted a football shirt in his favourite team's colours. A large Advent calendar had appeared in the kitchen on the first day of December and the children were taking it in turns to open the little doors, accompanied by gasps of delight at the tiny pictures thus revealed.

Not long after the calendar arrived, a huge tree was purchased from Fantastic Flowers one late afternoon after school. Uncle James had arrived home early from work and delighted the children by accompanying Auntie Molly to school and coming into the classroom after the bell to see their work displayed on the walls. A perfect family Christmas was being planned. Nanny and Grampy were driving down from the Lakes two days before the Big Day and would stay at the Kings Head in Mansford for a week. Nan and Pop were hoping to catch the train down from Scotland on Christmas Eve. They would stay in the spare room for four days before returning north for New Year celebrations.

The children's own dear Grandma and parents would not be forgotten either. After visiting Father Christmas, Auntie Molly and Uncle James were going to take them to the churchyard to put some lovely red and green holly in the pretty vase near Grandma's headstone with its sweet little angel. They had made Christmas cards for their mummy, daddy and grandma, which would be covered in plastic and stuck near the angel to help them have a happy Christmas in Heaven. Cards had also been carefully made for their grandparents in New Zealand. These had been posted the same day the Advent calendar started its countdown because, as Mark knowledgably assured them all, it was a long way to the other side of the world. Cathy wondered if it was almost as far as Heaven but Mark said he didn't think so because Heaven was on the other side of the Galaxy.

Adam Ward knew exactly what he wanted for Christmas, a real football and boots. He had been practising kicking a soft ball up and down the Gardens with young Mark in the few minutes of remaining daylight after school, but at weekends he played with the big boys. Mr Norris still took him to Mansford Park on Saturday mornings and sometimes his dad was able to go as well. When they returned, he and Sam liked to practise their passes and dribbles on the green, and they were usually joined by several other budding footballers. They didn't like it when girls wanted to play but their mums always insisted that they be allowed. Though Adam would never admit it to Sam, he had a grudging admiration for a couple of the girls who never cried when the ball hit them and were actually quite good players.

Hannah wouldn't have been seen dead kicking a dirty old ball but was hoping, with fingers and toes crossed, that Father Christmas would bring her a dolls' house. She had been going to ask for another Barbie but, three weeks ago, had seen the best dolls' house in the whole world in a Mansford toy shop and, from that moment on, had hardly been able to sleep in case her letter hadn't yet reached the North Pole. Her mother said it would surely have arrived by now, but as Father Christmas or his helpers never replied, it was hard to know. She was also worried that she hadn't explained well enough in her letter where that particular dolls' house was to be found, her writing skills not being too good as yet. She had confided her fears to Sally, Jenny and Amy who, having had their birthday were now older girls and assured her that Father Christmas was magic and always knew what children wanted. They themselves wanted more Barbie accessories and roller skates. Hannah thought it was amazing that all three wanted the same things but she supposed that, as all three looked and sounded alike, they must also think alike.

Sophia had found that one of the joys of being the Vicar's wife was the yearly assembling of toys for various village children whose parents were not particularly well off. This required great tact, which Sophia had in abundance. This year, being busy with dear little Maria and working extra days at Fantastic Flowers, she had been late gathering her hoard, but on the Saturday before the bazaar she had sallied forth on her mission to the Mansford shops, bearing a satisfying amount of money, being the interest from a small bequest made years ago by a wealthy and much loved Fairmead spinster. Sophia had bought a suitable present for each of the children on her list and the remaining money would be given to the Children's Christmas Party Committee.

Once home, the gifts had been wrapped and stored, awaiting distribution. John Fyne and his four brothers were each to receive a present and Sophia knew that their mother would be full of thanks. Her husband had been unable to work for two years after a serious car accident, and she herself had had to leave her part time job in order to care for him. The family got along as well as possible but it was not easy and every little kindness was much appreciated.

CHAPTER 27

At school, Miss Browning had made her decision and was testing herself as to whether it was the right one. She had often, in recent years, played this game and found it to be invaluable. When a decision was not immediately obvious, she set her mind to one course of action and observed how she felt. After a suitable time, she then set her mind in the opposite direction and observed herself closely. It was then clear which way to go and the exercise had never failed her.

On the first of December, she had made the decision to leave. That evening, she had written on a large sheet of paper all the many advantages of early retirement. This had been attached with holiday souvenir magnets to the fridge, in a very prominent position, and for the next week she had allowed its happy thoughts to wash over her and soak into her at every spare moment. The following week, she had completely changed her mind and replaced the first sheet with one detailing the advantages and joys of remaining in her position as Headmistress of Fairmead School, the culmination of her much-loved teaching career. These thoughts had been occupying her during the week, though in all honesty there was so much to do leading up to Christmas and the end of term that she had very little time for anything else.

The supply teacher who had been booked to take Joy's class for the last few days of term had broken her leg and, naturally, had to withdraw. At this short notice it was extremely difficult to find a replacement. Miss Browning had spent all the previous day until nine at night on the phone, trying to contact various names on a list helpfully provided by the office, but to no avail. She was contemplating informing Mrs Evans that they would have to split the babies between them, and their classrooms were cramped enough as it was. She also had no wish to spoil Joy's big day by causing her feelings of guilt.

Her last hope was a name she had never heard of. This teacher was the only one who had not answered her phone or replied to Miss Browning's message. The outlook was not hopeful. But other concerns were also occupying her mind, principally, the Christmas Concert. Thankfully, this year it was not a big event because of the fairly recent Open Day and concert for Bonfire Night. It had been decided to keep everything simple and have a Carols Afternoon on the day before the last day. This was to be held in the Hall and each class had prepared one song only. All the other carols and Christmas songs would be sung by everyone, children and audience, accompanied by Miss Whitehead on the Hall's piano. Mrs Evans had volunteered to work the overhead projector, so the words could be displayed on a white screen which usually lived in the storeroom near the trestle tables. Joy had been spared the task usually undertaken by the infants teacher of preparing a nativity play and Miss Browning had assured her that simply having the children dressed in nativity outfits and arranged around in suitable poses would be most satisfactory.

Having asked the Vicar to pull names out of a hat in order to ensure complete honesty, Alison Wood had been chosen as Mary and Dan Norris as Joseph. The youngest of the Turner children had been designated a shepherd and had declared that he would ask his dad to bring one of the sheep, as there weren't any lambs at the moment. Miss Taylor had had to use all her tact to dissuade him but, in the end, he had agreed to bring his pet rabbit, which was very tame.

Through all the extra pressures of end of term, not least of which was ensuring that every child had completed their knitting and wrapped it in jolly paper, decorated with holly during the last painting session of the year, Joy remained calm and slightly abstracted from everything. A feeling of unreality had enfolded her, as if she was being swept along in a delightful dream. Her dress was now hanging in her wardrobe, the covering plastic removed so she could look at it, feel it and smell it at frequent intervals whenever she was at home.

Final numbers had been sent to the catering people; almost all those invited had accepted. Joy's dad would soon be on his way from Singapore and would return to his London flat before travelling to Mansford and booking into the prestigious Crowne Royal Hotel. She was looking forward to seeing him again after his latest prolonged trip to foreign parts. Talking of which, the Australian honeymoon had been booked and paid for in the blink of an eye. Anthony had taken charge of tickets and itineraries, so all Joy had had to do was sort out summer clothes for packing. These were now laid out on the floor of the spare bedroom awaiting decisions. Anthony had recommended that she take as little as possible, leaving plenty of room for the fruits of Sydney shopping expeditions. Even so, Joy reflected happily, it was wonderful how many more light summer outfits could be squeezed in than bulky winter ones.

As far as the weather on the actual wedding day was concerned, she was taking no chances of developing pneumonia and had acquired a set of thermal underwear to act as a barrier between her new lacy undies and the beautiful dress. This stratagem had been heartily endorsed by Sophia and Megan and all three had decided to help each other divest themselves of this apparel in the Ladies as soon as possible after arriving at the Hall.

All the little girls in Fairfield Gardens were to be angels in the nativity scene and all were convinced that angels were synonymous with fairies. They were, therefore, thrilled to be able to wear their fairy wings. Miss Taylor had emphasised to the parents that no one was to go to the expense of buying a new dress, but the children should wear white and Miss Whitehead had kindly agreed to make little cotton white shifts for any angel in need. Megan Todd and Margaret Ward already had pretty white dresses for their daughters, bought only last summer, but Molly had nothing suitable for Cathy. However, being a handy sort of person she soon acquired an offcut of white satin from Salston Market and, borrowing a pattern from one of her customers, ran up a gorgeously old-fashioned dress in only two evenings. Cathy was entranced and knew she was the luckiest girl in the whole wide world. When the dress was tried on, together with the wings and tinsel halo, Molly knew that she was the luckiest mother in the whole wide world. Cathy looked such a picture that Uncle James rushed upstairs to find his camera and save the image for posterity. Even Mark admitted that she looked all right.

Isabella was having a particularly busy week. Not only was she planning a large family gathering for Christmas Day, entailing numerous extra visits to Mansford supermarkets and extensive shopping expeditions with a list as long as Santa's, but the Children's Christmas Party Committee required her attendance on two afternoons. This was by no means a chore, as they were held in Paul and Sophia's warm and comfortable sitting room. This was a considerable improvement on the extra choir practice, held in church on the coldest evening that year. Emily had apologised profusely but felt that the organ was essential to the Christmas pieces they were attempting to learn. One was a rather complex Medieval carol and the other a lovely piece from the *Messiah*. Fortunately, the other carols were well loved traditional ones but, as numbers were up a little this year, they were hoping to sing them in parts. Emily was very patient but it was easier said than done.

Paul was also busier than usual at this busy time of year, though he refused to allow excessive 'doing' to overtake the spirit of the Advent season. He always felt this was his favourite time of year, a time of stillness and waiting for God's love to be realized. He liked to imagine himself in a cave just before dawn, awaiting the golden rays of the sun spilling over the horizon. He tried to arise a little earlier on these Advent mornings, not always easy if Maria had had a restless night, and spend a little extra time at his prayers, before plunging out into the cold half-light with Lady. He loved Sophia and Maria more than anything else in the world but treasured his brief solitary times, times when he could think and pray.

As a vicar he was the servant of all and never begrudged anyone his time or help, but the physical part of his life would have been hollow without the spiritual. And Paul had needed all his inner resources during the last few days. Several parishioners had fallen ill and all had been visited daily, even those who couldn't remember their last visit to church. One had died, rather unexpectedly, and Paul had not only organised and performed the funeral but spent hours with the distraught family. Various committees and meetings were, of course, part and parcel of his life, including a special visit to see the Bishop on the Thursday afternoon. It was always a pleasure to visit his old friend Henry, one that didn't happen nearly often enough, so Paul was hoping their business could be swiftly concluded, leaving sufficient time for an erudite discussion of a new book on the teachings of St Thomas Aquinas over a cup of tea.

Sophia's thoughts were as far away from Aquinas as they could possibly be. That morning, as she was picking up bills and Christmas cards which had just dropped through the letterbox, the phone rang and it was her mother's cheerful voice on the other end. Monica had already informed them that she wouldn't be coming for Christmas as she usually did, thanks to her recent visit, but this morning she sounded particularly chirpy, saying without preamble that she had had a brainwave. Why didn't Sophia and family come to her for a holiday, as soon after Christmas as Paul could manage? The weather was so much nicer than in England and it might even be warm enough for swimming. Sophia had been charmed by the idea and promised to ask Paul to speak to the Bishop that very afternoon. She hoped he would remember, but rather feared his mind was on St Thomas Aquinas rather than Spain.

CHAPTER 28

The rain continued over the whole weekend. From mid-afternoon on Saturday it was torrential for eight hours, and though it decreased after that, it didn't finally stop until just before the beginning of school on Monday morning, leaving several areas around Fairmead flooded. Fortunately, the village itself seemed to have escaped relatively unscathed. During the worst of the downpour, Bridge Road had been a fast-flowing river, taking run-off from slightly higher ground, including Fairfield Gardens, but once the rain ceased, it soon became an ankle-deep stream and remained that way all day.

The village green turned into a pond, causing harassed council workers to close it off, both for safety reasons and to preserve the grass from being churned up by excited children. At school these same children were wild, having been cooped up all weekend. Miss Taylor, normally easy-tempered and cheerful, was hard-pressed not to loose her cool when John Fyne and Joel Norris started a full-scale fight in the reading corner, causing the bookstand to overturn, scattering the books everywhere and ripping her precious Fairy Tales volume, brought in only that morning to read as a treat for the class. Not only that but the two little girls who had spent a happy hour on Friday afternoon tidying and arranging the bookstand were so upset that they burst out crying in unison and couldn't be consoled for ten minutes.

If Joy hadn't been so grateful that she and Anthony hadn't chosen this weekend for their wedding, she might have allowed her temper to flare. As it was, she made the boys pick up the books, then sent them to distant corners of the classroom, by which time, of course, they were the best of friends again. The little girls were given a sweet from the jar each and allowed to suck them in the Toy Corner. Peace was restored as far as it could be on a morning when high spirits and loud voices reigned.

Miss Browning was having a surprisingly good morning. She had six children away, which always made the class quieter and easier to manage. The maths lesson had gone smoothly, being revision of decimals, a lesson given so frequently over the term that it was almost second nature. By mid-morning, the children were quietly writing in their journals and Miss Browning was free to consider yesterday evening's phone call from the remaining supply teacher. This lady had apologised for not replying sooner as she had been away for a few days, but she would be willing to come and speak to Miss Browning after school. Fingers crossed, she would be suitable and free to take the infants for a few days. Miss Browning sincerely hoped so.

No sooner had the rain stopped than a watery sun appeared and in an amazingly short time most of the roads around Fairmead were almost dry. Bridge Road took much longer to dispose of its water, pedestrians having to squeeze themselves against hedges to avoid being soaked by the tidal waves of passing cars. The green remained out of bounds for three days, much to the disappointment of the village children. Two of the boys in Mrs Evans' class were caught red-handed up one of the trees by no less than their Head Teacher, who informed their parents of the misdemeanour, resulting in severe reprimands and threats of Father Christmas watching them.

Regular dog-walkers through the woods and fields were slowed considerably by the mud, bringing much of it home on their clothes and boots. Mothers sighed at the extra washing. Doris Simmons seemed to be cleaning the school floors twice as often as usual, but she never complained and Miss Browning thanked her lucky stars that she'd found her. All being well, the supply teacher would prove equally valuable.

Miss Timms had arrived promptly and shown great enthusiasm for all Miss Browning had told her. She was a tiny lady of indeterminate age, neatly dressed and quietly spoken. She lived with her sister in Mansford, had taught in a large school there for thirty years and had decided to retire early, at the same time as her sister. This, she disclosed rather sadly, had been an unfortunate mistake. The two of them, used to busy lives, had rattled around the house, attempting one activity after another but finding no fulfilment in any. Her sister was returning to her job in the New Year and she had decided to take on supply teaching while looking for another position. She was quite willing to tackle the infants for the last few days of term and the first two weeks of January while Miss Taylor was on her honeymoon in Australia. Miss Browning had taken her along to speak to Joy and, over a cup of tea and digestive biscuit, offered her the temporary position.

Miss Timms had arranged to spend a couple of hours the

following morning in the infants' room, discussing lesson plans with Miss Taylor, observing the children and generally getting to know about everything. She would then return on Friday morning to take the class. Miss Browning was quite looking forward to knowing Miss Timms better and she smiled to herself as she realised that that lady was the final answer to prayer, in more ways than one. She was now perfectly sure of her own decision concerning retirement, and with a happy heart and renewed enthusiasm she began to plan for next term and, God willing, many more after that.

Joy was more relieved than she could say that her little ones would be left in capable hands. The next few days would now be trouble-free and enjoyable. The children would meet their new teacher, thus ensuring a smooth transition, and Joy could concentrate on her imminent marriage and trip to the other side of the world. Her father had arrived back in London and she had enjoyed a lengthy phone conversation with him the previous evening. Dear Anthony was working extra hours to clear up outstanding commitments before his extended leave. Over the last week or so, he had been bringing clothes over to her house and they were now hanging incongruously at one end of her wardrobe. Having lived for many weeks in a hotel, he had no furniture or household items, but was looking forward tremendously to having somewhere to keep his slippers and coffee mug, or so he laughingly joked. He had to work until the usual time on Friday but Joy had the day off to attend to various little matters, not least of which was having her nails done in Mansford before meeting Sophia and Megan for lunch.

As Joy concluded Maths Activities with a sharp clap of her hands, and mentally girded herself for a concert practice, Kate was balancing rather gingerly on the second-highest rung of a ladder in a corner of the children's ward. For the last two weeks they had been rushed off their feet and decorating had been continually postponed. Today, however, was much quieter and the two young nurses, who had both succumbed to heavy colds and couple of weeks ago, had now returned to duty, much to everyone's relief.

Though in normal circumstances they would have been the ones up the ladders, Kate had volunteered, but now rather wondered if it was a wise move. As she wobbled worryingly, fearing to look down, a jolly little fellow, just turned five, shouted encouragement to Nurse Kate and started dragging paper chains out of a large box with his one good arm, the other being rather the worse for wear after a fall from a swing. Risking a glance down at her helper and seeing the shining faces of all the others, forgetting their medical troubles in the magic and excitement of Christmas, she returned to her task with a glad heart. Soon the ward looked like Santa's Grotto.

Not a hundred miles from Mansford Royal, Molly and James were sipping coffee in the old-fashioned office of Timothy Miller in Queen Anne Parade, having just received the best Christmas present ever. Timothy had been working hard on their behalf and had just received word that the adoption had been approved by the court, all relevant reports from social workers having been received in what, to Timothy, was a miraculously short time. Not only that, but the legal system had also put its skates on and the Standings were requested to attend, with the children in question, at two-fifteen on Friday the sixteenth of December.

Timothy himself had various documents for signature, after which he sent for coffee and relaxed considerably, marvelling at the speed and lack of complication of the proceeding. With sincere congratulations, he arranged to meet them on Friday afternoon. Turning to his pile of correspondence, he discovered, to his surprise, that he was humming. Molly and James were positively singing as they crossed the busy street, James to return to work and Molly to return to Fairmead and a perm for Sarah Barnett.

By eight o'clock that night, Cathy and Mark had been informed of the happy news. Uncle James and Auntie Molly would love to be their new mummy and daddy, but it was their choice and nobody would force them to do anything. Cathy wanted to make sure that 'doption' meant they would all be together for ever and ever, and, having been assured of this, she flung her arms around Auntie Molly, cuddling into her lap with a happy sigh. Mark looked slightly worried, so Uncle James suggested he and Mark should make a cup of cocoa for the girls.

In the kitchen, after a little gentle pressing, the question of names came up. Should he and Cathy still say Uncle James and Auntie Molly or Mummy and Daddy? Uncle James ruffled his hair and said it didn't matter one bit. They could decide now or later. The main thing was that they would be a proper family for always.

Next day, for News, Miss Taylor's class learned that Cathy and Mark were getting a new mummy and daddy on Friday.

As children do, this was accepted without comment, though Hannah Ward wondered where they had lost their old mummy and daddy and John Fyne wished he could get new ones because his old ones were always cross with him. Cathy drew a picture of her family when she should have been practising her spelling words, and under each person, she carefully wrote their name: Cathy, Mark, Mummy and Daddy. With a smile, Miss Taylor told her to put it in her pocket and take it home.

Angie was teething and quite out of sorts. She had also started crawling in earnest, making Megan wish she had six pairs of eyes. The Christmas tree had been placed on the coffee table, moved for that purpose under the window. But Angie wanted the pretty coloured balls and had cried and grizzled for almost an hour that morning, trying to reach them. When she eventually fell asleep, Megan sank into an armchair, switched on a seldom-watched daytime soap and drank a steaming cup of coffee, hoping sincerely that all would be well for lunch tomorrow with Joy and Sophia, not to mention the following day.

Even the girls were not their usual easy-going selves, what with the excitement of Christmas, Miss Taylor's wedding and the imminent arrival of Miss Timms. They had each brought home a present for their mother, a closely-guarded secret wrapped in gaily-painted paper, the previous afternoon, but as space on the coffee table was limited, a long argument had erupted as to where each one should be placed. Still, Christmas was for children and Megan had tried her best to be patient and she had a very pleasant couple of days ahead of her.

Margaret Ward was thinking more or less the same thing.

She had made a trip into Mansford the previous day, taken thirty-five minutes to locate a suitable parking spot, negotiated the lunchtime crowds with Joey peacefully oblivious to the mayhem, and finally picked up Hannah's longed-for dolls' house. Thankfully, an assistant had carried the huge box back to her car. She had then wended her way to the sports shop to buy Adam's football gear, armed with exact details provided by her husband.

By that time, Joey was waking up and proclaiming his hunger lustily as his mum struggled to stow the pram in the boot. He was fed in the front seat of the car and Margaret barely had time to swallow a home-made sandwich before her two-hour parking time expired. Feeling like a wet rag by the time she finally arrived home, she was nevertheless pleased and relieved to have acquired the children's Christmas presents. To top off a satisfactory expedition, William suddenly appeared to help her carry the large box inside and upstairs. Where to hide it was rather a problem, but it now reposed in the main bedroom under a pile of ironing.

CHAPTER 29

Very early on Saturday morning, the weather changed and Fairmead was turned into a winter wonderland. The last few mild, cloudy days had given way to clear skies and frost. As the sun rose, Fairmead's white covering sparkled, and even shady corners seemed brighter. Children were entranced and their parents said it was a good omen for Miss Taylor's wedding. Long-time residents reminisced about the Hawton family and their pleasure at having Anthony Hawton back in the Village where he belonged, not in some foreign place on the other side of the world.

Almost everyone was planning to make the most of this morning's happy event, either squashing into the back of the church or standing in a suitable position outside. Elsie Summerton had even arranged to swap times with another village, so she could arrive in Fairmead a little earlier than usual and slip out of the van just as the newly-married couple were emerging from St Mary's. She was a great reader of romances and couldn't miss this most romantic moment. Besides which, she doubted if anyone would be changing books at that time.

Miss Browning and Mrs Evans were, of course, official guests but they had impressed on all their children that it would be lovely if they lined the path outside church to greet Mr and Mrs Hawton as they emerged. It was trickier to let Joy's class know of the plan but one day the previous week, during a rainy playtime when Miss Taylor had slipped out to make a coffee and Miss Browning was watching her class, she had imparted the secret to them, telling them it was a big surprise and they mustn't say anything to their teacher. How successful she had been Miss Browning didn't know, but apart from two or three older boys, she hoped the whole school would turn up.

Most of Fairfield Gardens was in a fever of excitement from an early hour, only the Standings missing the first glow of the sun. Their big, exciting day yesterday had caused them all to sleep in somewhat. James had taken the whole day off, but the children had both wanted to go to school in the morning to see their new teacher. Though Molly had been a little apprehensive as to how they would adapt to yet another change in their lives, her fears were unfounded, and when they were picked up at midday, they were full of enthusiasm for Miss Timms. That lady knew all about Cathy and Mark's important day and had gone out of her way to make them feel comfortable with her. Just before playtime, the class had sung 'For they are jolly good fellows' for their friends and Miss Timms had stuck a large, shiny sticker on their collars. Not much lunch was eaten because of the excitement, best clothes were put on and hair brushed till it shone. Even Mark submitted to these ministrations because Uncle James was doing the same.

In no time at all, they were in a warm office at Mansford

Court and a very nice old lady was talking to them. Auntie Molly and Uncle James had to sign some papers, while another lady was asking the children if they would like a lollipop from a large jar. Cathy chose a red and yellow striped one and Mark had a dark green one that made his tongue and lips turn green. The old lady had asked them both if it was all right to add the name Standing to the end of their own names and that was fine because Uncle James had already asked them. The lady didn't say anything about calling Auntie Molly and Uncle James Mummy and Daddy, but Cathy had told Mark in bed last night that she would like to because Sally, Jenny and Amy called their mother Mummy. Mark thought it would be all right as long as they didn't forget their first Mummy and Daddy and Cathy promised she wouldn't, though she couldn't actually remember them at all.

Once outside, Mr Miller had taken photos of them on the steps of the court before shaking everyone's hand and saying he would see them tomorrow at Anthony and Joy's wedding. Then they'd had a lovely afternoon at a children's play centre, having hot dogs and chips, followed by ice cream and cake at the café before enjoying two hours racing around the play equipment. Being a school afternoon, they had it almost to themselves, which was much better than during holidays when you had to queue for hours.

For the first ten minutes, Mark couldn't quite settle to enjoying it as he had something on his mind which he wanted to go away, so he left Cathy climbing up a ladder, ran over to where Uncle James and Auntie Molly were drinking cups of tea and asked Mummy and Daddy if he could go to the toilet. For a moment, neither answered, then Mummy flung her arms round him, giving him a lipstick kiss, and Daddy stood up, with a big grin on his face. Of course, Cathy saw them and came for her cuddle, trying to work out what Mark's wink meant.

They had arrived back in the dark, Cathy falling asleep in the back seat and Mark unusually quiet. On their front doorstep was a huge arrangement of flowers and an equally huge card, bearing the legend 'Congratulations' and signed by every person in Fairfield Gardens. Even the three babies had sent a kiss each. Laughing with pleasure, they tumbled inside and within five minutes were enjoying a delicious bowl of hot soup each. Within half an hour they were curled in their favourite spots watching their favourite film. It was, of course, the children's favourite film but their Mummy and Daddy were more than happy to watch it too.

As soon as it finished, a last important duty had to be fulfilled, namely, a phone call to their grandparents in New Zealand. Calculating for the hundredth time the hours' difference, Mark dialled the number and waited with bated breath until they answered. Nanny and Grampy and Nan and Pop had been rung just before leaving for Mansford, so this final phone call was the culmination of a wonderful day.

As the Standings were embarking on their happy evening, Joy and Anthony were making their way up to the Hall, accompanied by several cheerful friends. The Whist Club had agreed to hold its meeting earlier than usual and were ready waiting to offer their help and good advice. In no time at all, the tables and chairs were in place, balloons blown up and decorations organised, pink, white and silver being the theme colours. Joy had collected the snowy-white tablecloths from the catering people that afternoon. These were spread carefully and name cards placed according to a plan held in Joy's hand. This was to save them having to come up in the morning, the wedding being at eleven o'clock. Having arranged everything to their satisfaction, the friends departed for a couple of hours at the Farmer's Arms, while Anthony and Joy drove off to their favourite riverside pub for their last meal as an engaged couple.

The next morning, they awoke about the same time, though in different locations. Anthony had been invited to breakfast by Timothy Miller and his wife. Edward Smythe and George Hitchin had also been invited, making it seem more like an office meeting than a prenuptial celebration. However, the four solicitors managed to let their hair down somewhat and were soon engaged in dressing themselves to Mrs Miller's satisfaction.

Joy's morning was somewhat busier. She had barely put a slice of bread in the toaster before the phone rang. It was her father sending all his love and saying he would be over before ten. Five minutes later, it was Anthony to say he loved her and if she was free could she meet him in church at eleven o'clock. She had hardly swallowed her first bite when Isabella arrived, closely followed by Emily Whitehead, both saying that she couldn't be alone on her wedding morning. Slightly later than planned, Molly bustled in, full of apologies, and Joy's kitchen became a salon as she spread out her hairdressing paraphernalia on the table. Sophia arrived at the same time as her friend Anita from Fantastic Flowers, and Joy's sitting room turned into a florist's. Megan was the last to arrive, as Amy had been unaccountably sick twice in the night and had ended up sprawled in her parents' bed, with its two rightful occupants clinging for dear life to the edges. Amy was blooming this morning, but Megan and Jack were slightly the worse for wear.

Among these distractions, Joy remained serene, and by ten thirty all was in readiness for the short trip to church. William had been under all the ladies' feet for the last hour, trying to take artistic photos of the bride, but he had been finally shooed away by his wife and was now on his way to church to await the arrival of the bridegroom and best man. Emily accompanied him to St Mary's and Isabella rushed home to change. Molly had departed an hour ago, declaring that Joy was the prettiest bride she had ever seen. Andrew Ward had volunteered to drive the bridal car the short distance to the church and had been busy cleaning and polishing since early morning. The result was sparkling. All traces of children had disappeared and Margaret made a mental note to ask him to clean the car every Saturday morning. She had bought a length of white ribbon while Christmas shopping in Mansford, and this was carefully tied in a large bow at the front of the car. The result was extremely pleasing and Andrew proudly drove his vehicle from number ten to number two at exactly ten thirty. Sophia and Megan departed in style, leaving Joy and her father to spend a last few quiet moments together.

The morning still glowed with sunshine on frost and the air was clean and cold - like the Matterhorn, said Chloe, who had recently returned from a short break in Switzerland. She had arrived quite late the previous evening and had time only for a quick cup of cocoa before retiring to the spare bedroom. This morning, though, Kate thought her daughter's glow matched the glorious morning and was looking forward eagerly to having a satisfying heart-to-heart with her once the wedding festivities were over. Louisa had gone to help Margaret with the children, leaving Andrew free to concentrate on his car. Adam and Hannah had been allowed to help Daddy find the cloths and polishes. They really wanted to splash around with buckets of soapy water, but Mummy and Gran insisted that it was far too cold to get wet and they soon lost interest in cleaning out the inside. They were allowed to play out with Sally and Jenny and the Norris boys for a while, with strict instructions to return home by ten o'clock. Lots of people were going in and out of Miss Taylor's house, but the girls were very disappointed that they couldn't see the bride. Though Mark had come out with his ball, the boys had hardly started to kick it between them when they had to go and get dressed up in their best clothes. If it had been for anybody except Miss Taylor, they would have been very upset indeed.

Anthony and his best man, Timothy Miller, arrived early, to be greeted by a welcoming group of villagers, with more arriving every minute. It seemed as though, by the time Joy arrived, the whole of Fairmead would be present. Anthony had never seen so many children outside school before. They were everywhere, keeping warm playing tag and hide and seek around the churchyard. Their parents were chatting nineteen to the dozen in the sunshine, stamping their feet and breathing clouds of steam like racehorses. Official guests were also standing rather self-consciously in the sun as it was very chilly in the church, despite the heaters being turned on earlier by the Vicar.

Just before eleven, all whose presence was required trooped inside, forgetting the cold as they took in the beautiful flowers, delivered by Anita a couple of hours before and arranged by Jane Simmons and Sarah Barnett, and the softly sweet music floating from the organ.

At exactly eleven o'clock, Joy and her father stepped from their shining car. Surrounded by a sea of well wishers, they made their way to the church door where Sophia and Megan were waiting. A few moments later, Emily's quiet music stopped and the Wedding March burst forth. Everyone rose and turned to watch Joy, the very picture of a radiant bride, glide down the aisle on the arm of her handsome father. As she caught sight of her dear Anthony, she smiled so widely that he felt his heart turn over. What a lucky fellow he was to have found such a wonderful girl, and what an intricate path his life had taken to ensure that they would meet.

Many others in the church were thinking much the same thoughts about themselves. Angie Todd, however, was more interested in thinking about escaping from her daddy's arms and exploring this big house. She wriggled and screamed, much to Megan's embarrassment, and poor Jack had to hurry outside with her or nobody would have heard the marriage ceremony. For once, Liz's boys were behaving themselves and she could concentrate on admiring the gorgeous lace veil, now being worn by Joy, but, not so long ago, she herself had been the wearer and her thoughts turned to her own wedding and subsequent happy marriage. Tom had been marvellous during her illness and she thought she loved him more now than on their wedding day. She could only hope and pray that Joy and Anthony would be equally blessed.

These sentiments were echoed in every person both inside and outside the church. Everybody wished these two special young people the very best life could offer and several happy tears were shed, not least by Isabella, who was cuddling a sleeping Maria while her parents were otherwise engaged.

To the triumphant sound of the Wedding March, played by Emily with all stops out, and the church bells, switched on by Bill Hughes, Joy and Anthony emerged into the still frosty sunlight. Claps and cheers greeted them and the path to the car was lined by Fairmead children, standing two or three deep. William was waiting as the official photographer, but cameras were whisked out left, right and centre. William had, of course, the authority to arrange groups to his satisfaction, though many others used his groupings to snap their own reminders of the happy day. Andrew performed his role as chauffeur to perfection and soon the bridal pair and their guests were safely installed in the warmth of the Hall.

Coats, hats and boots were discarded in favour of more summery wedding outfits. A glass of sherry soon warmed the coldest toes and everyone relaxed in anticipation of a hot meal and a jolly afternoon. No one was disappointed. At four o'clock, Joy and Anthony slipped away in Anthony's own car, kindly left outside the Hall by his friend George Hitchin, to get changed at Joy's house. At four-thirty they were back in the Hall being officially bidden farewell by all their friends. By five they were on their way to the airport to catch a late evening flight to Australia.

CHAPTER 30

The evening turned very cold and once the sun had disappeared everyone had the same desire, to sit in front of their own warm fire and happily mull over the day's events. William wasted no time downloading his photos on to his computer, feeling quite relieved that he had fulfilled his role with no major incident. He had never forgotten a disastrous occasion, many years ago, when he had forgotten to put a film in his camera at one of his children's christenings. That particular son never failed to remind him every Christmas. Isabella was full of praise when she viewed the wedding photos. She had had a wonderful day, made all the better by the fact of being there simply as a guest and having no part in the organization.

The next day church attendance was rather meagre. Even the choir was reduced to three, apart from Emily who was there to play the organ, as always. She had left Snowball curled on her cushion while she herself had braved the uninspiring morning. Whereas the previous day had been cheerfully cold and invigorating, today was damply cold, with an unending grey sky. But Emily hardly noticed the weather, as she was greatly looking forward to an afternoon in Mansford with a friend she hadn't seen for twenty years. This lady was the wife of George Hitchin, lately of Miller Smythe Hitchin, solicitors. She and Emily had known each other well but somehow lost touch, for no apparent reason. They had become reacquainted yesterday at the wedding and Emily had been invited to afternoon tea. She was to be picked up at two o'clock and this treat was appreciated the more for its being unexpected.

Most of the other residents of Fairmead were content to spend a lazy day at home. In the early afternoon, some boys played a rather desultory game of football on the Green, but even they seemed to have been afflicted by the general sense of indolence and within half an hour they had wandered back home to watch television or play computer games.

At the Village Stores and Louisa's Café business was slow. Yesterday had been the busiest day for weeks, the lovely weather having brought people out from the city and surrounding areas. While Fairmead had been occupied with the wedding, Doris had been run off her feet with customers, as had Flo and Marjorie. All three ladies had been sad to miss seeing the beautiful bride, but business had been so brisk that they had had hardly had a minute to think about it. William had promised to show them everything on Monday morning and they were invited round for elevenses, so they were looking forward to enjoying Isabella's hospitality and seeing the wedding on William's new-fangled computer.

On Monday morning Sophia made a special trip into Mansford to book a flight to Spain. Paul had said he thought he could do it on the internet, but Sophia preferred to hold the actual tickets in her hand, and assured her husband that she also had some last minute Christmas shopping. Henry

Procter had been more than willing to agree to Paul's request for a week off after Christmas and had promised to ask a neighbouring vicar to take the Sunday service, though possibly at an earlier hour. Within a very short time, the Rev. Wilson had rung Paul and dates were arranged. They were to depart on December 27th and arrive back on January 3rd. Immediately, Sophia had rung the travel agent to make a booking and she had been fortunate enough to secure two cancellations, it being a very popular time for people to flee the cold weather. These seats had to be paid for on Monday and Sophia set off, armed with cash, having no faith in credit cards.

Miss Timms' day had not started as smoothly as Sophia's. Alison Wood's mother had rung to say she was awfully sorry, but her daughter had come out in spots the previous day. They didn't exactly look like chicken pox but they might be, so she would be off school for the last few days. Alison was to have played Mary in Wednesday's Carol Concert. Miss Timms consulted Miss Browning as she knew every other little girl had acquired an angel outfit, now hanging on a clothes airer in a corner of the classroom.

At that precise moment, Margaret Ward parked her pram near the school doorway, politely knocked on the door and entered the infants' classroom, bearing a school reader, lost for two weeks and recently found in a kitchen cupboard. With a purposeful look, Miss Browning strode over, introduced Miss Timms and explained their problem, asking if Hannah would be willing to exchange angel clothes for Mary's. Margaret assured her that it would be no problem at all and escaped into the noisy playground, feeling as if she had just been summoned to the Headmistress' office for a ticking off.

With that little difficulty solved, Miss Browning rang the bell and gathered their classes. Being experienced teachers, they knew that the only way to survive the last few days of term, particularly those leading up to Christmas, was to attempt to continue working as normally as possible.

William was determined to have an easy day, so after taking Scrappy for his walk, he settled down with the *Times* crossword and wasn't heard from again until morning coffee, when Doris, Flo and Marjorie bustled in to see the wedding photos. He put on a very professional show, resulting in many oohs and aahs and even a couple of tears from tender-hearted Flo. Once his duties were completed, he left the ladies to discussions of outfits, the gloriously frosty day, the afternoon's festivities, the honeymoon destination and the approximate time little Hawtons would start to arrive.

As soon as lunch was over, the three ladies having departed at ten minutes to twelve to attend to lunch at the café and, in Doris' case, help out with lunch at the Farmer' Arms, William began to prepare himself for the evening. It was to be the Cubs' Christmas treat, always much enjoyed by everyone, including the Cub Master. Most of the boys attended Fairmead School but a couple came from further afield, so they had arranged to meet outside Mansford Bowling at five o'clock. Several parents had agreed to drive their sons and other boys whose parents were not available. William was always grateful for this help and for the fact that they usually stayed to supervise the bowling. If truth be told, the parents probably enjoyed the outing as much as the boys.

Although uniform did not have to be worn, William was

always pleased at the good behaviour of the boys and was invariably proud to be their Cub Master. The very special treat within the treat was hamburger, chips and soft drink, which took the place of their usual boringly healthy teas and was consumed with much good humour on arrival at the bowling alley. William always blamed this weighty meal on his inability to make a strike, or indeed to touch the pins at all. It was always expected that the Cubs would score better than their leader and this outing was to prove no different. Sam, Adam and Mark had to work especially hard to maintain the honour of Fairfield Gardens.

Next day there were quite a few sleepy faces at the school and in the lower two classes at least, all pretence of normality had disappeared. Miss Timms' children spent the first part of the morning making Christmas cards for their families. Bits of coloured paper, cotton wool, glue and glitter spread like snowflakes on the floor and every surface of the classroom, but the results were surprisingly beautiful. Having taught older children for many years, Miss Timms was rather taken by surprise and even blinked back a tear when she saw Cathy Standing's effort. On the front was a robin, identifiable by its brightly crayoned red body, almost smothered in cotton wool snow and liberally sprinkled with glitter, as was its maker. Inside, in very best writing, rubbed out several times until perfect, were the words: 'To my best Mummy and Daddy, love from Cathy', followed by ten kisses and several hearts.

Though Mrs Simmons never complained about extra cleaning, Miss Timms was of the old school, believing it her duty to leave the room as neat and tidy as possible, so, twenty minutes before playtime, all work ceased and every child was delegated to a clearing-up task. Jenny Todd secured the coveted job of trying to sweep up as much stray glitter as possible with a dustpan and brush. Dan Norris found himself banished to a corner by himself, having been spied by his teacher's eagle eye tearing up scraps of paper into even smaller confetti-sized bits in order to make two of his friends laugh.

Just as the room was restored to its usual order, the bell rang and excess energy could be used up before the final carols practice. This was to be in the Village Hall, and the teachers collectively breathed a sigh of relief that the weather remained dry. A disturbing dampness had crept into the air that morning and the sky was threateningly grey. However, all managed to go as planned. At eleven o'clock, the three classes marched along Bridge Road to the Hall, recently vacated by the Ladies' Gentle Exercise Group. Excitement and confusion reigned for about two minutes as the children entered but was soon quashed by Miss Browning's raised hand. In no time at all, the infants were arranged in their nativity scene and the older ones assigned to their places. Miss Whitehead was already there ready to play for them and the practice was under way.

By midday, Louisa had been on the phone a dozen times to complain about the non-arrival of the milk delivery. Apparently the van had been involved in a minor accident on the Salston Road but it was expected in about half an hour. However, that had been the story since eight thirty, and Louisa was getting more frustrated by the minute. Only the calm appearance of Sophia at a quarter to twelve had prevented her blood pressure from skyrocketing. She had then seen the funny side of it and realised it was not the end of the world. Besides which, it was almost Christmas and she would be able to spend it with her dear family, the first time in several years and the first time ever with little Joey. It would be a really special time for them all, as Margaret's parents were also coming and Louisa got on well with her son's mother-in-law, though they had seen little of each other since the wedding. So, with a sincere smile, she explained to yet another customer that the milk delivery was due any time and she was so sorry for the delay.

But even if the Christmas spirit of goodwill had not already descended on Fairmead, not one person would have dreamed of blaming Louisa. Many took the opportunity of staying longer than absolutely necessary and having a chat about unreliable service these days, the terrible crush in Mansford at this time of year and the weather. The latter was, indeed, a major topic of conversation. Bill Hughes knew for a fact that it would be a white Christmas. Not only were his bones telling him that snow was on its way but that very morning he had seen two robins on his front gate, a sure sign of a wintry Christmas. Though Clarissa Jones didn't usually like to agree with Bill, in this instance she was forced to concur. Her old mother had been a great observer of nature and passed on the skill to her daughter, who noticed the change in the wind and feel of the air and declared that snow was imminent.

For this reason she had made a trip to the Stores, armed with two ancient baskets, to stock up on essentials in case they were snowed in for days. Louisa assured her that someone would deliver her milk as soon as it arrived and, at exactly one o'clock, the Vicar himself volunteered to be the milkman. He was actually on his way to discuss the Christmas hymns with

Emily Whitehead but had popped in to say hello to Louisa. Flo had waved through the café window but been too busy to have a word. As he hurried along the pavement, Paul felt a sharp tingle on his cheek, followed by another a minute later, and knew the childish joy of being outside when the first snow of the winter began. It wasn't much that day, just the occasional icy drop falling from a leaden sky, but it was a beginning and Fairmead held its breath to see what would happen over the next few days.

Fortunately, Alison Wood did not appear to have chicken pox and no other child came out in spots. Hannah Ward was still to play Mary, having warmed to the idea because she could take her favourite baby doll, Kimberly, to be Baby Jesus. At first she had wanted to dress her in the pink outfit purchased when leaving America, but Miss Timms had explained that Baby Jesus was a little boy and it would be better to wrap him in a white blanket.

As the weather was so cold on Wednesday, it was decided that Mr Blackett would take all the costumes to the Hall in his car, where as many mothers as possible would be waiting. The infants' class, suitably bundled up in coats, hats and scarves would walk to the Hall at about one-thirty and change there, the other two classes following soon after. As the older children had only streamers of red and green crepe paper to attach to their wrists, and hair in the case of the girls, it wouldn't take them long to get organised. The carols afternoon was due to start at two-thirty and was expected to take about an hour, after which parents could take their children and the remainder would walk back to school.

By two-fifteen the Hall was crowded and had warmed up

considerably. Excitement rippled through the children and noise reached into every nook and cranny. Miss Whitehead settled herself at the piano, Miss Browning raised her hand, quiet spread across the Hall and welcoming words were spoken.

As always, it was the infants who stole the show. The angels were so angelic that Bessie Crabtree was seen wiping tears from her eyes and even their mothers had lumps in their throats when they sang *Away in a Manger*. The little boys were more comical than sweet, in their tea-towel headdresses and towel clothes. Joel Norris was wearing a checked tablecloth, secured with a belt. This had come out of the belt and was trailing behind him like a cloak, but he seemed quite unaware of it and was singing his heart out, to his mum's great pride and pleasure.

James Standing had taken the afternoon off work, as had several other fathers. He and Molly were on the front row proudly watching Cathy and Mark, enjoying their first Christmas concert as real parents. Margaret Ward's attention was a little divided, as she stood near the back, ready to dart out of the door if Joey's grizzles erupted into serious crying. This she hoped she would not have to do, as it was bitterly cold outside and she wanted to enjoy her children's first carol concert in their new country.

Hannah was perfect as Mary, hugging her baby and singing with all the innocence of childhood. Adam was also obviously trying his best, though he had the worst sense of pitch his mother had ever heard. Little Dan Norris had everyone mesmerised as he balanced first on one leg, then the other, wobbling quite dangerously at one point, though fortunately

Hannah didn't appear to notice. By twenty past three, the carols drew to a close with a rousing rendition of *O come all ye faithful* and several of the older members of the audience were heard to declare that that was the best Christmas Concert they had attended for years. Miss Browning heartily agreed. It had been simple, gone to plan and required little preparation.

With great satisfaction all round, parents collected their children and teachers gathered the few remaining ones, while William stored the projector and screen in its hiding place and Emily packed her music into her neat little case. Soon the Hall was quiet and dark, chairs having been stacked by the bigger boys, but not for long. That evening the Whist Club was to hold its last session of the year and the following day the Hall was to host the Playgroup Christmas treat, followed by the much anticipated Fairmead Children's Christmas Party in the afternoon.

School was due to close for the Christmas holidays at one o'clock, so the children would be able to have a rest before the party, which started at three. As the teachers knew would be the case, almost every child turned up. Several mothers needed the morning to take their little ones to the Tiny Tots' Playgroup party, where every child received a small gift from Bill Hughes, dressed in his ancient Santa suit. As the children were so young, not one of them suspected that Father Christmas himself had not actually arrived. Some of the older babies were rather unsure and clung to their mummies, but most were intrigued and several tried to pull his rather untidy beard. Bill always enjoyed himself enormously, telling his cronies that it was worth getting old just for that occasion.

Those mothers without younger children made the most of their last morning of freedom. One or two rushed into Mansford for last minute shopping, while others hastily wrapped presents and secreted them away from prying eyes. Miss Browning's and Mrs Evans' classes had been told to bring books and board games but no electronic gadgets. Despite the prohibition, two had been brought in the senior class and one in the juniors, and these now reposed on their teachers' desks until home time. In Miss Timms' class, the children were happily playing with blocks, jigsaws and various other activities spread around the room. After an extra long playtime, which the teachers found a penance in the biting wind, all gathered in Miss Browning's class for a special Christmas Assembly, attended by the smiling Vicar. After that it was clean-up time, and by hometime, the whole school was spick and span, ready for Mrs Simmons' ministrations later.

From midday, Isabella and several helpers had descended on the Hall and put up a myriad of decorations, old and new. Sophia had brought Maria, asleep after her hasty feed, and was soon up and down the ladder, being by far the most able-bodied person there. She herself had had barely time to eat a banana after returning from Playgroup with Maria's little gift. It had been only her first visit, as she had been busy at Fantastic Flowers, but Anita had been adamant that she could manage today and she must take Maria to see Father Christmas. Bill had, of course, insisted that he had several extra presents, just in case, and there was to be no argument.

As Sophia was looping streamers, Isabella and her ladies were loading the tables with party food and William was staggering in with a large, old-fashioned, rather moth-eaten Christmas tree. This venerable tree had been used at the Fairmead Children's Christmas Party for so many years that even Clarissa Jones could not be entirely sure when it had made its first appearance. During the year it rested in an old cloth bag in the far recesses of the Hall's storeroom, gathering its strength for its annual Big Day. Once William had secured it in a large red pot, the ladies descended on it with coloured balls and miles of tinsel, soon transforming it into a beautiful tree that Santa Claus himself would be proud of.

With the money from the bazaar, Isabella and her Committee had bought a small present for every child who would be attending. These had been carefully wrapped and labelled during the last couple of weeks and were now arranged in satisfying piles around the base of the tree, awaiting distribution by the Vicar towards the end of the party. At two o'clock, all was in readiness and the helpers returned home for a quick bite to eat before returning in an hour.

All over Fairmead, excited children were demanding to know the time and mothers were exhorting them to keep their party clothes clean and tidy, at least until they arrived at the Hall. By a quarter to three, the village was on the move. Doors opened and children shot out, much faster than they usually did on a normal school day. All were well wrapped up, as the bitter wind was even more piercing than it had been in the morning. Once inside the warm Hall, mothers were hard-pressed to keep track of their offsprings' boots, gloves, hats and scarves as they were hastily discarded. Although it was not officially a school event, the Head Teacher was always present to keep some kind of order, as were the other teachers. Isabella shuddered to think what chaos could have erupted without them and they were treated as the most honoured guests, as was the Vicar, having cups of tea and cream buns thrust upon them frequently.

The party then proceeded on its much-loved, traditional way, starting with games, moving on to enjoyment of the scrumptious feast and ending with the orderly distribution of presents. The first game was always Musical Chairs. First the girls had their turn, then, with much pushing and shoving, the boys had theirs and, finally, the last remaining six from each heat had a playoff, accompanied by much shouting of support from friends.

The final game before tea was, without fail, Pass the Parcel. The large circle necessitated a huge parcel and the resulting torn wrapping paper almost filled one of the Hall's dustbins. After this excitement, Miss Browning indicated that calm should be restored and each child should find their name card at the table and sit quietly, waiting for the Vicar to say grace. It was ancient custom that older and younger children were placed next to each other, so the seniors could help the little ones and show a good example, which they invariably did, much to their parents' and teachers' satisfaction.

The adults usually had a cup of tea and as much or as little party food as they wished, seated at their own table near the kitchen. The children were not allowed to leave the table until the Vicar had said a short thank-you prayer, and were then expected to clear the tables. As tablecloths, cups and plates were all made out of paper, great fun was had squashing it all into large rubbish bags. Once this task had been completed to Miss Browning's high standards, all sat on the floor as near the Christmas tree as possible, infants to the front. It was then the Vicar's great pleasure to pick up each gift and present it to its recipient. No one was allowed to open their parcel until the last one had been found, and much prodding and poking and whispered guessing went on for the ten minutes this took.

The final part of the Party's well-known ritual was the singing of *We Wish You a Merry Christmas*, followed by three cheers and a clap for the Vicar and all who had contributed in any way to this year's celebration. By six o'clock, the Hall was tidy once more and the decorations were being carefully replaced in their box. Only the tree remained and would do so until just after Christmas.

The next day felt almost as though Christmas was over, the last few days having been so exciting. Several parents were a little later than usual setting off for work and most children slept in, enjoying the luxury of no school. For those mothers at home, though, the day before Christmas Eve was an important one. Whatever the plans for the next few days, every house had to be cleaned from top to bottom, as was Fairmead's immutable law. In vain might husbands and children say that they would be away all over Christmas or the house would be completely messy after all the relations had been there five minutes. Their words fell on deaf ears and by nine o'clock, housework had started in earnest all over the Village. Children were sent out to play and told not to reappear except in the most dire emergency. Fairfield Gardens was no exception and soon every child of school age was outside, armed with bikes, balls and skipping ropes. Fortunately, the wind had died down completely and the morning was still and grey.

Granny Isabella was nominally minding Cathy and Mark, while Molly continued with her Christmas hairdos. This morning she had promised to attend to the ladies' needs at St Mary's Home, and even Emily Whitehead had asked for a trim and set. She had been asked to spend Christmas Eve afternoon at the Hitchins' and, as usual would be going to Paul and Sophia's for Christmas dinner. Isabella and William were expecting the same large family gathering as at Easter, with the addition of two extra babies. It was always William's duty to clean as many windows as possible, inside and out, and to make sure the wintry garden was reasonably tidy. Scrappy was in his element with his master in the garden and the children rushing about noisily just outside the gate. He raced up and down and around in circles barking happily, despite William's threats of tying him up in the back garden.

By midday, Molly was home and after a quick lunch of homemade vegetable soup with toast, she and the children set off to meet Nanny and Grampy in Mansford, after their drive down from the Lake District where a few flakes of snow had been falling since breakfast time and heavier falls expected, spreading gradually south, over the next couple of days. The Standings found their family warming nicely in front of a cheerful log fire in the Kings Head lounge and, after many hugs and kisses, they all set off for the High Street where Father Christmas' helpers seemed to be on every corner and in every shop window. Though Nanny and Grampy would be staying the week in Mansford, they would be driving to

Fairmead almost every day and were greatly looking forward to meeting up again with Nan and Pop, due to travel down from a freezing Scotland by train the next day.

Kate was also looking forward with high anticipation to Chloe's arrival the following day, though she would be coming from the slightly warmer south. Her friend Chris (Professor Bradley), would come on Boxing Day, as he was spending Christmas with his own family in Devon. Kate had seen a rather blurred photo of him on Chloe's phone and couldn't wait to meet him in person, having heard so much about him. Her daughter had had so few boyfriends, concentrating all her energy on study and academic pursuits, that Kate hardly dared hope that she might have found someone at last. Time would tell.

Meanwhile, she had a few days leave to enjoy and, like most other Fairmead ladies, was hard at cleaning and polishing. Dear Louisa was far too busy with the Stores and Café to attend to household matters and would be working with her friends, Doris, Flo and Marjorie, plus Susie Blackett, until well after closing time on Christmas Eve.

CHAPTER 31

Christmas Eve, at last! Children woke early and attempted to be as helpful as possible, in case Father Christmas was still watching. Megan wryly commented to Molly, as they passed each other outside the Stores, that it was a wonder the girls knew where the laundry basket was as it was hardly used throughout the rest of the year. Still, it was nice to only have to ask for something to be done a couple of times, rather than a dozen.

Molly laughed and continued on her way to Clarissa Jones and then to Sophia's aunt, Sarah Barnett. She hadn't meant to work this morning but these two ladies had seen her yesterday and begged her to oblige them. James and the children had some secret business in Mansford, to which she was not invited, so she had nonchalantly announced her intention of working for a couple of hours. After which, she had plenty of work in the kitchen. Nanny, Grampy, Nan and Pop would all be coming in the early afternoon for a happy Christmas Eve get-together and the plan was for the ladies to prepare for the next day's feast, while the two granddads took the children for a walk and play on the green. Tom and Jack were also required to amuse the children for a few hours in the afternoon, while their wives prepared for the morrow.

Both Liz and Megan had less to do than some as family would be descending the next day, laden with contributions. However, the thorny questions of organising tablecloths and table-settings, not to mention available chairs and where to seat everyone, had to be settled. Margaret Ward loved Christmas but had been denied a white one for several years while living in Los Angeles. She was even more excited than the children, if that was possible, when she heard that morning's weather forecast. Light snow was expected to start falling by late afternoon. With fingers crossed, she put her camera in a handy position in a kitchen drawer. She had promised a good friend in California to take photos of their Christmas celebrations and, if possible, the snowy village.

Just as Isabella and William were settling down to their lunch of sausage sandwiches, the phone rang. It was Joy and Anthony, ringing from Sydney, on a balmy night near the Harbour. It was almost midnight and they were out celebrating with friends. They had had a wonderful week, had been invited to their friends' for a Christmas barbecue and would depart for the Great Barrier Reef the day after Boxing Day. They sent all their love to all their Fairmead friends and were looking forward to seeing everybody in a few weeks. With a huge smile, Isabella promised to pass on their good wishes and in turn wished them a very Merry Christmas, before resuming her lunch and sneaking little bits of sausage to an appreciative Scrappy.

For Paul and Sophia, it was a busy day. Paul had taken special care over his Christmas sermon and had spent almost an hour the previous day refining and pruning it, as he knew most of his congregation would have only half their minds on his words. He had also been busy attending to parish affairs, in readiness for his little holiday. In one way he would rather not have gone at that time of year, but he knew it meant a lot to Sophia and indeed to his mother-in-law. He would not forget Monica's invaluable help when Maria was born and would do all in his power to please her. Sophia had already packed their cases with summer clothes and swimming costumes and was hoping to buy some little outfits for Maria, though she rather suspected that her mother would have pre-empted her and that Maria would soon look like a little Spanish baby.

Sophia had spent Christmas Eve morning at Fantastic Flowers, while Paul looked after Maria. The afternoon, however, was for organising the church flowers which she had chosen herself. A couple of other ladies had volunteered to help and they met in the church porch at two o'clock. To Maria, the church was a second home and she fell peacefully asleep as soon as she was wheeled through the gate. All had wrapped up well, anticipating a cold church and a pleasant hour was spent arranging the red and white flowers, holly and ivy. The Christmas tree was wreathed in coloured lights, a great golden star decorating the top. At its foot was the Crib, lovingly made by parishioners more than a hundred years ago. The figures were intricately carved and the old paint was faded. but nobody had yet had the heart to adorn them with gaudy new colours.

When all was finished, the ladies paused for a few moments, overcome by the peace and beauty of the church which for so many centuries had been a haven while affairs outside its walls had progressed on their turbulent way. Maria was just waking as Sophia was locking the heavy wooden door and attention was, for a moment, on her. Then all eyes turned to the outside world and movement ceased. The drab grey afternoon had turned white. Gentle snowflakes were drifting down through the still air and had already settled on the grass and path. The stark outline of the bare trees was softened in the downy mist and snow was resting in the forks of some larger branches. How long they would have stood gazing at the wondrous sight no one knew, but Maria was hungry and her cries roused the ladies, so they hurried home, leaving footprints and wheel trails which remained for ten minutes, after which the snow once more ruled the silent world of St Mary-in-the-Mead.

If it were possible to increase the level of Christmas Eve excitement, only the snow could have done it. Apart from Maria and Joey, every child in Fairfield Gardens, and indeed the whole of Fairmead, was at fever pitch. Even Angie Todd was affected. Sally, Jenny and Amy forgot all about being nice and became decidedly naughty, chasing Rusty round the house, knocking over a vase of Christmas flowers and driving their parents crazy with the barking and general mayhem. It wasn't much better at number four. Dan, Joel and Sam had just been returning from the Green with their dad when the first flakes had begun to fall. Whooping and punching each other, they had arrived home like a tidal wave and rushed straight out into the back garden, attempting to make snowballs out of the thin covering and succeeding only in throwing clods of dirt and mud. Dan got hit on the cheek by a small stone, resulting in a satisfying drop of blood and a major fight between the combatants. Tom waded in to separate the warring parties, Liz cleaned up the wound, and all three boys were sent to different parts of the house for ten minutes, despite Joel's loud complaints that it wasn't fair if Father Christmas didn't come to him because he hadn't done anything.

Hannah and Adam Ward were entranced. They had never seen snow before. Although they had returned to Fairmead twice for Christmas, it had not snowed. Both children begged to be allowed outside to see what it felt like and, to Andrew's amusement, his wife was as excited as the children. While he and Joey remained cosily inside, the other Wards quickly found coats and boots, hats, gloves and scarves, and rushed outside for a tour round the changed village. The Stores was still open, lights shining out like a beacon, but the café had closed half an hour ago and they waved to Flo and Marjorie who were stacking chairs and mopping the floor. The old houses of Fairmead were becoming blurred and all colour disappearing as white snow and grey sky enfolded them. Though Margaret had brought her camera, the pictures had none of the magic of reality and she soon put it in her pocket, preferring to immerse herself in this special afternoon.

Cathy and Mark Standing had had a successful morning in Mansford buying a Christmas present for their mother. Their father was in the best of moods because he had found a good parking spot after only five minutes of searching and had been heard to hum a Christmas carol as they crossed the High Street and entered one of Mansford's biggest stores. It didn't take long for Cathy to choose some pretty hankies with 'Mother' embroidered on them and for Mark to choose a box, adorned with a picture of roses creeping up a thatched cottage, containing rose-scented talc and bubble bath. Clutching their purchases, they fought their way to the cafeteria, where more good luck awaited them. A family at a table near the door were just standing up as they entered and the Wards fell on to the three vacated chairs with cries of triumph.

They had chocolate milkshakes and doughnuts with rather violent-coloured pink icing which mummy didn't usually let them have. Then, satisfactorily refreshed, they set off to meet Nan and Pop at the station. The train was fifteen minutes late, but it was fun watching the trains pulling in and out and watching the crowds of people surging to and fro. There was a large Christmas tree at one end, with oversized shiny balls dangling from every branch, and this seemed to be a meeting place. People met, kissed and departed separately, with dizzying regularity. When Nan and Pop finally emerged from one of the trains and their own kissing and hugging had taken place, they found the car exactly where they had left it, rather to Cathy's relief, and headed home, hoping that Nanny and Grampy would already be there.

The grey day soon merged into grey evening and the gentle snow continued. Emily had been dropped home by some friends of the Hitchins who lived at Salston and was pleased she had left on her little heater. Snowball was curled on a cushion and appeared not to have moved a muscle since her mistress had left earlier in the afternoon. With a very thankful heart, Emily switched on the light and kettle and took off her heavy coat, whispering a little prayer for all those poor, unfortunate people who had no warm home to return to on this wintry Christmas Eve or who had nothing to look forward to at Christmas. She herself, though having had no close family for many years, had never had a lonely Christmas. She had just returned from a lovely afternoon with new friends and tomorrow she would go to Paul and Sophia's after Church. Earlier in the morning, she would visit several Fairmead homes and, on Boxing Day, she would entertain half a dozen older village residents in the Common Room downstairs. Bill Hughes and Jan Fletcher were each leaving for a couple of days with their families after the Christmas service and even Bessie Crabtree had been invited by her great-niece to spend Christmas with them.

While Emily was enjoying her peace and comfort, it was time to hang up stockings and pillowcases in Fairfield Gardens and all over Fairmead. Sophia had made and embroidered a sweet little stocking for Maria and this she carefully pinned to the mantelpiece. It seemed as though every parishioner had shyly slipped a little gift into her hand over the last week for Maria. These were placed beneath the tree, together with a small rectangular package for Paul and a large, soft one for her.

She had managed to obtain, after much searching, a book on the life of St Francis of Assisi that she knew he wanted. Fortunately, she had started her search early and a rather obscure little bookshop, away from Mansford's main bustle, had finally located it for her. She had been quite busy over the last few days but felt no sense of panic over her lack of preparation for tomorrow's Christmas meal and, as usual, her serenity ensured that everything needful would be done. Once Maria was settled and Paul had retired to his office to tie up one or two loose ends, she began to move about the kitchen with calm certitude that all would be well.

As usual Isabella and William would be having the biggest family gathering, which was wonderful but sometimes a little bit of a trial if the weather was not suitable for the children to play out. During the evening, Isabella was constantly jumping up and running to the window to check on the snow. She half wanted it to continue and half didn't. William said she let in cold air every time she moved the curtain and Scrappy became excited with the possibility of an extra walk. The snow continued, neither very heavy nor very light, the whole evening. Children knew this was Father Christmas' ideal weather, though Hannah Ward was a little worried that he would either forget that they had moved from Los Angeles or that he might get lost in a blizzard. She didn't mention these fears to Adam because he would laugh at her and call her a baby. He seemed in no doubt at all that the Great Man would deliver his football gear as requested and cheerfully left his new blue pillowcase conveniently near the Christmas tree before skipping upstairs to bed half an hour before his usual time.

This pattern was repeated in several neighbouring houses. Sally, Jenny and Amy had become their usual placid selves and were only too willing to brush their teeth and get ready for bed. They had stockings to hang up on hooks stuck on to the mantelpiece, huge red ones made out of felt and decorated with holly and stars. Jack hoped the hooks would hold, at least until the girls were in bed. The Norris boys were a little later settling than the girls and there was some good-natured rivalry as to where the special Christmas pillowcases should be positioned. This was a sore point every year. Dan and Joel were quite content to leave theirs near the tree but Sam wanted his at the bottom of his bed, so he could try to keep awake and catch Santa leaving his presents. In the end, as always, Mummy and Daddy said if they didn't get to bed and go to sleep, Father Christmas wouldn't come and nobody would get any presents. So Sam gave in, determined to get his way next year, and soon peace descended. Of all the Fairfield Gardens children, Cathy and Mark were the latest going to bed. Being their first Christmas with the Standing family, none of the adults really wanted to see them go.

They played little games, read stories and chatted until almost nine o'clock, but by that time Cathy was almost asleep and Mark's eyes were heavy. Soon the only child awake was Joey Ward, demanding attention whether it was Christmas Eve or not. For almost an hour, his weary parents tried to soothe him and eventually, wonderfully, quiet returned, allowing the last hour of the day to be spent drinking a glass of wine and relaxing into the feeling of a real Christmas, with the snow gently covering the village outside.

CHAPTER 32

In the very early hours of the morning, Hannah woke with a start. She had been dreaming of lying in bed inside a huge dolls' house, as Father Christmas was dropping it down a vast, dark chimney which seemed to have no end. In a moment, she was wide awake and quietly leaving her soft, warm bed for the chill of the shadowy bedroom. Bravely conquering her fear of the dark and even greater fear of finding no presents, she tiptoed past Adam's and Mummy and Daddy's rooms, down the stairs and into the room where the outline of the Christmas tree could be seen near the window. Suddenly she stopped, tingling with excited relief as she plainly saw a huge square shape, among many others, less easily defined, parcels. For two minutes, she didn't move, then with a hop and a skip, she scampered upstairs and dived back into bed, which was now decidedly cooler than when she had left it. Hugging to herself the delightful surety that Father Christmas had not forgotten her, she was soon sinking back into peaceful sleep.

Maria woke for a feed at exactly six o'clock, but she was by no means the first Fairmead child to be awake in the cold darkness of an early Christmas Day. In Fairfield Gardens, the only two to remain asleep were Cathy and Mark Standing, who had had a very busy Christmas Eve and a very late bedtime.

In Louisa and Kate's household they too had remained up, chatting to Chloe, until almost midnight, and were making the most of a lie-in.

Sam Norris had woken at five-thirty but still not early enough to catch Santa Claus. With a shout, he had woken his brothers and the commotion had brought their father to his bedroom door, dressing gown unfastened and hair standing on end. With finger on lips, he quelled the excitement and ordered them back to bed until seven o'clock, so Mummy could continue to sleep. It seemed a cruelly long time to wait but, being thoughtful boys at heart, they submitted to the imposition. Sleep was, however, impossible and many laughs, shouts, bumps and bangs could be heard emanating from the boys' room for the next hour and a half. Liz heard it all, though she pretended to be asleep, for Tom's sake. He was so solicitous of her welfare and so kind in all he did for her, that she felt a lump rise in her throat. Almost imperceptibly, she moved closer to him and was soon cuddled up to his back. For the next hour, they remained this way, one wide awake and the other gently snoring.

During the night snow had continued to fall, covering all Santa's tracks, but he had certainly been to almost every house in Fairmead and before the sun had even thought about rising, piles of wrapping paper mounted in bedrooms and around Christmas trees. Shouts of surprise and delight filled the small houses and noisy toys started to give parents a headache before the day had really begun. In Fairfield Gardens, Maria and Joey were the only children relatively unaffected by the general mayhem. Even the animals had not been forgotten by the ever generous Father Christmas. Lady had a new red collar, wrapped and labelled, under the tree, while Rusty found a packet of his favourite treats and Scrappy had a thick plaid blanket, bestowed on him by Isabella, at Santa's request. William always marvelled at his wife's ability to purchase what seemed like hundreds of presents with an unerring intuition of what each person would like. Gifts for all their many children and grandchildren were now piled high as near the tree as possible. In addition, there was a present for him and for every child in Fairfield Gardens. His own gift to her was placed near the perimeter of the present zone, so he could find it easily and give it after breakfast before the hoards descended at midday.

As darkness slowly and silently gave way to daylight, a Christmas card Village came into view for those not immersed in presents and paper. Wrapped in an old white dressing gown, Emily sat by her window with Snowball curled on her lap, gazing in awe at the transformed garden. The snow had stopped falling and now adorned every branch and bush. The lawn was a pure white blanket and the fields beyond merged into the lightening sky. Then, imperceptibly, the clouds dissolved, the wintry sun began to send its rays over the horizon and the world seemed caught in a gossamer web of sparkling light. Emily's prayer that morning was a faithful echo of the Angels' Gloria and that great song of praise was still in her heart as she began to prepare herself for Church.

Paul was also filled with the glory of Christmas, as he plunged through the snowy woods with a rather surprised Lady whose ears and tail were on full alert in this strange environment. Though they appeared to be the first dog-walkers that morning, other creatures had certainly been there before them. In the clearings were bird prints and several unidentified larger tracks. Paul rather wished he could remember his tracking-lore from long ago in the Scouts but the magic of the morning soon dispelled all conscious thought and he became a tiny part of the magnificent whole for a blissful thirty minutes. As Fairmead came in view once more, he remembered that he was a husband and father and indeed, the Vicar, in which capacity he would play an important role in reminding others of the true, most wonderful meaning of Christmas. Hurrying down his garden path, the door swung open and Sophia greeted him with a laughing kiss and the mouth-watering smell of a slowly-cooking turkey.

In many homes around Fairmead, the same delicious smell was being released from ovens large and small, gas and electric. Many a mother was thankful for Clarissa Jones' capacious pinafore covering her best church outfit satisfactorily as she started preparing vegetables and all the trimmings of a traditional Christmas lunch. Husbands were dispatched outside to clear the snow from the front path, with strict instructions to sprinkle plenty of salt in case it remained slippy for Great Aunt Edna, who was known to be unsteady at the best of times. Children were requested to tidy up somewhat before being allowed outside for an hour or so.

By nine o'clock Fairfield Gardens had come to life. William and Jack set off about the same time with Scrappy and Rusty, commenting cheerfully on the progress of a large snowman under construction near one of the trees on Hawton's. Sam Norris seemed to be the supervisor of this mammoth effort, the other children being his willing slaves. At frequent intervals Joel and Dan stopped to throw snowballs at each other and, even better, the girls, if they weren't looking. The resulting screams started a full-scale skirmish, boys versus girls and Sam had trouble reasserting control over his minions, not made any easier by the fact that he was sorely tempted to join in the fight.

Eventually order was restored, Cathy and Hannah were sent indoors to beg or borrow accessories for the snowman and work continued until various dads appeared with the news that it was time to come in and get ready for church. Amidst many groans and protests the children trailed inside, vowing to come out again as soon as they got home.

Louisa, Kate and Chloe were the first to leave their house, looking forward to the Christmas service and the delights of a day to be spent with family. Adam and Hannah had already been round to wish them a Happy Christmas and tell them about all the lovely presents Father Christmas had brought. Louisa knew how worried Hannah had been and was delighted to see her joy. How different this Christmas was to previous ones, when a phone call to America had been the best that could be expected.

The younger Wards were also preparing for church but were at least ten minutes later setting off. This was partly due to the fact that Margaret had felt impelled by the beauty of the morning to set out with her camera but the intended five minutes had stretched to forty and when she had arrived home, Joey had been sick and required a complete change of clothes. The other two children had also needed a complete overhaul, as they were soaking from their activities on

Hawton's. Miraculously, every child in Fairfield Gardens emerged into the sun-filled, snow-covered morning, dressed in their Sunday best, several sporting new woolly hats and colourful scarves, looking like angels on their way to church. It was a picture-perfect day: the pale sun was shining in a pale-blue sky, snow covered every surface and drifts had collected against walls and fences. On Hawton's, rooks circled around the three large elm trees and, at the foot of one of them, a large snowman, complete with hat, carrot nose and pebble eyes, smiled his pebble smile in satisfaction.

On this beautiful Christmas morning, every person from the little cul de sac of Fairfield Gardens was present in church. Only Joy and Anthony Hawton were missing, but they had not been forgotten by their friends. As the vestry door opened and Paul prepared to enter the church, he paused for a moment. Before him were all his dear Fairmead friends and neighbours: Liz Norris, looking so much better now, thank God, sitting with Tom and her three mischievous boys; Megan and Jack, hanging on to Angie as she tried to shuffle along the seat, making the triplets giggle in unison; dear Isabella and William, so much a part of village life, everything that good neighbours should be; Molly and James, sitting proudly with their new family, ready to join the choir as soon as the Vicar appeared; Louisa and Kate, surrounded by family, baby Joey asleep in his father's arms; dear Emily Whitehead, still thought of as belonging to Fairfield Gardens, playing the last few notes of her favourite Bach, with a gentle smile on her calm face; and last but very much not least, his darling wife, Sophia, cradling their beautiful little Maria, the light of their lives.

With a prayer of thanks for all the blessings of the past year, Paul gathered his thoughts and stepped into the church of St Mary-in-the-Mead, which was filled with light on this special morning and which had witnessed all of Fairmead life through countless centuries.

The End

Lightning Source UK Ltd.
Milton Keynes UK
UKOW03f1634240214

227047UK00001B/67/P

9 781782 810278